Praise for

Changing Faces

and

KIMBERLA LAWSON ROBY

"Juicy saga of sister-friendship with all its twists and turns."

—*Essence*

"A refreshingly new page-turner filled with comedy, love, mental illness, and loads of drama."

—*Library Journal* (*Starred Review*)

"Vicious, compelling fun."

—*BookPage*

"Roby's fiction . . . [addresses] issues that are important to women today."

—*Memphis Commercial Appeal*

"Women everywhere will relate. . . . Roby . . . writes in an engaging, conversational style, like a long chat-fest between best girlfriends . . . Roby dishes up enough drama, heartbreak, violence, and redemption to keep the pages turning."

—*Washington Post*

By Kimberla Lawson Roby

Changing Faces
The Best-Kept Secret
Too Much of a Good Thing
A Taste of Reality
It's a Thin Line
Casting the First Stone
Here and Now
Behind Closed Doors

And in Hardcover

Love and Lies

KIMBERLA LAWSON ROBY

Changing Faces

AVON BOOKS
An Imprint of HarperCollins*Publishers*

A hardcover edition of this book was originally published by William Morrow in February 2006.

This is a work of fiction. Names, characters, places, and incidents are products of the author's imagination or are used fictitiously and are not to be construed as real. Any resemblance to actual events, locales, organizations, or persons, living or dead, is entirely coincidental.

FIRST EDITION

ISBN: 978-0-06-078080-7
ISBN-10: 0-06-078080-0

The William Morrow hardcover edition contains the following Library of Congress Cataloging-in-Publication Data

Roby, Kimberla Lawson.
Changing faces / Kimberla Lawson Roby.
p: cm.
1. African American women—Fiction. 2. Female friendship—Fiction.
3. Conduct of life—Fiction. I. Title.

PS3568.O3189C47 2006
813'.54—dc22 2005041479

08 09 10 11 RRD 10 9 8

This book is dedicated to all of my readers everywhere

Acknowledgments

EACH YEAR, THERE ARE always so many people who continue to show me such amazing love and support, but of course, I must begin by thanking God for everything.

Will, for being the love of my life for fifteen years; my mom, for being such a huge blessing when she was alive and even now that she is gone; my brother Willie, for suggesting the title *Changing Faces,* and my brother Michael, for recommending my work to readers online and everywhere else; my stepson and daughter-in-law, Trenod and LaTasha, for being so caring toward me; my aunts, uncles, cousins, nieces, and nephews for all their love and support; Lori, Kelli, and Janell, the women in my life who are there for me daily and have been for twenty-plus years. There is nothing in the world that compares to family and true friends and I love each and every one of you.

My agent, Elaine Koster; my editor, Carolyn Marino; my publisher, Lisa Gallagher; and all the other wonderful people at HarperCollins/William Morrow who work hard at elevating my career.

My website designer, Pamela Walker Williams, at Pageturner.net and my freelance publicist, Tara Brown, for all that both of you do to promote my work.

My author friends whom I communicate with regularly.

Dr. Betty Price at Crenshaw Christian Center for such tremendous encouragement and support. What a blessing you have been to me over the last couple of years.

All of the bookstores who sell my books, every person in the media who publicizes them, and all of the FABULOUS book clubs and individual readers who read my stories. I am indebted to all of you.

Much love and God bless,
Kimberla Lawson Roby

Changing Faces

Chapter 1

Whitney

MY NAME IS WHITNEY, and while it shames me to say it, I'm a compulsive overeater. I don't want to be, but that's just what I've been since I was a child and I can't seem to change it. Of course, I've *tried* changing my eating habits a great number of times, specifically over the last fifteen years, but none of my yo-yo dieting has ever worked—at least not for long. And believe me when I say that I've tried the very best of them, one right after another. Jenny Craig, Ornish, The Zone, Fit for Life, Slim-Fast, Herbalife, Atkins, and every other low-carb, no-carb, low-calorie weight-reduction fad on the planet. I've even gone as far as starving myself completely, which was actually working until that night I passed out in the middle of aerobics class. Good God, I must have been entirely out of my mind.

But insanity is not uncommon for women like me who are at least one hundred pounds heavier than they should be—women like me who spend every waking moment planning their next delicious meal and then promising themselves that they really will *restart* their diet this coming Monday. Sure, there are many overweight women who love themselves just the way they are and who walk around proudly with their heads held high, but most of us are not happy with the way we look. More importantly, we are not happy with the way we feel or the way some of us tend to be treated. Like the other day, when I was sitting at the mall in the food court section wolfing down a colossal meal from Taco Bell, and the couple sitting a few feet away looked over at me in disgust. They never said a word, but I knew immediately what they were thinking. They were wondering why I had the nerve to be eating anything at all, let alone two large burritos, a salad, and a large drink. I could read their minds as clear as day, and while I wanted to beg for their understanding, I never looked in their direction again. Instead, I pretended that they didn't even exist.

But actually, this was a huge part of my problem. I've always searched for acceptance from others and I have my "wonderfully loving" mother to thank for it. From the time I was eight, she was already criticizing the way I looked, the way I walked, the way I did anything. Nothing was ever good enough. She demanded perfection, but I never gave it to her. Tina, my younger sister, on the other hand, did whatever it took to make Mother happy, and Mother has always loved her more because of it. Mother had even slipped and told me so a few years back during an argument we were having, but now she denies ever saying it. Still, I know what I heard and it is the reason our relationship has been terribly strained ever since.

I drove my SUV onto I-94 West and immediately came to a complete stop. Traffic was bumper-to-bumper the same as always, and I couldn't help wondering why I did this every day. Obviously, I needed to work for a living, but why I drove all the way to downtown Chicago from Covington Park, the south suburb where I lived, didn't make much sense. Not when I could have easily taken the Metra train round-trip. But to be frank, I just didn't feel comfortable doing it. The Metra was nice enough, but for some reason I'd always had this weird phobia about traveling on anything relating to the rail system. Of course, no one understood it, but it was just who I was.

I continued on my journey and realized I was barely a few miles from the exit that would take me to my favorite Krispy Kreme location. Each day I fought tooth and nail trying hard not to go there, and sometimes I actually didn't. Sometimes I drove past the exit and even felt good about it, but it was always a major struggle.

I slowed my acceleration and waited for the flow of traffic to start up again. When I did, my phone rang.

I rolled my eyes toward the ceiling when I saw that it was my sister.

"Hello?" I said.

"Where are you?"

"In traffic, on my way to work. What's up with you?"

"Why on earth do you keep doing that?" she said, ignoring my question.

"Doing what, Tina?"

"Driving all the way downtown."

"I do it because this is a free country and because I want to."

"Whatever."

"Whatever is right. Now, did you want something in particular or were you just calling to harass me?"

"I'm calling for two reasons. Well, actually, three. First, I wanted to tell you that I got promoted yesterday to purchasing manager."

"Well, good for you. I know you've been wanting that to happen."

"I have, and it's going to pay me fifteen thousand more dollars a year. Then, on top of that, Riley Jackson asked me out. You know, that fine-as-wine anchorman on Channel Eight."

"That's nice."

"*Nice?* It's fabulous. He's a huge local celebrity and that means I'll be going to the best parties that Chicago has to offer."

I couldn't believe how shallow Tina was. She was so, so my mother and every bit as appalling.

"What's the third thing you wanted to tell me?" I hurried to say because I didn't want to hear any more of my sister's bragging.

"That I'm planning a surprise birthday party for Mother."

"Oh really? When?"

"Duh. On her birthday."

"I know, Tina. But on her birthday, near her birthday, when?"

"Her birthday falls on a Saturday this year, so that's when I'd like to do it."

"Actually, my twenty-year high school reunion is in November, but I didn't pay much attention to the date. I'll have to make sure it's not the same day."

"Well, it's not like some reunion is more important than Mother's birthday, now is it?"

"And it's not like we can't have Mother's party on a different date, now couldn't we?"

"You are so selfish," she said.

"No I'm not. I've never been selfish when it comes to you and Mother. I've always gone along with the program and made my own life secondary. And anyway, the reunion date is already set and it's not like I can make the committee change it."

"Well, maybe it's not on Mother's birthday after all."

"But if it is, we need to have Mother's party that Friday or Sunday."

"I don't think so."

"Then I won't be there."

"What?"

"You heard me."

"You are so pathetic, Whitney. And it's not like you should really want to go to some class reunion anyhow—not unless you're planning to lose some of that weight you're walking around with."

I didn't know whether to cry or curse Tina out. I wanted to do both. I wanted to tell her how much I hated her and how I honestly didn't want anything to do with giving Mother a party in the first place. I wanted to tell Tina to . . .

"Tina, you know what? Go straight to hell!"

I pressed the off button and tossed my phone on the seat. I was fuming. I was as angry as ever, the same as every other time I finished a conversation with my sister. The only time I became more irritated was when I, on rare occasion, spoke to my mother. They both made me cringe. In a word, they made me sick.

I just couldn't understand why they treated me as if I didn't matter, but I knew it was mainly because they were ashamed of the way I looked. It didn't matter that I wore the best clothing a plus-size woman could buy, that most men swore I had a beautiful face or that my hair was never out of place. They didn't care about any of that. All they cared about was that I didn't look like them: thin. They despised the fact that I didn't act uppity the way they did or that I didn't care that much about status. They despised me for caring a great deal about food.

Traffic picked up a bit, and while I tried to forget about my sister, I thought about Jarrett, the gorgeous man who'd dumped me just eight weeks ago—which wouldn't have been so bad had I not fallen in love with him. He'd seemed so into me the first three months, but it hadn't been long before his daily calls began to lessen and he began wanting to see me only at my apartment. I soon realized that this was all because he didn't want to be seen with me in public. You see, I was good enough to give him sex and a well-cooked meal, but I wasn't the person he wanted to spend the rest of his life with. I know this because he'd told me exactly that, word for word. I remember crying for two days straight over a weekend, all the while consuming two whole pizzas, two twelve-packs of soda, and three-fourths of a German chocolate cake.

Now, here I was all depressed but still had at least thirty minutes left of my downtown commute. What was a girl to do? The only thing that would certainly make me feel better for the moment—exiting the highway and heading toward Krispy Kreme. As I drove closer, I could already see the bright red light illuminated inside the window, and that meant that the "originals" were warm and fresh. So, I rushed inside and purchased one full dozen. I ate two of them in the car before starting the ignition. I ate four more during the rest of my drive to work and took the remaining six up to my office. I wasn't proud of it, but I knew I would indulge in the rest of those before lunchtime. And why not, because it wasn't like I had anything else to comfort me. Food was a very necessary part of my life, and right now I just couldn't see a reason to go without it.

Truthfully, I simply didn't have the willpower.

Chapter 2

Taylor

I SWERVED MY BMW into the far left lane of the Dan Ryan Expressway and tried to gain my composure. The driver of a large black SUV had suddenly slammed on his brakes and I had almost crashed straight into the back of him. Even now, as I peered through my rearview mirror, I couldn't understand why he'd stopped so abruptly and was now causing a noticeable traffic jam. Then again, maybe he'd had some medical emergency and couldn't help it.

Although the more I thought about it, I wasn't feeling all that well myself, even light-headed, and I wished that this legal conference in Los Angeles had been scheduled for another time. Specifically, not close to my infamous menstrual cycle. But with the conference being a very important one and one that the senior partners had been encouraging me to attend, I hadn't been in a position to argue about it. I did what they expected in hopes of becoming one of them, and I wanted my promotion to happen as soon as possible. The thing was, I was already thirty-eight, and I just couldn't see waiting until I was forty before I saw more career advancement. Lord knows I worked much too hard and much too competently to have that happen. I was truly the dedicated one and my bosses had praised me many times for being their expert when it came to very nasty divorces. I also second-chaired personal injury and malpractice cases, so I guess I had a knack for representing any client who'd been wronged unjustifiably. I worked hard at representing my clients to the best of my ability and I enjoyed doing it.

I continued on my way to O'Hare International Airport in what was mostly stop-and-go traffic and I was glad that I'd left home as early as I had. I lived in a south suburb, but at eight in the morning, travel to any Chicago destination took a lot longer than it should have.

After finding the *Tom Joyner Morning Show* on the radio, I heard my cell phone ringing. It was Cameron, the man I was deeply in love with, the man I'd been dating for almost two years. He was also the man who was taking much too long to ask me to marry him, the man I was starting to become impatient with.

"Hey, sweetie," I said.

"Hi, baby, how are you?"

"Just trying to make it through traffic."

"I can only imagine, and I apologize again for not being able to take you to the airport."

"Don't worry about it. Work comes first and you know I understand."

"But I'll definitely go pick up your car this evening when I get out of here."

"I keep telling you, you don't have to do that."

"I know, but I never leave mine there either, because I'm always worried that it'll be vandalized."

"Cameron," I sang, smiling. "Thousands of people leave their cars at O'Hare every single week and nothing ever happens to them."

"Maybe. But I'd rather be on the safe side, Taylor. You know that."

"Whatever you wanna do is fine with me."

"So, what time are you arriving at LAX?"

"Around one Pacific Time."

"Do you have any events today?"

"Just early registration. The sessions don't actually begin until tomorrow."

"But you're flying out as soon as they're over on Friday, right?"

"Yeah, I'll be back around eleven."

"Man, I'm missing you already, you know that?"

"I miss you, too," I said, and wanted to ask him why we were still doing this dating thing and didn't seem to be moving toward a more permanent commitment. I wanted to know why he was satisfied with the existing conditions and why he didn't seem to mind this idea of living in separate households—even though we were clearly in an exclusive relationship. It wasn't that I wanted to shack up with him, because I didn't. But he claimed he loved me and I certainly loved him, so I just didn't see what the problem was when it came to getting married. I didn't understand what his delay was in making me his wife. I wanted to ask him a great number of questions, but I didn't want to complain or cause any unnecessary tension between us. Not when we'd always gotten along so well. Still, it was getting to the point where an ultimatum was going to be inevitable, regardless of what the consequences might be. The bottom line: I was ready to settle down and start a family because my biological clock was ticking pretty loudly. It was time Cameron proposed or else. It was time he played the game correctly or forfeited by default. And I would tell him so when the time was right.

"Why don't we do dinner and a play on Saturday?" he said.

"Sounds good to me. Do you know what's playing?"

"Not in particular, but I'll find out before you get back."

"Oh, and hey, did you get the tickets for the Prince concert?"

"As a matter of fact I did, and they cost me five hundred dollars, too."

"What!"

"I waited too late to order them, and all the decent seats were gone, so I had to get them from this web site."

"Is that legal?"

"I don't know," Cameron said, laughing. "You should be telling me."

"Please. I handle divorces, not ticket scalping."

"Well, actually, it is legal in certain states, and of course the Internet allows free rein with stuff like that."

"At five hundred dollars, our seats should be right on the stage *with* Prince."

"I don't know about that, but they are second row center."

"Really?"

"Yep. You like that, don't you?"

"I won't even deny it."

"I didn't think so. I know how much you love him, though, so they were well worth every dime."

"You're too much."

"Well, hey, I'd better get going. We're meeting with some city officials today about this multimillion-dollar housing development they're wanting to build, and hopefully we'll be presenting them with a proposal in a couple of weeks."

"This sounds like a big one."

"It is. Business has been great ever since I went out on my own, but this would definitely make it better than ever."

"I'm sure you'll get the job. You're one of the best architects in the area, and you've got tons of references to back it up."

"We'll see. Anyway, baby, wish me luck."

"You'll be fine. I'm sure of it."

"Love you."

"Love you, too, and I'll call you when I get settled."

Traffic was now moving much more steadily, and I was maybe about twenty minutes from my exit. My cramping, however, was beginning to accelerate and all I could hope was that I wouldn't start bleeding. If only I could make it through another day, and even better, until I returned home. Especially since it had only been three weeks since my last painful cycle. I'd actually bled straight through the super-size tampon I was wearing, the two overnight maxi pads, and ultimately through my clothing. I had even soiled my leather executive-style chair, which I'd hurried to clean before anyone saw it. And the more I thought about it, I'd been bleeding excessively for more than six months, and it was getting worse all the time. It was starting to make my life completely miserable and I didn't know what to do about it. Maybe it was something minor and could be corrected, but regardless, I knew I had to see a doctor. There was no way I could go on the way I was.

After about twenty minutes I drove into the airport parking ramp and found a space to leave my car in. But right when I did, my phone rang again. My first thought was to ignore it, but when I saw that it was my mother, I answered.

"Hello?"

"How are you this morning?"

"I'm fine, Mom. What about you?"

"I'm good. Just taking a vacation day today since it's so beautiful outside."

"I don't blame you, because this *is* unusual weather for the month of September."

"I know."

"And how's Daddy?"

"He's at work, but he's doing fine. Still complaining about how his twenty-eight-year-old supervisor doesn't know what she's doing and how he's going to make up his mind and retire without notice."

Mom and I laughed. "Daddy cracks me up. But at the same time, I'm sure reporting to someone who is that much younger than him must be hard."

"It is. I've never seen your father more upset than he's been lately. He's been with the bread company for over thirty-two years and he's always loved it. But now I think he's serious about coming out of there."

"Well, he should if he's not happy. You guys have more than enough money saved and life is much too short to keep doing something you don't enjoy."

"I agree, and that's why I'm retiring next year myself."

"Right, Mom. You've been saying that for how long?"

"I'm serious. I really am. I love teaching, but it's time. Children are not what they used to be, and the last thing I want is to get hurt or end up in jail."

"Why do you say that?"

"Yesterday, one of my ninth graders stood toe to toe with me and cursed me out right in the middle of class."

"You've got to be kidding."

"No. Earlier in the day, I'd seen her in the hallway with some boy, practically having sex with their clothes on. So I broke it up. But when she came into the classroom, she told me that if I didn't stay out of her business, I might as well start expecting an ass-whippin'."

"What?"

"Isn't that something? And you know I wanted to snatch that little girl and throw her against the wall as hard as I could, but I didn't. Which is why I know it's time for me to stop teaching. This sort of thing is going on all the time all over the city, and depending on who the parents are, they can be worse than the children. Some of them will defend those little brats until the very end, even when they know how wrong they are. It's almost like Mitchell High has become a war zone between the faculty and the students."

"Then I don't blame you, you should retire. And to be honest, I wouldn't wait until next year. I would do it at the end of this semester."

I couldn't help wondering how so much trouble could be

going on in Mitchell, a city ninety miles away from Chicago and populated with only a hundred fifty thousand residents.

"We'll see," she said.

"Well, Mom, I don't want to rush you off the phone, but I'd better get inside so I can get checked in."

"I'm sorry, honey, I thought you were still driving. I'll let you go then."

"I'll call you back when I get up to the gate."

"If not, I'll talk to you later. I just wanted to call you before you took off, because you know how nervous these planes make me ever since 9/11."

"Mom, you were afraid of planes even before then."

"I know, but now I'm terrified, and I'll be worried sick until you get back here safely."

"I'll be fine."

"And I'll be praying for exactly that. That's the other reason why I took the day off."

I smiled. My mother was so cautious, but I did appreciate her.

"I'll call you as soon as I land."

"I love you, sweetheart."

"I love you, too, Mom. And kiss Daddy for me."

I stepped out of the car, pulled my garment bag from the trunk, and locked the doors. Then I headed inside the airport and over to American. The building was already full, and thankfully I'd purchased an electronic ticket and had the option of checking myself in. It was so much more convenient than having to wait in a line that had easily sixty people in it.

I stepped up to the terminal, swiped one of my major credit cards, and waited for my information to appear on-screen. I saw my first initial and last name, but the system wanted the first three letters of my destination city or the acronym of the airport. I typed in LAX and my flight itinerary displayed pretty quickly. Then, shortly after I answered a couple of other questions, my boarding pass printed and I proceeded up to the counter. The representative checked my photo ID and asked me to place my luggage on the platform next to her.

"Do you have any film in your bag?" the representative asked.

"No."

"Is it locked?"

"No."

"Then that's all we need. Have a nice flight."

I left the area and headed through security, which was sort of an ordeal in itself. I'd placed my laptop and coat on the rubber belt and walked through to the other side, but the metal detector had beeped and they'd asked me to remove my shoes and then scanned my body with a plastic wand. I wasn't happy about the delay or all the personal scrutiny, but I knew this was all very needed and I actually felt somewhat safer.

When I'd gathered all of my belongings, I took an escalator down to the lower level and another one up to a different area. I strolled toward one of the delis, preparing to grab a bite to eat, but suddenly I stopped in my tracks. Blood was gushing into my underwear, and I hurried to the nearest restroom. Thankfully, I'd brought my oversized tote and had packed a number of tampons and sanitary napkins. Actually, I'd put on a pad this morning, just in case, and I was glad I had.

But I hated this. It was one thing for this to happen at home, but not out in public. So, what was I going to do? How was I going to make it four hours on a crowded flight? What if I bled straight through my clothing again and onto my seat? I would never be able to live that down. The humiliation would be unbearable. On the other hand, I knew my bosses really wanted me to attend this conference and I couldn't have them thinking that I'd skipped out on it—especially not because of female problems. It would be all the reason they needed to believe I couldn't cut it as a partner. As it was, one of them, Skyler Young, already had these preconceived notions about women in the first place.

I wanted to cancel the trip, but I decided to just make the best of it. And while I was in fact concerned about my career, I realized that this medical issue was starting to frighten me. In the beginning, I'd thought maybe the bleeding might be the result of fibroid cysts, but now I worried that maybe I had some form of cancer. Uterine. Ovarian. Cervical. It could be anything. It happened to women all the time. Even women like me, who were in their late thirties or younger. I knew my failure to see a physician hadn't been in my best interest, but for some reason I just hadn't found the courage to do so before now. It hadn't helped that my longtime gynecologist had moved her practice to a different state and I wasn't thrilled about searching for a new one.

When I finally pulled myself together, I left the restroom. But as soon as I did, something dawned on me. I don't know why exactly, but suddenly I realized that I'd been blessed with just about everything. Great parents, a man who loved me, a satisfying career. To put it plainly, I just didn't have a whole lot to complain about. Of course, I wanted to be married and I wanted to have children, but overall, my life was pretty happy.

So happy that I guess something was bound to go wrong eventually.

Chapter 3

CHARISSE

CHARISSE STIRRED the home-style grits one last time, removed them from the stove, and poured them into a ceramic bowl. It wasn't very often that she found time to prepare a full-course breakfast for her family, but she always tried to do so every Wednesday, her day off. As a matter of fact, Wednesday was also the day she had lunch with her two best friends and the day she attended Bible study in the evening. Although with Taylor being out of town on business, Charisse and Whitney had agreed to postpone their get-together until next week. Which actually was a good thing since for some time now Charisse had wanted to accompany some of the older women of the church when they visited members who were in nursing homes. Charisse worked hard at being a faithful and obedient Christian but she'd never felt that Sunday school, Sunday worship, or various evening services was enough. She wanted to be more involved with outside ministries. She wanted to share God's Word with people who weren't able to spend as much time at church as she did.

Just as Charisse lined the round glass table with scrambled

eggs, grits, sausage links, wheat toast, and a pitcher of orange juice, the children walked into the kitchen and took their seats.

"Good morning, Mom," Brandon said.

"Good morning," Brianna repeated.

"Good morning," Charisse said, sitting down at the table with them. "Where's your dad?"

"Right here," Marvin said, strolling into the room, *Chicago Tribune* in hand.

"Do you wanna say the blessing?" Charisse asked him.

"No, you go ahead," he said, and flipped open the sports section.

Charisse wanted to strangle him. It was almost as if he rebelled against church and anything to do with God just so he could piss her off. Damn him.

"Dear heavenly Father," she started. "Thank you for all the many blessings you have bestowed upon us and for the food we are about to receive. In your son Jesus' name, Amen."

"Amen," Brandon and Brianna said, and reached toward the center of the table, helping themselves to what their mother had prepared for them.

Marvin took a sip of orange juice, never looking up from his paper.

"Hey, B," Brandon said to his sister. "I wonder if your girl Nina is coming to school today. Especially, since she got that booty whipped so badly."

Brianna frowned. "She's not *my* girl. I can't stand Nina with her ugly self."

"Awww. You're just mad because she took your little boyfriend from you."

"Whatever."

"What boyfriend?" Charisse asked.

"Nobody," Brianna hurried to say.

"Liar," Brandon teased. "You know you like Halston."

"I don't! And I wish you would stop saying that."

"Yes, you do. You've been liking Halston ever since we were in elementary school. Admit it, girl."

"Whatever," she said, rolling her eyes at him.

"Okay, that's enough," Charisse interrupted.

Brandon laughed in a taunting way and Brianna made a face at her brother.

"You are so childish to be in the eighth grade," Brianna continued.

"And you're too silly to be in the seventh," he shot back.

"You make me so sick, Brandon."

"You're just mad because I busted you out about that boy in front of Mom and Dad."

"You didn't bust me out about anything. So, now."

"I *said*, that's enough," Charisse added.

"Sorry, Mom," Brandon apologized.

Brianna didn't say anything one way or the other.

"Did the two of you finish your homework?" Charisse asked.

"Yes," Brandon answered.

Charisse waited for her daughter to respond but she didn't.

"Brianna, did you hear me?"

"I finished my homework right after school the same as I always do."

"Are you getting smart with me?"

"No. I just answered your question."

Her tone was curt, and Charisse had to stop herself from grabbing her out of that chair. Ever since Brianna had turned twelve, their relationship had become a fiasco. Of course, by no means had they ever been close, not even when Brianna was a small child, but now things were much worse.

As of late, Brianna rarely smiled, she seemed almost irritated whenever Charisse said anything to her, and she was, for the most part, cocky. Although since she was Daddy's little girl, she never treated her father that way, but acted as if Charisse was her enemy. To be honest, Charisse felt the exact same way about her daughter. She wasn't proud of it, but she wished with everything she had that Brianna had never been born.

The Richardson family quietly ate their food until Marvin broke the silence.

"One of my coworkers is leaving the company and we're giving him a send-off celebration after work."

"Really?" Charisse said. "And where is this *send-off*?"

"At Tommy's."

"The sports bar?"

"Yep."

"And you think that's the right kind of place for a Christian man to be hanging out at?"

"I don't know whether it is or not, but I'm going."

"Oh, is that right? But you can't go to Bible study on Wednesday nights, though?"

Marvin drank more of his juice and picked up another section of the newspaper, openly ignoring her.

Charisse wished he was dead. He was so different now that he'd been promoted to area manager at the gas company and was now making noticeably more money—even more than she made as a surgical nurse. It was almost as if that little job of his had gone straight to his head and that he thought he could say or do whatever he wanted. He didn't even go to church on Sundays anymore. Not to mention he acted as though he despised her, and he barely said more than a few words to her on any given day. Which was why it was hard to believe there had been a time when he had done any and everything she'd told him to do, no matter what that any and everything had been. For fifteen years she'd been able to control him completely, but now that control was nonexistent. It was almost as if she was married to a total stranger who didn't care about her in the least.

The children glanced at each other and Charisse got up from the table and went over to the sink.

"You guys had better finish up," Marvin said. "Your bus will be here in fifteen minutes."

"Okay, Daddy," Brianna said, smiling.

Charisse hated both of them—her husband and her daughter.

"Dad, are you coming to my game tomorrow?" Brandon asked.

"Of course. You know I don't miss any of your games."

"And we're still going to the high school game on Friday, right?"

"Yep."

"I wanna go, too," Brianna said.

"Girl, football games are for men," Brandon bragged.

"Then why are you going?" she spat.

"Just shut up, Brianna."

"Didn't I say that was enough?!" Charisse yelled. "All you two ever do is argue, and I'm sick of it."

Brianna stood up and kissed her father on the cheek. "Bye, Daddy.

"See you, Pops." Brandon balled his hand into a fist and bumped it against his dad's.

"You guys have a good day in school."

Brandon pecked Charisse on the cheek. "Bye, Mom."

"See you when you get home," Charisse said, but her heart wasn't in it. She loved her children—well at least she loved Brandon, but right now she was more concerned about Marvin and his decision to go out partying.

"Well, I guess I'm out of here, too," he said, standing.

"You know, Marvin, you and I really need to talk. Things are very different between us and I'm not the least bit happy about it."

"The only difference is that I'm not letting you treat me like a child anymore."

"What are you talking about?"

"Charisse, don't even get me started."

"No. I want you to tell me what you mean."

"I'd really rather not."

"Look, Marvin. I want to know why you're acting like this and I want to know now."

"Okay, fine. You wanna know why? Well, for one, you've always told me where I could go, where I couldn't go, and pretty much how I should feel about everything. You even hated Ronnie and Charles even though you knew they were like brothers to me. You were so short with them every time they called that they finally just stopped calling altogether. And of course, whenever I wanted to go visit either of them, you always went into a rage. So, even though I didn't want to lose their friendship, I decided that our marriage and your happiness were more important. But even worse was the way you ruined the close relationship I had with my parents. You never liked them from day one and you did everything you could to keep me away from them. But in all fairness to you, I take the blame for that because it was I who allowed you to treat them so terribly. I will never forgive myself for letting you schedule that trip to Jamaica when you knew it was the same weekend as their fortieth wedding anniversary. And to think I was stupid enough to go along with what you wanted just so you wouldn't be upset with me."

"I can't believe you're saying all this." Charisse tried explaining, but she knew he was telling the truth about everything. She truly hadn't liked his parents, his friends, or anyone else who had tried to interfere in their lives. She'd wanted their lives to be only about the two of them, and if it hadn't been for her belief that God wanted women and men to procreate, she never would have considered having children either. It was also the reason she'd only wanted one child and not the two she'd ended up with.

"I'm saying it because it needs to be said. I allowed you to control my every move for all these years, and for some reason I was crazy enough to believe you when you said that I could never make it without you financially. Every time we had an argument, you kept reminding me of the fact that you worked ten-

and twelve-hour days, that you had a master's degree in nursing, that I only had an associate degree, and that you made almost six figures. Remember the time you told me that we could never have the lifestyle we have if it wasn't for you and all the money you earn? Remember? Well, what you don't know is that your criticizing me was the reason I decided to go back to school. The whole time I was working toward my bachelor's, you never knew that you were my inspiration to keep going. All the horrible things you said, trying to diminish me as a man, trying to keep me under your thumb, and trying to convince me that I should forget about going to school, was all the motivation I needed."

"Oh, so now that you have your little degree and that little management position, you think you can treat me any way you want to?"

"First of all, that little degree and my twenty years of experience is the reason I now have that *little* management position. It is the reason I was promoted three times in the last six years. It's the reason I now make more money than you *ever* will."

Charisse felt like a pot boiling over. It was a slightly cool day toward the end of September, but her body felt like it was on fire. If it wasn't for all the Jesus she had in her, she would take the long, sleek-looking butcher knife from the dish rack and stab Marvin multiple times with it. She would pay him dearly for the way he was speaking to her. She would kill him and then laugh about it later.

"You are so full of Satan, till it's not even funny," she said.

"No, I'm not full of anything. But what you need to know is that you're not running the show with this marriage any longer. You're not going to control my every move the way you always have. Those days are over."

"Dear Lord, I can't believe this is happening."

"Well, believe it, Charisse, because I mean every word I'm saying."

"Hmmph. I guess the next thing you'll be wanting is a divorce."

"If you try to stand in my way when it comes to anything—anything at all—that's exactly what we'll be getting."

"And I'll take you for everything you've got, too. I'll get everything that's coming to me. Child support and alimony."

"And I won't have one problem paying you so long as I don't have to live with you anymore."

"You asshole. You are so full of shit."

"Listen at you. Calling me an asshole and screaming the word *shit*, but always claiming to be such a Christian. You're incredible."

"I *am* a Christian. And if you were, too, we wouldn't be having this sinful discussion."

"Please. You treat Brianna like she's some stepchild you can't stand, you scream out curse words whenever you don't get your way with something, and I won't even go into some of the dirty stuff you've done to people at work."

"Brianna walks around here like she can't stand the ground I walk on, so I treat her the same way back."

"Can you blame her? I mean, if I had a mother who acted like she despised me all the time, I wouldn't have anything to say to her either."

"Well, regardless of what you say, I *am* a Christian."

"Why? Because you run to church 24/7? Because you run around quoting scriptures to people who don't do things the way you want them to?"

"No, it's because I turned my life over to Christ a very long time ago and because I'm saved for all eternity."

"You know what? It's time for me to go to work," he said, picking up his briefcase.

"Not until we finish this conversation," she said.

Marvin headed toward the doorway.

"Did you hear me?" She spoke loudly.

"I can't talk to you when you get like this, Charisse, so I'm through with it."

"I'm warning you," she said, moving toward him.

"Warning me about what?"

"You'd better not walk away from me, Marvin."

"Please," he said, heading out of the kitchen.

Charisse jumped in front of him and struck him across his face as hard as she could. Marvin immediately grabbed the side of his cheekbone. The blow was even harder than the time she'd slapped him right after he'd told her that he didn't want to go to her hospital's Christmas party. It was almost as hard as the time she'd slapped him silly because he'd told her that he liked her hair better when it was longer.

"Are you crazy?" he said, yanking hold of her arm.

"No. You are. And if you know what's good for you, you'll let me go."

She tried twisting away from him.

"Stop it," he yelled, grabbing her other arm, too. "Just stop it."

"Let me go, Marvin."

"Not until you stop acting crazy."

"I'm not playing with you. Let . . . me . . . go," she said, gritting her teeth.

"Fine. But if you raise your hand to me again, expect the same thing back."

She jerked away from him. "I wish you would. I wish you would even think about laying a hand on me."

"I'm advising you to stop while you're ahead."

He tried walking away again.

But Charisse pushed him from behind with all her might and his body slammed into the wall in the hallway. She watched him grab his side and then try to balance himself, but she had not an ounce of remorse or sympathy for him. She wished that she had hurt him much worse.

Marvin turned around and charged toward her, clasping his hands tightly around her neck and forcing her head against the wall. "Didn't I tell you to stop?"

Charisse gasped for air, trying to call out his name and trying to remove his fingers, but he wouldn't budge. He squeezed even harder but then finally released her.

Charisse coughed uncontrollably, both of them completely out of breath. She had never seen Marvin act this way before and wondered if maybe he was abusing drugs or something. Had to be if he thought he could stand up to her this boldly without any possible consequences. He was acting very different, and while she'd thought this change in attitude was a result of his latest promotion, something told her that there was much more to the story.

But for his sake, she hoped this sudden confidence he was exhibiting was only temporary.

For his sake, she hoped she wouldn't have to hurt him.

Chapter 4

WHITNEY

ANOTHER DAY, another irate caller. For the life of me, I could never understand why certain customers thrived on being so difficult. It was almost as if their wretched little lives desperately depended on it. It was as if they longed for the opportunity to ruin someone else's day and couldn't wait to laugh about it when they hung up.

Which is why I sometimes wondered why I hadn't resigned from this wonderful life of luxury, my position as customer service manager, a very long time ago. But who was I fooling? My staying on had absolutely nothing to do with job satisfaction and everything to do with the sixty thousand dollars that Telecom Wireless was paying me to be there. They paid me well enough that for the most part I didn't mind listening to brainless wonders like Tacquinisha Bell, the woman who had asked to be transferred to "someone with authority" only a few minutes ago. She was making me wish I had purchased one extra dozen Krispy Kremes, because after this I was definitely going to need them.

"Ms. Bell, I'm really sorry that you've been experiencing so many dropped calls over the last few days."

"Sorry? Sorry my ass!" she said, and I raised my eyebrows by reflex. "You people don't feel *sorry* when you send out those high-ass bills every single month, now do you?"

"Ms. Bell, I hear everything you've been saying, and I completely understand your frustration. But at the same time, I'm going to have to ask you to refrain from using those obscenities."

"What? I just know you ain't tryna' to tell me how to speak. Because in case you forgot, I'm the customer and the customer is *always* right. You got that? *Always*."

"I agree with you one hundred percent, but I am not obligated to listen to any forms of vulgarity. So, I'm asking you as nicely as possible not to use any."

"I'll say whatever the hell I feel like sayin', anytime I get ready. And you bet not hang up on me either."

"I don't want to, but company policy does allow us that option if it becomes necessary."

"And I just hope you do, too. *Whitney Todd*. Yeah, that's right, I wrote your name down as soon as you said it, and I'm gone make sure your ass is fired on the spot if you end this conversation."

The verdict was in. This woman was mentally insane. She was being unreasonable and it was time I ended this debate of ours before I ended up saying something I wouldn't be able to rescind.

"What we can do, Ms. Bell, is credit your next statement for a full month of service. Which I think is very fair considering the fact that the problem just started happening this week."

"So, what you sayin'? That my bill for October won't have no balance?"

She was sounding more pleasant already. Ghetto, nevertheless, but pleasant. What I wished was that someone would carjack her.

"That's correct. Your bill won't show any charges due until November."

"I don't know why you ain't offer me that in the first damn place."

"Because we don't normally credit customers a full month when they haven't had a full month of problems."

"Well, you should. Especially when there is so many other choices out there when it come to cell phones. That's why my boo says he won't touch y'all wit' a ten-foot pole."

See, this was the reason I agreed with Bill Cosby and the comments he'd made about black children of today. I despised Ebonics and I couldn't help wondering what kind of parents had actually raised Ms. Taco Bell in the first place. I mean what kind of name was that anyway? Had her mother been watching a Taco Bell commercial and decided that it was the only name she could come up with?

And I wondered what kind of rules she'd been taught, too? What moral values? What family values? The importance of getting a proper education? It was all so degrading. Not just to the black race but to the human race as a whole.

"Is there anything else I can help you with today?" I asked.

"Well, after all the clownin' you just made me do, some free minutes would be good. Five hundred to be exact."

Incredible.

"Ms. Bell, once again, I apologize for your inconvenience, but I really have done all I can, regarding restitution."

"Is that right? Well, then maybe I'ma need to go over your head, because apparently you ain't got the authority to help me with the rest of my concerns."

"You know what, Ms. Bell, you do whatever you think is best. And to make it easy on you, I'll transfer you to my supervisor right now. His name is Thomas Kennedy."

I clicked the phone and dialed the number.

"Tom Kennedy," he said.

"Tom, I've got a real live one on the phone for you today. I've been dealing with her for almost twenty minutes and Renee was on with her before that. She complained about multiple dropped calls, and after listening to her curse at me more than a few times, I eventually gave her a full month of credit, thinking that would shut her up. But it didn't. And now she wants free minutes to go along with it."

"What's the length of her contract?"

"Two years."

"What's her payment history like?"

"She's had her service suspended three times already."

Tom sighed because it was common knowledge at our company that customers who never seemed to pay their bill on time always had a list of things to complain about.

"Well, chances are she's not getting any free minutes," he said.

I couldn't help laughing. "I wish I could be on the phone when you tell her that, because when you do, she'll be calling you every vicious name she can think of."

"Maybe, but that's just the way it is. You can let her through now if you want."

I connected the call.

"Ms. Bell, I have Thomas Kennedy on the line, and he'll be assisting you from here."

"Good, because I've had more than enough of you anyway, Ms. Thing. I don't usually be gettin' down like this with people this early in the morning, but that little ignorant attitude of yours made me go there. I can't believe you were so unprofessional."

I dropped the phone on the base and did what that stress management instructor had told me to do a few weeks ago when I'd taken his half-day class. I breathed deeply, in and out, for an entire minute. Women like Tacquinisha Bell made me crazy. They made me want to tell them a number of things, words they would never forget. But to my disappointment, Telecom maintained that stupid recording procedure, and it, of course, had stopped me dead in my tracks on many occasions. You know the one where all customer calls are recorded for quality purposes? It was the one procedure that held my staff and me under hostage-like surveillance even when customers like Tacquinisha treated us like common criminals. They spoke to us any way they wanted to, knowing they could get away with it.

I leaned back in my plush leather chair, inhaling through my nose, exhaling through my mouth. I did this for a couple of minutes but now I was daydreaming about pizza. Romano's was maybe three blocks away, but I could still picture everything on their menu without even seeing it. I could practically taste the onions, peppers, mushrooms, and extra sausage plastered on their deep-dish creation—so much so that I could barely contain myself.

In the end, however, I was ashamed. Ashamed of the way I longed for lots of food. The way I worshiped anything that could slightly fancy my taste buds. There was no denying that I was a compulsive overeater and I hated it. Sometimes I even hated myself and wondered why God had allowed me to be conceived in the first place.

I wondered why He had blessed my sister and my mother and even my two closest friends with normal-sized bodies, but had given me something more similar to Humpty-Dumpty's. It just wasn't fair and I wanted an explanation for it. Charisse insisted that I had no right questioning God and that I would burn in hell for doing it, but I needed some answers. I needed to know why I'd been chosen to carry such a tiresome and loathsome burden. Why I was chosen to walk around with 250 pounds of unattractive, well—blubber. Because there just wasn't a better way to describe it.

After fantasizing about the delectable pizza I was going to devour in less than two hours, I signed off on a few vacation requests, reviewed yesterday's incident report, and called Renee into my office. When she walked in I asked her to shut the door behind her.

She was wearing that fitted black dress of hers that made her look a lot slimmer than she actually was. But I wasn't mad at her.

A little envious maybe because she was fifty pounds lighter than me, but I didn't mind that she'd learned a few tricks of the trade. Tricks that I went out of my way to execute daily with my own attire.

"What's up?" she said.

"I don't know about you, but after dealing with that witch Tacquinisha, I need a break."

"Isn't that the truth? She was truly a piece of work and as ghetto-fabulous as they come."

"I tried dealing with her, but finally I gave her to Tom. Can you believe she wanted free minutes *after* I offered her a full month's credit?"

Renee and I both laughed.

"It's amazing how the customers who really do have valid complaints can be as cordial as can be and the ones who really don't tend to act like fools," she said.

"I know. But unfortunately, in customer service you get all kinds."

"I knew from the moment I called up her account and saw that her name was Tacquinisha we were going to have problems."

"Sad, isn't it? I hate stereotyping anyone, but in this case, her name complimented her personality and her intellect. Which is too bad because people like her send the wrong message about any person who has been given a name that sounds black. I mean, not every person with a quote-unquote black name is illiterate. Some are very well educated and very intelligent."

"That's true, but a couple of weeks ago, one of the evening network shows did a special on names and they proved beyond a doubt that your name really can make a difference when it comes to getting a job."

"Really?" I didn't see it.

"Yep, there were two black women who sent out identical résumés to the same corporations, except one was named Amy and I think the other was named Kiesha. Anyway, after a period of time, Amy received calls one after the other, all day long, but Kiesha never received even one. Amy received so many calls that she became irritated with them."

"Wow. And the thing is, it's not just white people who pick up on names that sound black, because we do the same thing. We've all been conditioned to think the worst when we hear long and unusual names, almost like they're foreign, and that's the very reason my mother named me Whitney. I mean, who would ever guess that Whitney Todd is a black woman? And I promise you, if I have children, they'll have ordinary names, too. You will never be able to guess who they are until you see them in person. And by then they'll have a fair shot at giving a true first impression and the opportunity to discuss their overall qualifications."

"I agree. But it's unfortunate that we can't be culturally inclined when we choose baby names."

"Yeah, but it's not even about culture. I mean if it's an African name with some sort of special meaning, then I can understand it. But you and I both know that Tacquinisha is hardly African or any other nationality."

Renee chuckled. "And let's not forget about those babies who are named after certain types of liquor. Alize, Tequila, Cabernet. Unbelievable."

"Unbelievable is right. But girl, enough about that. What I wanna know is if you're still thinking about having surgery."

Renee and I chatted about weight-loss possibilities just about every single day, but recently she'd become extremely interested in the gastric bypass procedure. I was still somewhat hesitant, though.

"Yep," she said. "I've been researching it more and more and my plan is to schedule a few consultations with maybe four or five doctors, probably next month."

"It seems to be working for a lot of people. Plus you only need to lose fifty pounds, so that's not nearly the same as me having to lose a hundred."

"Yeah, but I think it could work for you, too. Especially since you don't have any medical problems. I have high blood pressure and diabetes, so I need to take extra precautions just because of that."

"Well, I do know one thing. I have got to lose this weight. Because more and more, it's making me miserable. And I'm starting to feel like I don't have a life outside of food and work. There are days that I do enjoy my work, but when it's all said and done, food is my greatest pleasure. It's the one thing that puts a smile on my face. Lately it has given me more enjoyment than any man has. And that's a doggoned shame."

"I know the feeling," Renee agreed. "Roger pretty much only calls me when he wants sex or when he doesn't have anything else better to do. And it's so humiliating."

"I know. I've been treated that way so many times that I can't even count them."

"And that's why I'm not putting this surgery off any longer. Our insurance will cover most of it, so once I find a doctor who thinks I'm a good candidate, I'm going for it. I'll be thin in a matter of months, and I'll finally know what it's like to have people treat me with a certain amount of respect and have men truly be attracted to me."

"I know what you mean," I said. "Although I gotta say that I still want men to like me for me and not just because of the way I look. I want them to love me as a person. My mother never showed me that. I've never known my father, and my sister doesn't love anyone except herself."

"Not me. I don't care about any of that. I just want to be beautiful and have men raving over me. I want them to notice me as soon as I walk into a room and then take me straight to their bed if they want to. I want them to want me simply because I look that good."

I didn't bother responding because Renee's mind was already made up. We both wanted to lose weight, but we wanted it for different reasons. Renee wanted to attract as many men as possible even if they didn't care anything about her, because she had this dire need to feel gorgeous. I, on the other hand, wanted to attract decent men who would love me unconditionally and I terribly wanted to feel better about myself. I wanted to know what it was like to walk up even one flight of stairs without gasping profusely and trying to catch my breath. I wanted to know what it was like to shop in the regular misses department.

More importantly, I wanted to know what it was like to truly love myself and live happily ever after with my soul mate.

I definitely didn't want to be like Renee, a woman willing to settle.

I wanted so, so much more than that.

What I wanted was *the* grand prize.

Chapter 5

Taylor

I COULDN'T BELIEVE this was happening. The conference had begun barely two hours ago, it was now eleven o'clock, and already I was rushing back to the restroom for the second time. I'd arrived in Los Angeles yesterday afternoon, but because I'd been up and down throughout the middle of the night, I was starting to feel weaker as time went on. Right now, it was a major task putting one foot before the other.

In the ladies' room, I slid into one of the stalls and hung my belongings onto a hook. But just as I prepared to remove my clothing, I started feeling dizzy. I even grabbed the side of the wall and closed my eyes, waiting for this spell to pass, but when I opened them, all I saw were huge, blinding stars. My head twirled and I wondered when I would ever feel normal again.

This all lasted for more than a minute, but when it stopped, I left the restroom and headed up to my suite. I decided that the conference, at least for the remainder of today, would have to do without me, and the partners would just have to understand that I wasn't feeling well.

When I arrived inside my quarters, I dropped everything I was carrying on the sofa and walked into the bedroom, where I removed my shoes and blazer. I then proceeded into the bathroom, cleaned myself up, and found something comfortable to put on. Finally, I lay across the bed, trying to rest my nerves. I still felt pretty weak, but my mind raced back and forth, hoping that I wouldn't have to be hospitalized away from home. What an ordeal that would be. My parents would be worried sick, hopping on a plane immediately, and I didn't want them going through so much trouble.

I relaxed for maybe an hour but the problem occurred when I tried to stand up. I felt dizzier than I had earlier, and without warning, I fell to the floor. I tried to lift my body up, but I couldn't. I tried again and again until finally I just decided to lie there. I prayed that God would take care of me and that it wasn't my time to die.

When I stood up and sat on the side of the bed and saw that it was four o'clock, I realized that I must have passed out or something. But the thing is I felt stronger because of it. Admittedly, I wasn't my old self, but I didn't feel as bad as before. Yet I decided it was time to call Charisse to see what she advised. I'd told Whitney bits and pieces of what I'd been experiencing, but I hadn't shared anything with Charisse because I knew she was going to chastise me. She would insist how irresponsible it was for anyone to bypass seeing a doctor when they knew something was probably wrong with them. So until now I hadn't wanted to hear it, but after obviously falling unconscious, I really didn't have much choice.

I dialed her number but knew it might be hard getting in touch with her, especially if she was in surgery.

"This is Karen," a woman said.

"Hi, is Charisse Richardson available?"

"She just walked down the hallway, but can you hold?"

"Sure."

I switched the phone from one ear to the other and flipped on the television. I waited two minutes before Charisse answered.

"Hey, girl," I said. "Did I catch you at a bad time?"

"No, actually, I don't have to go back into surgery for another hour. We've already done three but we still have two more to go. But hey, how's the West Coast?"

"Beautiful as usual, but to be honest, I haven't felt well since I got here."

"Why, what's wrong?"

"I've been bleeding way too much and now I'm having dizzy spells."

"Oh no. When did this start?"

I could tell she was already hyped up.

"Well, the bleeding has been going on for months, but I assumed it would get better."

"Why would you assume something like that? I mean, if you haven't always experienced heavy bleeding, then you had to know something was wrong, right?"

"Maybe, but when I had the dizziness today, I knew I needed to see someone."

"Well, it's my guess that you haven't been taking those iron pills that your doctor prescribed for you. Am I right?"

I was already wishing that I hadn't called her. Charisse was one of my best friends, but she always knew how to get under my skin. She did the same thing with Whitney, but for some reason we kept tolerating her year after year. We'd been doing it since college and maybe it was because we'd always been able to depend on her when we needed to. She was more critical and judgmental than we liked, but we still loved her like a sister.

"Taylor?" she said when I didn't answer her question.

"No, actually, I haven't been taking them. I keep meaning to, but it just hasn't worked out that way."

"Then the dizziness is all your fault. Because you and I both know that when a person suffers from anemia, they need to take their medication."

"I realize that, Charisse, but what I need you to do now is refer me to a good gynecologist. Mine is no longer in town so I need to find a new one."

"Dr. Green is one of the best, and if you want I can get his number."

"You go to him, too, right?" I said, picking up the pen from the nightstand, preparing to jot down his information.

"Yes, as do quite a few other nurses on staff here," she said, and recited all seven digits.

"Is the area code 7-7-3?"

"Yes. His office is only two blocks away from the hospital. And when you call him, tell the receptionist that you are out of town with an urgent situation and that I thought you should speak to Dr. Green directly."

"Will he be okay with that?"

"He'll be fine. He's one of the nicest doctors I know and he has the best bedside manner."

"Sounds good. I'll call you back later to let you know what he said."

"Make sure you do."

"I will. Talk to you later."

I pressed the button and dialed the number Charisse had given me.

"Covington Obstetrics and Gynecology," someone answered.

"Hi. I'm a good friend of Charisse Richardson's and she suggested that I call and speak to Dr. Green. I'm out of town with a pretty urgent medical problem and I really need some advice."

"Your name?"

"Taylor Hunt."

"Let me see if he's available. Please hold."

I sighed when I tried to imagine what that idiot Skyler was going to say when he learned that I hadn't been able to attend most of the legal sessions after all. He was my worst rival and neither of us made any excuses for not liking each other. Skyler disliked me mainly because he thought I was way too career-minded to be a woman and because he felt that only men should be assigned certain high-profile cases. I disliked him because he was a male chauvinist and was ridiculously arrogant. I also disliked him because he was one of the most attractive men I'd ever seen. I, of course, would never tell him that, but I couldn't deny what the truth was.

"Ms. Hunt, this is Dr. Green," the voice said.

"Thank you so much for speaking with me. I won't take up too much of your time, but I do need some advice."

"No problem at all. What can I do for you?"

"I've been bleeding pretty heavily for quite a few months, and this afternoon I became dizzy and then passed out."

"Have you had dizziness before?"

"No. Not really."

"Have you had any problems with anemia?"

"Yes."

"For how long?"

"Almost ten years."

"Are you taking any meds for it?"

"Well, actually, no. I have a prescription for iron, but I haven't taken it like I should."

"Then, that's probably where the dizziness came from. Are you also feeling weak?"

"Yes. Very."

"My receptionist said that you were out of town, but do you have any pills with you?"

"No, I don't."

"Who's your primary care physician?"

"Dr. Cilletti."

"Well, what you need to do is call her up and ask her to prescribe just enough iron to get you through the weekend so that you can begin taking it this evening. And hopefully that will help you at least some. Then, when you're back, I'd like to see you regarding the heavy bleeding that you're experiencing. I'd like to do a complete exam and any tests that I think are necessary."

"I appreciate that, and I'll be sure to make an appointment sometime next week."

"You take care of yourself."

"Thanks again, Doctor."

I felt so stupid. I mean what did all of this really say about me as a person? Knowing that I had a problem, knowing that I had prescribed medication yet I didn't even have the intelligence to take it? I didn't like the way Charisse sometimes talked down to me, but she'd been right when she'd said that my recent symptoms were all my fault. And then there was this whole idea of not seeing a doctor and pretending that nothing was wrong with me. Pretending that changing sanitary products every hour on the hour was somehow completely normal.

Now I wondered how I'd been able to breeze through Yale Law School as if it were nothing but didn't seem to have the sense enough to seek medical attention. My grandmother, God rest her soul, had always talked about people who had book sense but no common sense, and I was ashamed to say that maybe I had fallen into that category. Because the truth was I knew better. I knew that the earlier you caught cancer, the better your chances were of surviving it. I didn't know if I had cancer or not, but who was I to take a chance on it? Who was I to decide that my bleeding just wasn't that serious?

But when it was all said and done, I knew that I wasn't stupid and that I certainly had my share of common sense. I knew that my hesitation toward seeing a doctor had everything to do with fear. I was scared to death that I really did have a terminal illness. Sure, I knew it might simply be endometriosis or some other common disease, but my pessimistic thoughts were forcing me to think otherwise. I was known to be a true optimist when it came to family, my career, and life in general, but when it came to sickness, I'd always thought the worst. Even as a small girl I'd always assumed that a slight headache definitely meant

I had a brain tumor. I assumed that any ache or pain was a sign that I needed emergency surgery.

But as I grew older, gained a lot more wisdom, and experienced life specifically on life's terms, those particular thoughts began to cease. I no longer worried about what horrible thing could or might happen to me. I never worried about anything like that until now. But starting today, I was going to do whatever I had to do in order to find out what was ailing me. I would do whatever it took to get well.

Chapter 6

Whitney

"WHITNEY?" Charisse said when I answered the phone. "Did you know that Taylor was having all these bleeding problems?"

"No," I lied, and didn't even flinch because I never told any of Taylor's business to anyone. Not even Charisse. We were all best friends, supposedly, but the fact that Charisse regularly judged both of us whenever she had the opportunity was reason enough for me not to tell her anything. Plus, I enjoyed knowing something that she didn't. I wasn't sure why, but it probably had something to do with her constantly acting like she knew everything.

"Well, she called me today, saying that she'd been having dizzy spells and that she'd been bleeding real heavy for a long time."

"Really?"

"Yeah, and it's up to you and me to make sure that she goes to see her doctor. And can you believe she hasn't been taking her iron medication? I mean, that's just crazy."

"Well, I wouldn't say it's crazy, because there have been many times that I've stopped taking medicine way before my doctor told me to."

"Yeah, but you weren't taking any medicine that you'll probably need for the rest of your life. Taylor knows that she's anemic and that she can't do without it, but for some reason it's no big deal to her."

We were barely two minutes into the conversation and Charisse was already getting on my nerves. She was sounding too much like she was badmouthing Taylor behind her back, and I wasn't going to continue listening to her. Although to be fair, I must say that, knowing Charisse, she probably wasn't saying anything she wouldn't say straight to Taylor's face, but I still didn't like what I was hearing.

"I'll have to call her when we hang up," I said, hinting that I wanted to end our conversation.

"I hope you do. And I hope you tell her how irresponsible she is for blowing off her health condition. And if that man of hers was worth anything, he would see that she took better care of herself."

"Charisse, please. Taylor is the last person you should be calling irresponsible. And as far as I can tell, Cameron is a good person. So, let's talk about something else."

"Okay, then let's talk about you and the fact that you're not doing a single thing to lose any of that weight. I mean, we're talking at least a hundred pounds, Whitney. And you know how dangerous obesity is because I've told you a thousand times about all the health problems you're setting yourself up for. I mean, what is it going to take? A heart attack? A stroke? What?"

"You know, Charisse, most of us do the best that we can and not everybody can be as flawless as you are."

"Meaning what? Because I've never said that I was perfect. But at the same time, I want you and Taylor to do the right thing. I don't want to lose either of you before it's time."

"Well, you've said yourself that God has all of our destinies determined and that's what I believe, too. So, the bottom line is that we're not going to die until it's time for us to anyway."

"Maybe. But the Bible also says that we ourselves are God's temple and that God's Spirit lives in us. And that if anyone destroys God's temple, God will destroy him for God's temple is sacred and we are that temple."

Good grief. I'd known it was just a matter of time before Charisse doused me with a few of her favorite scriptures. She always did this when she couldn't get me to agree with what she was saying. But today, I had my own scripture ready and waiting.

"The Bible also says that he who conceals his sins does not prosper, but whoever confesses and renounces them finds mercy."

"And what is that supposed to mean?"

"Do I have to tell you? Because I think you know exactly what I'm talking about."

"I can't believe you would even bring that up."

"Well, I wouldn't have, Charisse, but I get so tired of you judging Taylor and me. Maybe you mean well, but when you say some of the things you say, it sounds like you never do anything wrong and that we're basically a couple of heathens."

"But you know that's not true. And if I offended you, I'm really sorry. God forgive me."

She did this all the time, too. Saying she was sorry and then asking God to forgive her for stuff she was certainly going to do again. She was so predictable.

"Don't even worry about it," I said. "And as a matter of fact, let me get off of here so that I can call and check on Taylor."

"Tell her to call me later, okay?"

"I will."

"And Charisse, I'm really sorry that I upset you."

"Like I said. Don't even worry about it."

"Talk to you later."

I hung up and smiled. I wasn't a cruel person, not by a long shot, but I loved reminding Charisse about her skeletons—those that were dangling silently and eternally. I loved reminding her that I knew a whole lot more about her than even Marvin, Taylor, or any of her church members did.

Of course, I would never tell another living soul for as long as I lived.

Not when Charisse was one of my very best friends.

I would never tell another living soul unless she forced me to.

Chapter 7

Charisse

CHARISSE TURNED to the last page of Matthew, read a couple of lines, but then slammed her Bible shut. For two hours she'd been trying to calm herself and figured maybe reading a few scriptures just might help. She'd even spoken a couple of prayers, asking God to deliver her from all the anger she was feeling. She'd asked Him to remove the horrid thoughts she was having and the hatred that was consuming her. But this was all Marvin's fault. First it was this brand-spanking-new personality of his, and now he'd actually stayed out past 1 a.m. She hadn't approved of his going out after work last night anyway, but staying out until the next morning was unforgivable. He'd never done anything like this before, not the entire time they'd been married, and it was more than she was willing to put up with. All she could hope was that he would never do this again and that she wouldn't have to keep hearing that voice screaming inside her, begging her to punish him. Begging her to punish him for all his wrongdoing.

And then there was Whitney, who'd had the audacity to drag up antique news—something that God had already forgiven Charisse for a long time ago. How dare she bring up anything about anybody, looking like Miss Piggy. But Charisse was going to let it slide this time because she knew miserable people craved new company and Whitney was definitely a miserable soul. Had to be, given all the fat she was hauling around, and Charisse felt sorry for her.

Charisse closed her eyes and recited another prayer until she heard someone walking up the stairway. She knew it had to be Brianna because Marvin and Brandon were still at Brandon's football game and wouldn't be home for at least an hour.

"Brianna, is that you?"

"Yeah."

"Girl, what have I told you about saying 'yeah' whenever I ask you something? When you answer me, you answer with 'yes' and nothing else."

Brianna didn't bother responding and Charisse heard her walk into her bedroom and close the door behind her.

Charisse jumped up from the chaise, stormed out of her room and into her daughter's.

"Brianna, did you hear what I said?"

"Yeah."

"What did you say?"

"Yes," she finally said.

"And you'd better wipe that silly frown from your face, too, before I do it for you."

When Charisse stared at Brianna, she became livid when she noticed too many of Marvin's facial features. It was another reason she couldn't stand her. Daddy's little girl. Daddy's little sweetheart. Daddy's precious little gift. It was enough to make Charisse ill. She wanted to like Brianna, but she just couldn't. Not when she hadn't wanted to have her in the first place. Even today, she still wondered why she'd been so careless, having sex with Marvin barely eight weeks after Brandon was born and not taking any birth control pills. It had been so stupid of her. And it wasn't like she'd had any options because she certainly hadn't believed in abortions. The idea of it all was so ungodly and she hadn't seen herself committing such a despicable sin.

Thus Brianna had been born and Charisse had never gotten used to it. And how could she when Brianna had been the reason she'd had to waddle around knocked up, back-to-back with only two months in between? Instead of the normal nine months, her second pregnancy had felt more like twenty. Not to mention having to care for a newborn baby and then carrying another one inside her stomach simultaneously.

And it wasn't like Marvin had been any real help to her either. He'd made a ton of dim-witted mistakes and he hadn't done one thing a real man would have done in his situation. It was almost as if Charisse had become a single parent, and it was the reason she'd decided to wear the pants in their household from then on. She decided that she would run the entire show and that Marvin could, for the most part, take it or leave it. Of course, he had tried to rebel a few times in the very beginning, announcing that he was a grown man and that he wasn't about to have his own wife bossing him. But Charisse had told him in no uncertain terms that he could either go along with the program or pack his rags and get out, and it wasn't long before Marvin had given up the battle. Charisse had won and become his ultimate ruler.

Then, five years ago, she'd even stopped him from purchasing the black Cadillac that he'd always wanted, partly because she preferred silver and would only agree to that particular color, but mostly because she had become a pure, unadulterated control freak. And she never allowed Marvin to go anywhere after work unless he was running specific errands, those that she had instructed him to take care of. She did this because, according to her mother, it was the only way to guarantee a permanent and happy marriage. It was the only way to make sure that her husband never had an opportunity to sneak off and be with other women.

After returning to her bedroom, Charisse pulled an armful of underwear from her dirty clothes basket, took them down to the laundry room, and tossed them into the washer. She poured liquid detergent into the dispenser, set the cycle to delicate, and closed the lid. When she opened the dryer and saw Marvin's workout clothing, she got angry all over again. Just the thought of him going to some fitness center, working out with a roomful of women, made her want to lose it. It was the reason she'd gotten an attitude every time he'd gone there last year and then accused him of committing adultery when he arrived back home. Eventually, she'd caused so much trouble between the two of them that Marvin had finally stopped going altogether and then simply canceled his annual membership.

Charisse had learned early on that the best way to handle Marvin was to cause a major production. So, she did it every time Marvin tried to involve himself in anything that didn't include her or the children. But yesterday, for the first time ever, her usual dramatics hadn't worked. Marvin had done what he wanted to do and hadn't cared what she'd had to say about it.

Charisse walked into the kitchen and heard the phone ringing. She hoped it was Taylor because she really needed someone to talk to. She would never let on about what was happening with her and Marvin, but if she could just hear Taylor's voice it would help her. If she could talk about Taylor's problems, it would take her mind off of her own.

But it wasn't Taylor at all, it was her mother.

"Mama? How are you?" she said.

"Why haven't I heard from you in the last couple of days? A daughter should check on her mother every single day no matter what's going on."

"I'm sorry, Mama, I was going to call you tonight."

"So, how are my two grandchildren?"

"They're fine. Brianna is upstairs and Brandon had a football game."

"And what about you, how are you doing?"

"I'm okay, I guess."

"You don't sound okay."

"Marvin went out last night with his coworkers and he didn't come home until after one this morning."

"Excuse me?"

"I know. I still can't believe he did this."

"But what did you do about it?"

"We argued before he left for work yesterday morning and then again when he got home from the club, but Mama, he's changed. He told me that he'll do whatever he wants to do and that if I try to stand in his way, he'll file for a divorce."

"And you should've pulled out a butcher knife and stuck it right against his throat, too. Didn't I teach you anything, girl?"

"I wanted to, really, I did, but I was afraid that if I picked it up, I really would have used it. Plus, I just believe that if I keep praying, God will take care of this. He'll bring Marvin to his senses and everything will go back to the way it used to be."

"Are you that naïve or just plain stupid, Charisse?"

"No, Mama, I'm not."

"You and that church mess of yours. And where has it ever gotten you anyway? No, what you need to do is handle Marvin the way I taught you to handle him. About thirty years ago, your crazy father got bold enough to stay out one night, but I waited up and then met him at the back door. And after all these years, that fool still gets nervous when he sees even the smallest pot of boiling water. I scorched the skin off that Negro, and I promise you, he won't ever forget it . . . ain't that right, Roy?" Charisse heard her mother asking him.

Tears streamed down Charisse's face as she remembered the night her father had cried out in excruciating pain. She'd only been seven years old, but she still remembered his violent screams and the way he'd begged her mother to call an ambulance for him. "Mattie Lee, please. I didn't mean it. Please call them people so they can take me to the hospital. Lawd, Mattie Lee, please."

Charisse remembered how her mother had scolded him for at least thirty minutes before she'd finally decided to have mercy on him. But when she did, her mother had told him that he'd better tell the police what really happened: that he'd been boiling some water, preparing to make some mashed potatoes, and had accidentally spilled the water all over himself. She'd told him that if he mentioned her name even slightly, that he would have hell to pay a thousand times over. Charisse remembered how her father had done exactly what he'd been told and how she herself had feared her mother from that day forward. Charisse had worked hard at being a good girl so her mother wouldn't have to beat her, but sometimes Charisse hadn't been good enough. There were times when her mother had whipped her so brutally with an extension cord that Charisse's skin had welted all over. She could still feel the pain as if it had just happened hours before. Then there were the few times her mother had punched her with her fist, twice in the eye, but she'd only done it during the summer months when school was out. That way her teachers and schoolmates couldn't question anything.

"Charisse, this is what you're going to do," she continued. "When that bastard gets home, I want you to treat him real nice-like . . . hell, even have sex with him if you want to. But then when that joker falls asleep, you go downstairs and boil you some water and then you yell at the top of your lungs like somebody's breakin' in. And when he comes flyin' down those stairs, you toss that scaldin' hot water all over his ass. You hear me?"

"Yes, Mama."

"Because that's the only way for you to get back the upper hand. I don't know how you lost it in the first place, but now you have to do whatever it takes to get it back. If you don't, you can kiss that marriage of yours good-bye."

"I think he's pulling into the driveway now."

"Then I'll let you go, but tomorrow I want to hear a progress report."

"Okay, Mama. I love you."

Mattie Lee dropped the phone on the hook without saying another word, the same as always, and Charisse wondered what she was going to do about Marvin. She was standing by the kitchen sink, trying to figure out her next move, when the door to the garage opened.

"Hey, Mom," Brandon said. "We won 27–0."

"Good for you," Charisse said. She almost hugged him, but suddenly remembered that her mother had told her that hugging children too much showed a true sign of weakness and shouldn't be done that often.

"I'm starving," he said.

"There's some spaghetti and fried chicken on the stove, but you probably need to microwave it."

"Cool," he said, and ran upstairs.

When he did, she turned her attention to Marvin.

"So, Brandon played well, huh?" she said.

"Yep. And he made one of the touchdowns, too."

"Marvin, why are you doing this?" she said without warning.

"Look, Charisse, please don't start with me. I went out, I came home, and that's that."

Charisse was hearing those voices again, telling her to do bad things to Marvin. But she also heard her mother telling her to treat him "real nice-like."

"Okay, honey, I'm sorry," she said. "Let's not argue. As long as you weren't out with another woman, then I guess I can accept you being out with your friends."

"And that's all it was. Me hanging out with some of my coworkers and having a good time. I know you don't approve, but Charisse, you really are going to have to get used to this. And the other thing is that I can't ever go back to being one of your children. I can't ever go back to doing only what you allow me to do."

Charisse nodded, pretending to agree with all he was saying. She bit her tongue and put on a happy face the way he expected. She smiled the way she knew her mother would want her to. She did this to set him up for the kill.

"Fine," she answered, and then reached her arms out.

"I want us to be happy again," he said, embracing her. "My first thought was that I should just leave, but I realized today that I really do care about you, Charisse. I don't like some of the things you say or some of the things you do, but I do want us to stay together. And it might even help if we saw a marriage counselor. And eventually a counselor for the whole family, because I don't like what's going on with you and Brianna."

"Counselor?" she said, pulling away from him. "For what? Are you saying that I'm crazy?"

"No. No. I'm not saying anything like that. But what I am saying is that we all have a problem with the way we interact as a family and maybe a third party can help us with that. You and I argue all the time. You and Brianna don't get along and the kids don't get along all that well either."

Charisse turned her back to Marvin and walked out of the kitchen. It was better to just ignore him because if she didn't she might end up blowing things out of proportion. She might end up boiling that hot water the way her mother had commanded her to. She could picture Marvin lying in the hospital with third-degree burns right now.

But what stopped her were those terrifying flashbacks from the past. She hadn't experienced such haunting memories in a long while, but now those memories were badgering her and she had her mother to thank for it. If only her mother hadn't reminded her about the time she'd scalded her father. If only she'd kept her mouth shut about that entire episode.

Charisse walked back into her bedroom, closed the door, and kneeled on the floor.

She prayed that Marvin would come back to his senses.

She prayed that Taylor's medical condition wasn't serious.

She prayed that the voices in her head would stop whispering.

They were starting to work her last nerve.

Chapter 8

WHITNEY

THANK GOD IT WAS FRIDAY. My favorite day of the week. Sometimes I did work on Saturdays, depending on how full my to-do list was, but not tomorrow. And it was payday, too. I couldn't wait to head over to Oakbrook Mall in the morning. I couldn't wait to check out all the department stores and specialty shops that carried clothing for big women. I knew with me planning to lose weight, it was ill advised to keep buying droves of plus-size apparel, but shopping, like eating, made me happy. Yes, I was heavy-duty, but I figured dressing up, doing my hair, and perfectly applying my makeup was the very least I could do. Truthfully, it was all I had going in the looks division. And sometimes it worked because I could still remember William, this guy from Charisse's church, complimenting me on the way I carried myself. He'd been extremely impressed with my pants suit, up-do, and apparently the new foundation I'd been wearing from Lancôme, but still not impressed enough to keep seeing me. He'd been cordial enough, but like all the others, he'd quickly bowed out and moved on, I was sure for someone a lot smaller. Someone who wasn't larger than a size 10.

I exited the freeway, drove around the ramp, and turned left toward McDonald's. I was now only five minutes from my house, and while I usually treated myself to a more expensive dinner on weekends, I had a taste for a fast food burger.

When I entered the parking lot, I drove around the building and joined the line leading up to the drive-thru speaker. There were maybe six cars or so in front of me, but they were moving pretty quickly. So, I sat patiently until my phone rang. It was my loving and devoted sister, Tina, and all I could hope was that she wasn't about to ruin the rest of my evening.

"Hello?" I said.

"Hi. Did I catch you at a bad time?"

"No."

"Well, I'm calling to see when we can get together to plan Mother's party."

"Did you change the date?"

"No. And why would I?"

"Because my class reunion is on her birthday."

"And you're still thinking about going to that?"

"No, Tina, I'm not thinking about it, I'm actually going."

"I can't believe you."

"Well, you might as well start."

"And what am I supposed to tell Mother?"

"Tell her whatever you want, but if you really want *me* to be there, you'll change the date."

"You know how Mother loves surprises, and what better time to do it than on her actual birthday? I mean, this will make her so happy."

"Like I said, you need to change the date."

"I'm not doing that."

"Then there's nothing else to say."

"You know what, Whitney, you go to your little reunion. You go there so that everyone can tell fat jokes about you and then laugh right in your face."

I flipped my phone shut. I did it because I didn't want to hear any more of Tina's malicious comments and because it was now my turn in line.

"Welcome to McDonald's, would you like to try one of our new salads this evening?" the male voice rang out.

"No, thank you," I said. "I'll have a Big Mac Value Meal, a Quarter Pounder with Cheese Value Meal, and two apple pies."

"And what drinks would you like?"

"Coke and lemonade."

"Will that be all?"

"Yes."

The cashier repeated back my order, gave me my total, and then asked me to drive around to the second window. The cars in front of me pulled forward one by one, but as I sat there waiting, I felt a little embarrassed. And I'm not sure why because I'd done this for years—order two drinks whenever I ordered two meals because two drinks made it seem as though I was buying for two people. I did this because I didn't want those drive-thru people thinking bad thoughts about me. It was a trick I played time after time, but deep down I knew the joke was on me. I knew I was only fooling myself no matter what I tried to make others believe.

After driving away from the restaurant, I opened the paper bag and pulled out a few French fries. It was amazing how good they always tasted. Hot, greasy, salty, and loaded with plenty of carbohydrates. If only those highly advertised low-fat, low-calorie foods could deliver the same satisfaction, my struggle with weight gain would be over for good. It would be over for every person in America and we'd all be healthy again. Because while I currently didn't have any known health problems I was aware of, I knew Charisse had been right about my risk of having a heart attack or stroke. I knew it was just a matter of time before my excessive eating habits caught up with me.

Inside my house, I kicked off my pumps, shed my blazer, unbuttoned my pants, and plopped down on the sofa. I flipped on the television and reached for my bag of food. First I ate the rest of the fries that I'd already started on and then I pulled out the Big Mac. Between bites, I sipped on my Coke, and surprisingly enough, I suddenly felt full, almost fatigued even. My plan had been to eat the Quarter Pounder right away, but I could tell that I didn't have any room for it. That is, without completely stuffing myself. Which actually was a good thing because normally I never knew when to stop. Especially when I knew I was gearing up to spend another evening all alone. I was also proud of the fact that I hadn't touched that second set of fries either, which was another shocking discovery.

I stood up, took the rest of the food into the kitchen, sat it on the counter, and then poured the lemonade down the drain. And then it dawned on me. I was full because barely two hours ago I had stopped at the food stand just outside of Telecom's building before heading up to the parking ramp. I'd bought and eaten a pretty thick polish sausage, a bag of potato chips, and drunk a twenty-ounce bottle of Sprite.

What was I thinking? And how had I forgotten about eating an entire meal so quickly? Was I now stopping at fast food places simply by reflex? And doing it whether I was actually hungry or not? Was I no longer able to distinguish between being hungry versus eating just because I could? Had I stopped at McDonald's because I couldn't imagine not stopping somewhere after work?

Before I could continue with my self-interrogation, tears flooded my face. I was a complete mess, and I desperately needed help. This was no longer about the foolish choices I was making, it was about me and what was making me act so compulsively. What made me think differently than women who ate normally, or more important, what made me the total opposite of women who were anorexic or bulimic? I'd read an article once that declared that my way of eating was an addiction. It had gone on to say that eating properly and exercising regularly was easy for some people, but that there were others who mentally couldn't help themselves. For some, there were deep-rooted emotional issues causing them to act out irrationally. Some people gambled, some drank too much, some did drugs. But others, like me, ate everything they could get their hands on. They did what they had to do in order to satisfy a certain emptiness. They tried filling a void that forever nagged at them.

I walked back into the family room and lay across the sofa. I closed my eyes, and while I tried not to, I shed a lot more tears. I was so ashamed, so miserable, and disgusted with myself. I wanted to call Taylor, but when I'd spoken to her first thing this morning, she'd told me that she'd decided to take an early flight and would be in around six. And since it was only six-thirty, I knew Cameron had already picked her up from the airport and they were probably on their way home. It would have been nice if I could have phoned Charisse instead and told her how I was feeling, but I just couldn't take any more of her criticism. I needed someone to build me up and not tear me down and I knew Charisse couldn't help me with that. Plus, I'm sure she wasn't all that happy about me bringing up her past the way I had yesterday.

I tried pulling myself together by searching for a decent movie to watch, but I stopped when I saw a commercial claiming that a certain pill could eliminate unwanted belly fat. It even claimed that the pill worked so well and so quickly that it wasn't recommended for people who only had maybe twenty pounds to lose. I admit that it seemed unbelievable, but I had to try something.

Next, I found another channel broadcasting an infomercial claiming that their workout and eating program would give anyone the perfect body in just six weeks. Call me silly, but I sat down the selector on this one. Everything I'd heard so far definitely sounded too good to be true, but still I was all ears. My class reunion was happening in eight weeks, and if I could lose even fifty pounds by then, I'd be a happy sister. I'd still have to find an outfit tagged with double digits, but at least I wouldn't have to look in the 20s section. Because at two hundred, I might even be able to wear a 16W. Not a 16, but a 16W, because there was a noticeable difference.

I listened closely, paying special attention to the personal testimonies and obvious success stories. One woman had previously been about my size and height, but now had a gorgeous six-pack. Her arms and legs were beautifully sculpted, too. She looked great and I could see myself looking just as good in the future.

I watched the entire thirty-minute segment, admiring both men and women who had accomplished their goals, and then immediately picked up the phone and dialed the 800 number. A representative answered on the second ring, and I placed my order. She asked for my general mailing information and whether I wanted rush delivery, which I did. Lastly, I gave her my credit card number and expiration date and she said that I should receive my package by the end of next week. I sure hoped that this was true, because as it was, I would then only have seven weeks to work with. Although in the meantime, on Monday, I would drop my carb intake to no more than twenty grams per day and I would start back walking on my treadmill. I would also do as many sit-ups as I could muster and lift a set of free weights every other day. That way, I wouldn't be so out of shape by the time I started my new program and I could probably lose close to ten pounds in the process.

I felt better already. I knew the road ahead wasn't going to be easy, but this time I was determined to make it. This time, I was doing it for me and not for anyone else, and that would be a benefit in itself. I didn't care what my mother or sister would have to say and I wouldn't let either of them discourage me—the way they had so many times before. They constantly complained about me not losing any weight, but whenever I tried, they always predicted that I was destined to give up. It was almost as if they enjoyed seeing me suffer. As if they wanted me to fail.

But not this time. Not if I could help it. I was in this for the long haul, and I had faith in what I was doing.

Yes, this time I would lose all the weight I needed to lose and I would keep it off forever. I would eat the two apple pies that I'd purchased a bit earlier, but I would pitch the other fries and burger in the trash. Tomorrow I would eat whatever I wanted to and do the same again on Sunday. But come Monday, everything would be different. My whole way of thinking would be changed and I would be a much better person because of it.

I was finally ready to rumble.

More than anything, I wanted to win.

Chapter 9

TAYLOR

IT WAS SO GOOD to finally be home. The bleeding still hadn't stopped, but at least I wasn't flowing nearly as much as before. My doctor had called in my iron prescription, so maybe it was already helping me. Either that or I was feeling better because three days had passed and my period was halfway finished.

"I can't believe you went all the way to California and didn't go to Santa Monica Beach," Cameron said, setting down my garment bag.

"I wasn't feeling well," was all I said. I wanted to tell him the real reason, but I had this crazy idea that my news might change things between us. Which was interesting, because how could I ever doubt his understanding? Not the man I loved, trusted, and wanted to marry. The man who swore he loved me back. "But you're better now, though, right?" he said, smiling and pulling me into his arms.

"I am. I'm still a little weak, but definitely better."

"Good," he said, caressing my buttocks and kissing me.

The strong passion between us made me quiver. We kissed wildly and forcefully and my body felt like exploding. Oh, how I wanted to make love to this man. How I wanted to feel him inside me. How I wanted to show him that I could be all he would ever need me to be.

"I want you so badly," he said.

"I know, baby. I want you, too." I sighed. "But I can't."

"Why?"

"It's that time of the month for me."

"What?" He groaned.

I could tell he was disappointed. "I'm sorry. It'll be over in a couple of days, though."

"Why didn't you tell me?"

"I don't know. I guess I just forgot."

"Is that why you were sick?"

"Probably so. Sometimes I feel ill when I get my period. But it's no big deal."

"Well, it kind of *is* a big deal, because I've spent the entire day thinking we were going to be together."

"And we still can be."

"But not intimately."

"Is that all you care about?" I said, wishing I hadn't because I didn't want to start a fight with him.

"Is that what you think?"

"No, but you're making it seem like we can't have a nice evening together without sex."

"That's not what I meant at all, but I guess I'm just a little disappointed. And I'm also pretty exhausted. I had a very stressful day at work, so what I should probably do is just head home and get some rest. And after flying all afternoon, you should probably do the same."

"You're kidding, right? I just got back to town and you're planning to leave already?"

"All I'm saying is that we both need some rest so that we can get together early tomorrow."

"You know, Cameron, you do this all the time, but to keep peace between us, I never say anything."

"What are you talking about?" he said, frowning.

I hated this. Over the last couple of years, we'd had a few minor disagreements, but never any major blowups. And I preferred it that way. The thing was, I didn't like confrontations. Of course, I didn't mind having them in the courtroom, but not when it came to my personal associations. I avoided all arguments with family members, close friends, and men I dated, but Cameron was trying my patience. His lack of compassion and commitment to our relationship was really beginning to tire me.

"Why are you so upset?" he asked when I didn't answer his first question.

"If you don't know, then let's just forget it."

"Women," he said, grabbing his keys.

Then he kissed me on the forehead. "I promise I'll be over first thing in the morning, okay?"

"Sure. Whatever you say."

"I can't believe you think I don't want to be with you," he said, laughing.

But I didn't see anything funny. There was nothing humorous about any man making lame excuses the way Cameron was doing now. I loved him and I wanted to marry him, but I would never be his fool. I would never be any man's fool because I didn't have to.

"See you later," I said nonchalantly.

He walked toward the front door. "You know I love you, right?"

I smiled, but not genuinely.

"See you tomorrow," he said, and then left.

I locked the door and then picked up the mail that was lying on the glass and wrought-iron sofa table. I had brought it inside when Cameron and I had first gotten home but I hadn't taken time to look through it. Most of my bills came toward the middle of the month, so mostly what I saw were magazines and junk mail. There was also a package from Victoria's Secret, though probably the clothes I'd purchased for Brianna. It wasn't her birthday or anything like that, but when she'd spent the night with me a couple of weeks ago, she'd been looking through the VS catalog and had become ecstatic over some of their new apparel. She'd fallen in love with this black knit dress and a cute worn-looking denim pants outfit. Actually, I was loving the jeans outfit myself and was thinking about ordering another one.

Miss Brianna was my heart. For the most part, Charisse was like a sister to me, so I loved Brianna like a niece. I took her lots of places, even out of town on occasion, and there were months when I bought her things she hadn't even asked for. Although there were times when I knew Charisse didn't like it. I wasn't sure if maybe she was a little jealous of the relationship that Brianna and I shared or if it was that she and Brianna didn't get along with each other. But either way, I didn't understand because Brianna was a good girl. She was beautiful and smart and to me she was a mother's dream. But Charisse just didn't feel that way. And I had even asked her in a roundabout way why they weren't that close, but Charisse had suggested we talk about something else. She'd told me to mind my own business without saying the actual words, and that's what I had done.

But still it worried me because sometimes Brianna seemed awfully sad and I didn't know what to do about it. Over the years, I had tried to question her, too, asking her what was wrong, but she always told me it was nothing. So, finally, I'd decided to stop the inquiries and just be there for her whenever she needed me.

I pulled my luggage across the black marble flooring, down the hall, and into my master suite. This was one of those days when I was glad Mom had talked me into purchasing a house with at least one first-floor bedroom, because I couldn't imagine dragging this bag of clothing up a tall flight of stairs. I remembered not caring one way or the other whether I had first-floor accommodations or not, but Mom had insisted that it would definitely come in handy. That is, if I ever broke a leg, had major surgery, or lived to be ninety. As always, she was cautious about possibilities like that.

I opened my bag and separated my clothing into three piles. Dry cleaning, regular laundry, and those that I hadn't gotten a chance to wear. I pulled out my shoes and toiletries, placed them where they belonged, and took off the Ralph Lauren suit I was wearing. It was my navy blue one and hands down one of my favorites. Next, I removed the pure white pointed-collar shirt along with my panty hose, and as Cameron had so conveniently suggested, I decided that lying down might be a good idea. But before I did, I went into the bathroom, washed up for the evening, and slipped on a cotton lounging two-piece. I felt a little on the hungry side, though, so I went into the kitchen and fixed myself a cold-cut sandwich. This, however, was teeing me off because I'd been sure that Cameron and I would order in. I'd been sure that we would do the same as we did every Friday night, but so much for assumptions.

I bit into the smoked turkey with mayonnaise, drank some diet Mountain Dew, and realized Charisse had been right about it not having an aftertaste. I couldn't believe how good it was and I was already feeling that wonderful caffeine sensation. Although I wasn't sure that this was the best thing to have just before bedtime. Then again, I did need a pick-me-up.

When I finished, I went back into the bedroom, made myself comfortable, grabbed the phone, and dialed Whitney.

"Hey, T," she said. "I'm glad you made it back safely."

"Yep. Got in about an hour ago. What's up with you?"

"Well, actually I just ordered this great weight loss program. I was watching the infomercial and suddenly I had this huge revelation. And you know how I get when that happens."

I smiled because Whitney was always trying a new gimmick. Especially those that promised to make you thin.

"Really?" I said.

"Yeah, and it'll only take six weeks. Maybe not to lose everything, but I really think I can shed fifty by then."

"Well, you know I'm behind you regardless."

"Thanks, girl. Because I know you have to get tired of hearing me talk about my weight all the time and how I'm trying to lose it."

"Hey, we all have something and we all need someone to talk to about it. It's no different than me talking about my medical situation, my work, Cameron, and everything else I go through."

"I know, but I always start these diets and then I quit and move on to another."

"Well, I have faith in you and maybe this will be the one that you'll really be able to stick with."

Whitney didn't say anything and I knew immediately that she was having one of her moments.

"Okay, Whit, what's wrong?"

"You just don't know how much your friendship means to me. No matter what I say or what I do, you never judge me. You always encourage me, and my own mother and sister won't even do that. I don't know what I would ever do without you."

"Please. I'm here for you the same as you're always here for me."

"I love you, Taylor."

"I love you, too. Now, let's talk about somethin' else before you get me to crying over here."

We both laughed.

"So how have you been feeling today?" she asked.

"Better. I don't know if those iron pills are helping or not, but I'm going to keep taking them just in case."

"Good. And your girl Charisse will be happy to hear that, too, with her critical behind."

"I know. And as a matter of fact, I'd better call to let her know that I made it home."

"Well, I don't want to be on when you do. Remember I told you this morning how she and I had some words on Wednesday night."

"Come on now, don't hang up. The three of us haven't spoken by three-way in a long while."

"That's because Charisse is always saying something stupid."

"But you and I both know that Charisse is just Charisse and you either love her or you hate her."

"Well, right now I'm more close to hating her."

"Girl, just hold on, okay?"

"I guess."

I pressed the flash button, dialed Charisse's number, and connected Whitney.

"Hello?" Charisse answered.

"Hey, whatcha doin'?" I said.

"I wondered when you were going to call."

"I haven't been home that long. Oh, and Whit is on the phone, too."

"Hi, Whitney," she said.

"Hi, Charisse."

They were cordial but I could tell there was tension. I detested playing referee and it was starting to happen a lot more often than it used to. They just couldn't seem to get along with each other the way they once had.

"So, where's my little Brianna?"

"She went to the high school game with Marvin and Brandon."

"Well, tell her to call me when she gets in because I have a surprise for her."

"What is it?" Charisse asked.

"I ordered her some clothing from a catalog she was looking at when she was over here."

"I don't know why you do that, Taylor, because Brianna already has way more than she needs."

"I know, but I like buying her things."

"You should be glad that somebody loves your child well enough to spend that much money on her, because that means you don't have to do it," Whitney added, and I knew there was going to be trouble.

"Actually, Whitney, I wasn't talking to you. I was speaking to Taylor about *my* daughter."

"Oh. Well then, I won't say another word."

"Will you two stop it," I pleaded.

"Taylor, why don't you just call me later?" Whitney suggested.

"First Cameron disappoints me and now you guys are doing the same thing. What a mess I came home to."

"What do you mean Cameron disappointed you?" Charisse asked.

"It's nothing serious, but right after we got here, he left to go home."

"Just like that?" Whitney asked.

"Well, not just like that, but when I said I couldn't have sex with him, he all of a sudden started talking about how tired he was and how he needed some rest."

"Hmmph," Charisse said. "I don't know why you keep wasting your time with a man like that anyway. Especially someone who won't marry you."

"Because I love him," I said, now wishing I hadn't brought the subject up.

"But it's like Tina Turner says, 'What's love got to do with it?' " Charisse continued. "Plus, if he loves you the way he claims, then why hasn't he put a ring on your finger?"

"Why do you always have to be so negative?" Whitney chimed in.

"I'm just being real, because the Bible says, 'He that committeth fornication sinneth against his own body.' God doesn't want any of us—"

"Taylor, you know what?" Whitney interrupted. "Forget Charisse. You do what you feel is best for you. If you're not happy with the way things are going, then sit down and talk to Cameron about it. But don't just end your relationship with him."

"You're right," I said. "And Charisse, just for the record, I do know that fornicating is wrong, and it's not like I'm proud about doing it. But I'm not perfect either. I wish I could be, but I'm not. I have to pray about the sins I commit just like everyone else does."

"Charisse isn't perfect either, are you, Charisse?" Whitney said.

"Taylor, I'll tell Brianna to call you and I'll talk to you later, okay?" Charisse said.

"Fine," I said, and Charisse hung up.

"Can you believe that witch?" Whitney said. "I'm getting to the point where I can't stand her."

"I can see that, but what's really going on with you guys?"

"Nothing. I'm just sick of Charisse talking down to you and me like we're children. She does that crap to Marvin all the time, right in front of everybody, but I'm not putting up with it anymore."

"Yeah, but what did you and she argue about yesterday, because things seem a lot worse than usual."

"I wasn't planning on telling you this, and that's why I didn't bring it up when I called you two nights ago. But Charisse was saying how crazy and irresponsible you were for not taking your medicine and that Cameron wasn't worth a thing if he wasn't making sure you took care of yourself. And then when I wouldn't discuss anything about you, she started ragging on me about my weight."

"Oh really?"

Maybe I shouldn't have been shocked, but it really bothered me that Charisse had spoken so rudely about me behind my back. Especially when I had always defended her to people who didn't like her or who thought she had mental issues.

"That's why I let her know that she hasn't always been the saint she claims to be now," Whitney said.

"Meaning what?"

"Meaning that I know things about Charisse."

"Like?"

"Like things you won't want to believe."

"Is it that bad?"

"Trust me, you won't ever look at her the same again."

Chapter 10

CHARISSE

BRANDON? Brianna? Let's go."

It was already eight-thirty, and for as long as Charisse could remember she had never been late for Sunday school. Even as a small child, she'd never arrived at church even once after nine o'clock, and these children of hers would not change her tradition. Sunday school, like her pastor's sermon, was nourishment for the soul and she didn't want to miss any of it. As a matter of fact, she was considering the idea of teaching the adult women's class herself. The superintendent had asked her about it just a few weeks ago, but now it was time to think more seriously about it. She loved reading the Bible, she loved being in church, and she loved discussing God's Word. So, it was only fitting that she would take on this type of responsibility. As far as she was concerned, she was the perfect person for the job.

Charisse grabbed her keys and saw Brandon hurrying down the stairs. But Brianna walked slowly, practically dragging her feet. It was almost as if she did it just to irritate Charisse, and Charisse wanted to yank her by her throat. And she just might have done it if today hadn't been the Sabbath. Like the fourth commandment outlined, she remembered the Sabbath and kept it holy. But tomorrow would be different. Tomorrow would be Monday and Charisse wouldn't be so lenient. Instead, she would chastise Brianna the way Proverbs 22:15 had instructed her to. "Foolishness is bound in the heart of a child, but the rod of correction shall drive it far from him."

It was one of her favorite scriptures and it was unfortunate that thousands of parents were ignoring it. There were far too many who were sparing the rod and spoiling the child, and Charisse refused to be one of them. She would not go to hell for that or any other reason.

"See you guys later," Marvin said when they all walked into the kitchen. He was sitting at the table reading his stupid newspaper.

"I don't know why you can't come with us," Charisse said.

"I'm not going because I don't feel like it. And if you want to know the truth, that pastor of yours is not someone I wanna listen to anyway. All he does is speak about money and prosperity and it just seems to me that he should be more concerned about saving souls."

"He preaches about that all the time."

"Not when I used to go."

"Well then, you just weren't there enough."

"Maybe. Maybe not. But I still don't care for him."

Remember the Sabbath day to keep it holy. She recited those words in her head over and over so that she wouldn't have to curse Marvin out. She was trying her best to stay calm.

"Kids, let's go," she said, walking toward the garage.

"Bye, Daddy," Brianna said, kissing her father.

Brandon followed suit. "See ya, Dad."

"See ya."

"Will you be here when we get back?" Charisse asked.

"More than likely."

"Look, Marvin, either you will or you won't."

"Like I said, more than likely."

"Brandon, you and your sister go get in the car and I'll be out in a minute."

Marvin folded his arms and stared at her.

She shut the door behind the children and asked, "Why are you doing this?"

"Why am I doing what, Charisse?"

"Why are you acting this way? Like you don't care about anything. Like I'm your worst enemy."

"Because you don't care anything about me."

"How can you say that?"

"Remember last week when I told you that I cared about you but that I wanted us to get counseling? And you refused?"

"So because I won't do what you say, you're going to punish me for it?"

"Call it whatever you want, but just know that I'm only here because of my children. If it weren't for them, I would have left you a while ago."

Charisse glanced at her watch and saw that it was eight-forty. She couldn't believe she was actually going to be late. It was obvious that Satan was causing these problems on purpose. He didn't want her to be on time and he was using Marvin, clearly one of his head warriors, to distract her.

"Marvin, I guess I don't understand what's going on. Is it another woman? What?"

He laughed and shook his head in disbelief. "Another woman? Charisse, please. This is all your fault and your fault only. So don't try to blame this on someone else."

"Look, Marvin, I'm not stupid. Nobody changes overnight the way you have. Not after having the perfect marriage the way we did."

Now he laughed even louder.

"Perfect? Is that what you think? Charisse, the only reason our marriage was perfect to you was because you controlled everything."

"But why are you all of a sudden complaining about it now?"

"Baby . . . I woke up. It's as simple as that."

How in the world could this be happening? And why hadn't she seen it coming? How could she have been so blind and not paid any attention to what had been evolving? This was such a hard reality to take, and while she hated Marvin for changing on her, she felt sad—a feeling she'd rarely felt in her whole adult life. She had always been so much stronger than that. So much more confident and in control of her situations. And the idea of this man leaving her all alone with Brandon and Brianna made her uneasy. She certainly would never want her mother finding out. She would never want anyone, not even her friends, learning that her marriage was a lie. That it was no longer happy and Christian-like.

She didn't want anyone to know that Marvin was now possessed by the devil.

"Tell me what you want me to do," she said.

"I told you before. I want us to see a professional."

"What about Pastor? He counsels people all the time."

"You just don't get it, do you?"

"Marvin, what better person could we talk to? Pastor is a true man of God and right now that's what we need."

"No."

"Why not?

"Either we find someone with a real counseling degree or just forget it."

"Pastor does have a degree."

"What kind? An honorary one?"

"It's still a degree."

"But it's not good enough for me. Plus, I don't trust that man as far as I can throw him. I don't trust any man who has a history of picking up prostitutes."

"That was twenty years ago."

"I don't care if it was a hundred."

"But—"

"But nothing. Either we find a reputable therapist or we continue living just like we are."

She glanced at her watch again. She wanted to leave the house right now, but it was time she set Marvin straight once and for all. She'd been pleading with him like a child, doing something she had never done before, but enough was enough. It was high time she put him in his place the way her mother had taught her to. It was time she stopped playing this little game of his and reminded him that she was in charge.

"Marvin, I want you to listen to me and I want you to listen real good. We're not seeing any therapist, you're not going out to any bars again, and this ridiculous idea about you doing whatever you want to do is over with."

"You think so?"

"I *know* so."

"Well, if I were you, I'd think again."

"Don't push me, Marvin. I'm begging you not to do that."

"And if you know what's good for you, you won't push me either."

"Push you to do what?"

"Tell your mother about that insurance policy your brother left for her."

Charisse was stunned. Her heart raced and she tried diligently to catch her breath. Marvin's news flash had knocked the wind out of her.

"Yeah, that's right. I know all about that. You thought you had me so trained, but girl, I know more than you realize."

"My brother left that policy for me."

"No he didn't. He left the whole two hundred thousand dollars to your mother and somehow you collected all of it. To this day, I don't know how you got them to send it to you. And then you were slick enough to open an account in your name and your mother's, deposit the check in it, transfer it out, and then close the account like it never existed."

"You don't even know what you're talkin' about. There was never any joint account, and I'm telling you again, Johnny left every dime of that money to me."

"Charisse. I saw the paperwork with my own eyes."

He couldn't have. And if he had, how could she have been so careless? How could she have misjudged what he was capable of? He'd had no right snooping around in her personal files or anything else that belonged to her.

"My mother will never believe a word you say," she warned.

"Really," he said, walking over to the phone. "Why don't we call her and see what happens. Let's just call up Mommy Dearest and see how this plays out."

Charisse jumped in front of him. "No, Marvin. Please don't do that."

"That's what I thought."

"I can't believe you're doing this to me. Your own wife."

"I can't believe a lot of things, but that's beside the point. What matters now is that I know what I know, and if you don't change your attitude, I'm calling your mother."

Charisse thought long and hard, trying to figure out how she'd allowed this to happen. How she'd allowed Marvin to slip right through her fingers and get the best of her.

"It's not like you have any proof," she said, preparing to head up to the attic where the evidence was stored. If only she could get to it and get rid of it, she wouldn't have a thing to worry about.

But Marvin stopped her in her tracks. "I made copies weeks ago."

Charisse turned to look at him. She was violently enraged, but the thought of her mother discovering the truth quickly settled her down. Her mother wouldn't think twice about killing her, especially over such a large sum of money. She would call the police and tell them what she'd done like it was nothing. As it was, she had killed some boy during her teen years, claiming that he'd tried to rape her, and she had gotten away with it.

"I hate I ever married you," she said.

"Believe me, the feeling is mutual."

"Then I guess you were lying every time you said you loved me."

"No, I was telling the truth. And even now, I do still love you, but only as the mother of my children. I stopped loving you as my wife a long time ago. Even when we had sex I only gave it to you because you wanted it."

Brandon opened the door and stuck his head through it. "Mom, what's taking you so long? It's almost nine o'clock."

Charisse dropped down in one of the chairs. "We're not going."

"Why?"

"We're just not. So go turn off the car and tell Brianna to come inside."

Brandon stood for a few seconds, obviously confused, and then went back outside.

"So, where does this leave us?" she asked Marvin.

"I keep telling you. We have to get counseling. It might not make a difference for our marriage, but it will for the kids."

Charisse stood and walked out of the kitchen. She walked upstairs to their bedroom and slammed the door behind her.

What was she going to do? If only she could dispose of him and get away with it. But she would never be so lucky. If only she could kick him out of the house and then file for a divorce. The only problem was he knew her secret. And she believed him when he said he would squeal to her mother about it. She could tell from the way he'd looked at her that he was serious. He was thrilled that he had something to threaten her with.

And she was scared to death. She would never let on that she would do just about anything to keep him quiet and that she would, against her will, go see a marriage counselor. She would even see a family therapist for the four of them. She despised the whole idea of it, but she knew she didn't have a choice. Her mother, of course, wouldn't be happy about her new marital arrangement, specifically the part where Marvin was now telling *her* what to do, so she would never tell her mother the truth. She would tell Mattie Lee that she'd boiled the water as planned but how Marvin had fallen to his knees and apologized to her, begging for her forgiveness. That way her mother wouldn't have anything to complain about or criticize her for. She would pat Charisse on the back for handling her business the way any real woman should have.

Charisse slipped off her shoes and dress and then sat down on the side of her bed. She thought about her brother and how she'd pleaded with him to add her to his insurance policy, but he'd never gotten around to doing it. Not because he hadn't wanted to but because he'd been lazy and irresponsible the same as most other men she knew. If only he'd done what she'd advised him to do, she wouldn't be in this predicament to begin with. She would never have to bow down to Marvin like she was spineless.

But as far as she was concerned, bowing down was only temporary. She would pretend that she truly wanted to work things out with him and she would even try to get along with Brianna in the process. She would be the pleasant little wife that Marvin was forcing her to be.

She would do all of this, but in the end, he would be sorry. He would wish that he had stayed out of her business. He would never threaten any one person he could think of ever again.

Chapter 11

Taylor

IT HAD BEEN FIVE YEARS since I'd joined Martin, Sable & Wesson, but no matter how many years passed by, I still felt proud each time I walked through those glass double doors. This was one of the top firms in downtown Chicago, and it was an honor just to be employed by them. Let alone be considered for a partnership. Although it was for that very reason that Skyler and I had always been at odds with each other. He'd been hired maybe twelve months before me and had made partner just one year ago, but I deliberately upstaged him during every staff meeting. Which he didn't like because it made him look bad in front of the other partners and there was nothing he could do about it. That is, except harass me every chance he got.

I strolled through the reception area, speaking to the receptionists, and continued down the long, plush-carpeted hallway to my corner office. About a month ago, I'd won a marital settlement for a woman who'd caught her millionaire husband sleeping with her sister, and the partners had been grateful. As a token of their appreciation, they'd replaced my old furniture, which had still looked untouched, with upscale contemporary pieces. Mahogany was my favorite wood grain, so I was loving my desk, bookcases, and file cabinets. The black leather chairs and sofa finalized the package. It was another sign that I would eventually be promoted.

I read a couple of interoffice memos and then picked up a case file that Jim Sable had left on my desk. There was a note attached asking if I could review it and then outline a possible strategy. The case involved a woman who'd lost two fingers on the job, but as soon as I saw that she worked for the same company as my father, I knew I was going to pass on it. The partners wouldn't see a problem with it, but for me, it was total conflict of interest. For all I knew, my father might be a witness and I couldn't take a chance on it. I never mixed business with personal situations, not even remotely.

I was skimming through some other items on my desk that needed attention when Skyler walked into my office. He was wearing a sharp navy blue suit and I could tell he'd paid a pretty penny for it, probably nothing less than seven or eight hundred dollars, and it was worth it. To put it plainly, his attire looked good on him.

"So, how was the conference?"

"Fine."

"Did you learn anything?"

"Don't I always?" I knew I'd missed eighty percent of it, but what Skyler didn't know wouldn't hurt him.

"Did you see the file Jim left for you?"

"Yeah, but I can't do it."

"And why not?"

"Because my father works for the company that we're planning to sue."

"And?"

"And, I'm not doing it."

"You know, for someone who hasn't made partner, you sure do call a lot of shots around here."

"Well, if I were you, I wouldn't worry about it. Jim is the person who gave this case to me, and he's the only person I need to discuss it with."

"But in case you've forgotten, I'm a partner, too, and I have just as much say-so over what happens at this firm."

"Maybe in your dreams."

"No, I'm talking reality."

"Skyler, look. I have a lot of work to catch up on, so if you don't mind, I'd like to get back to it."

"You're just mad because I'm already sitting in the place where you want to be."

"But what good is it doing you? You might get paid more, but it's not like you're more knowledgeable than me. And you certainly don't receive any more attention than I do from the people who work here."

"You're just jealous, Taylor. You've always been jealous and I feel sorry for you."

"Feel whatever you want, but right now I need you to do it outside my office."

Skyler laughed sarcastically, looked at me, and then left.

Geez. What a jerk. And after all this time, why did I always let him get to me? He was really starting to annoy me, but no matter what happened, I would never let him know it. I would smile and pretend that I looked forward to our daily insults.

After meeting with two of my clients and making an appointment with Dr. Green, I decided to phone Whitney. Today was the day she was starting her new diet and I wanted to see how she was doing.

"This is Whitney, can I help you?"

"So, how's everything going?"

"Girl, don't even ask."

"That bad, huh?"

"You know it always is. Especially the first day."

"Well, what did you have for breakfast?" I asked, opening a client's file.

"Some low-carb bar that I read about in a magazine, but it hasn't done a thing except piss me off."

I couldn't help laughing.

"Well, maybe you should eat something else."

"Like what?"

"I don't know. What can you have?"

"Meat, cheese, eggs, and a few other things, but that's pretty much it."

"Oh, that's right, you're giving up carbs. Well, why don't you run out and get a steak."

"I guess. But it's amazing how the last thing I want is what I can actually have. And don't get me started on my sugar cravings."

"Well, just hang in there, because this will all be worth it in the long run."

"That's what I keep telling myself, but I gotta be honest, I don't know if I can do it."

"Yes, you can. I know it's hard, but if you can just make it through tonight, things will be a lot easier tomorrow."

"Maybe. And hopefully I won't murder me somebody in the process. I saw one of my coworkers eating some potato chips and all I could think was how I wanted to attack him. Girl, I could actually see myself wrestling him to the ground and grabbing his little snack from him."

We both laughed. Whitney was hilarious.

"Well, I'm glad you didn't," I said.

"I am, too. It would be a shame to get fired over some junk food, wouldn't it?"

"That it would."

"So, how's work?" she asked.

"Busy. I was only gone three days, but it feels like thirty."

"And what about Skyler? Did he mess with you today?"

"He tried, but I pretty much blew him off."

"He's a trip."

"Don't I know it," I said, removing my earring.

"And what about Cameron? I know you saw him Saturday, but what about yesterday?"

"We drove over and went to church with my parents and then to dinner. So, I guess everything is okay. Actually, he seemed fine."

"Maybe he was just having a bad day on Friday."

"Maybe. Who knows."

"And hey, did you make your doctor's appointment?" she asked.

"I did it right before I called you and I go on Friday."

"That's good. Because maybe now you'll be able to find out what's going on."

"I hope so, because it's really starting to stress me out."

"I can imagine."

"You know, this is off the subject, but I still can't believe what you told me about Charisse," I said, still pretty shocked.

"Most people wouldn't. Not with the way she acts."

"To be honest, I feel sorry for her."

"I used to, but not anymore. Not with her treating me the way she does."

"I hear what you're saying, but Whit, the three of us have been friends for a very long time and nothing is worth losing that."

"But T, she does the same thing to you, too."

"I know, but it's just not that serious. I don't like a lot of things that Charisse says or does, but I still care about her. And while I know you don't want to hear this, I still want us to get together on Wednesday, the same as we always do."

"Unh-unh. I'm not dealing with Charisse right now."

"Whit?"

"I'm not."

"Not even if she apologizes?"

"Not even if she apologizes."

I could tell that Whitney wasn't going to budge, so it was time I reminded her of a few things.

"Do you remember the time your mother got mad at you and said she wasn't sending you any more spending money? And how Charisse went to the bank on campus, drew out half of her own money, and put it into your account?"

Whitney didn't say anything. But I continued anyway.

"Or what about the time she gave you her credit card and let you buy five complete outfits because your mother said she wasn't buying you anything. It was just before we left home to start our junior year, remember?"

"And you're telling me all of this because . . . ?"

"Charisse is a real friend to you."

"I know she *used* to be a real friend, but I wouldn't say she is now."

"You're just being stubborn."

"No, I'm tired of her self-righteousness. I'm tired of her whole attitude."

"But you know she's always been this way."

"Yeah, but now she's worse and I can't take it."

"Okay, then what about ten years ago when she loaned you the rest of the down payment you needed to buy your house with? If I'm not mistaken, she gave you five thousand dollars."

"But you loaned me the same amount," Whitney said.

"Yeah, and why did I do it?"

"Because you love me."

"And Charisse did it because?"

"She wanted something to hang over my head."

I tried not to laugh, but I couldn't help it.

Whitney laughed with me.

"But seriously," I said, "you know Charisse cares about you and that she's always been a friend to you. She's always been a friend to both of us."

"Do we have to talk about this?" Whitney asked.

"Yeah, we do. And I'm calling Charisse and telling her that we'll meet her at the restaurant for lunch."

"Fine. But if she says anything out of the way to me, I'm leaving. And then I'm not speaking to her again."

"You don't mean that."

"You don't think so?"

"No. I don't."

"Well, come Wednesday, just watch me. If Charisse criticizes me in the smallest way, I'm going off."

"I'm sure you won't have to do that."

"Then, you'd better warn her up front . . . especially with me not being able to eat like I want to. Shoot, I'm just dying to tear someone's head off."

"You're too much."

"I'm serious, T, so if I were you, I'd tell her to watch how she treats me."

"Okay, I'll talk to her. But in all fairness, I don't want you scrutinizing every single thing she says and trying to make something out of it. Because you know how you do."

"Yeah, I can be a trip when I want to, can't I?"

"Oh, let me count the ways," I teased her.

"I'm only like that because I've taken so much crap from so many people and I'm not doing that anymore. From now on, I'm not trying to satisfy anyone except myself."

"You know I've always told you to do that anyway. I've always told you to stop worrying about what other people think or what they have to say. It's the only way you'll ever be happy."

"Well, I'm finally taking your advice."

"I'm glad. Because you should have done it a long time ago."

"Better late than never, though."

"This is true. Well, I hate to cut this short, but I'd better get back to work. I have court all day tomorrow and I need to make sure I'm ready."

"I need to get going myself, but call me later tonight so I can tell you how my visit to the health club went."

"I will."

After hanging up the phone, I worked straight through lunch, stopping only to grab a sandwich from the vending machine. Thankfully, I felt back to normal, because it was now five o'clock and I still felt strong enough to work a few more hours. Cameron and I had made plans to go out for dinner, but it was obvious that I wouldn't be able to make it.

I dialed his office to inform him.

"This is Cameron."

"Hey, you."

"Hey, yourself. You getting ready to leave?"

"Actually, no, and that's why I'm calling. It looks like I'm going to be here for most of the evening."

"Oh, okay. Do you want me to bring you something?"

"No, I'm fine, but thanks."

I wanted to ask him why he didn't sound all that disappointed. But maybe I was just being paranoid because of the way he'd acted on Friday.

"Maybe we can do dinner tomorrow instead," he offered.

"Yeah, that should be good. I have court, but chances are I won't be coming back to the office when I leave there."

"Then let's plan on it."

"I'll give you a call later."

"Don't work too hard and, hey, I love you."

"I love you, too, Cameron."

I hung up the phone and wondered why I couldn't shake the eerie feeling I was having about us. Cameron hadn't said anything suspicious but it just seemed to me that our not getting together wasn't a major concern to him. It was almost as if he was fine one way or the other.

But the thing is, I didn't have time to focus on whatever was going on with him. My clients expected top-notch work from me and I couldn't allow my personal matters to interfere with that. I couldn't allow distractions of any kind to hinder my reputation.

All I could hope was that Cameron wasn't seeing another woman.

Chapter 12

Whitney

I WALKED INSIDE the health club, swiped my ID card, and proceeded toward the locker room. My original plan was to work out at home until my weight loss package arrived, but since Telecom paid for all management staff to have their own membership, I decided to make use of it. And it wasn't like I hadn't been here before, because I'd come here three weeks straight when I'd first become a member, but then I'd given it up for no apparent reason. Although I hadn't been all that comfortable with working out in front of people I didn't know—specifically in front of men. But I'd also been ashamed to undress in front of some of the women, who'd looked like Halle Berry. Women who'd had tiny waists, flat stomachs, and curves in all the right places.

Inside the humid locker room, I found an empty locker and opened up my duffel bag. I pulled out a pair of double X sweatpants and a T-shirt that had my company's logo on it. Then I waited for some of the other members to clear out. When there were only two of us left, I quickly removed my street clothing and put on my athletic ensemble. The woman down the row from me was actually bigger than I was and I couldn't deny that

I was happy about it. It was a relief to know that I wouldn't be the fattest person out there huffing and puffing on a treadmill, praying that I wouldn't pass out.

I forced all of my belongings into the locker, shut the door, and locked it. Then I went out to the equipment area. There were easily fifty people riding bicycles, stair-stepping, walking, rowing, using the elliptical machine, and lifting weights. All of the treadmills were being used, and now I wondered if coming here straight from work had been a good idea. I wasn't thrilled about the option of showing up at the crack of dawn, though, either, because it was bad enough having to be at work by eight.

After waiting five minutes or so, I hopped onto one of the bicycles, but what a grave mistake that was. The seat couldn't have been more than three inches wide and my butt quickly swallowed it whole. The woman next to me looked on in horror and I was so humiliated. Still, I decided to show her just how brave I was. I gripped the handlebars, set the digital timer, and starting pumping like a mad woman. I rode the machine for so long that I broke into a thick sweat. Then I started panting like the dog in my neighborhood. I did this after riding for all of two minutes and the woman next to me looked worried. I'm sure she thought I was threatening cardiac arrest, but once again, I showed *her*.

I got off and walked away while I was still able.

But now what was I going to do? I still wanted to tackle the treadmill, so I guess I would just have to wait. And wait. And wait. Until someone finally got off of one of them. It was amazing how some of the patrons were walking at least three to four miles per hour, yet they were watching television or reading a book. Some of them were even chatting and, get this, laughing with their workout partners. They actually looked like they were having a good time. Oh, how I wished I could be in their shoes. How I wish I could do any exercise for more than a half hour and leave this place feeling good.

After more waiting, I turned and went over to the water fountain, but when I arrived some guy blocked my path and smiled at me.

"Want a drink?" he said.

"Well, that was the plan," I responded. I spoke in a salty manner, but it was only because I was self-conscious and didn't want him seeing me this way. The man was breathtaking and I wanted him to see me *after* I lost my weight.

"Oh," he said, moving out of the way. "I'm sorry."

I leaned over and drank at least a gallon of water, hoping he would be gone when I raised up. But no such luck.

"You must be new," he said.

"Not really. I used to come here a long time ago."

"Well, I'm glad you decided to come back."

Wait a minute. Was this Negro making a fat joke? If he was, being tall, chocolate, and beautiful wasn't going to help him.

"What are you trying to say?" I finally said.

"That I'm glad you came back so I could have this chance to meet you."

It was obvious that I'd jumped the gun. Either that or he'd seen the perturbed look on my face and was trying to fix what he'd insinuated.

"What did you *think* I was saying?" he continued.

"I wasn't sure."

"Well, I'm sure."

"About what?"

"How beautiful you are and how I'd like to take you out if you're not seeing anyone."

He couldn't have been serious. Not with me standing here looking like a big blimp. I mean, was his vision impaired or was he simply trying to be funny? And just in case, I looked around for hidden cameras. For all I knew, this random meeting might have been intentional. Worse, he might have been recruiting for some fat girl reality show.

"You don't even know me," I said.

"But I can get to know you, right?"

I looked away from him because he was sounding too serious.

"Does that bother you?" he asked.

"What?"

"The fact that I'm attracted to you and that I'm so straightforward?"

"No. Not really."

"Good. Because this is the way I am. I say what I mean and mean what I say."

I was starting to feel awkward and I wasn't sure how to respond to him.

"What's your name?" he asked.

I paused until I remembered what it was.

"Whitney."

He reached out his hand. "It's nice to meet you, Whitney. I'm Rico."

"It's nice meeting you, too."

"So, are you waiting for one of the machines?"

"The treadmill, if it ever becomes available. What about you?"

"Nah. I've been here for almost two hours and I'm all worked out."

"Oh."

"So, when can we get together?"

I tried to control myself, but I could feel myself blushing.

"I don't know."

"What about tonight?"

"No, I don't think so."

"Why, because you don't know me?"

"Yeah, that's part of it. But it's also because it'll be late when I leave here."

"What if I just wait on you and then we can grab a bite to eat when you finish?"

"Maybe another time," I said.

"Okay, Whitney, look. I think it's time for me to explain my intentions. I'm really attracted to you and I don't care that you're heavier than you want to be. You're a beautiful woman and I can tell you have a beautiful personality."

I was speechless. I had had this happen many times before, men claiming that they didn't care about the weight and then eventually realizing they couldn't handle it.

"So, what do you say?" he said.

"I don't know. And to be honest, I don't think you know either. I mean have you ever dated a heavy woman before?"

"No, but does that matter?"

"Yeah, sort of. Because at least if you'd dated someone like me before, you would know what to expect."

"I disagree, because size doesn't have anything to do with who you are internally."

I glanced across the room and saw two treadmills opening up.

"Like I said, maybe another time. Maybe I'll see you again and we can exchange phone numbers or something."

Rico didn't say anything but he stared at me in the sweetest way. He leaned his body against the wall and folded his arms, watching me walk away.

I straddled the treadmill, set the speed and time, and began the workout I'd come here for. I tried not to look in Rico's direction, but I couldn't help myself and gazed over there. To my disappointment, he was gone.

Now, I wondered if I'd made a huge mistake. I wondered if maybe he might have been the man of my dreams and not at all like the rest.

I strode for ten minutes without any real difficulty, but only because I'd set the speed fairly low. I took one determined step after another, occasionally looking toward the water fountain, but there was no Rico. I could have kicked myself for not taking him up on his offer. I'd been worried about being hurt again, but now I wished I'd given him a chance.

Although now it was too late and it was best just to forget about him.

Back in the locker room, I didn't have the courage to remove every stitch of clothing and jump into the shower. Not in front of so many women. As a matter of fact, I didn't even have the nerve to change back into the outfit I'd worn here. So, I gathered everything together, stuffed it inside my bag, and headed out to the parking lot.

The night air whipped a sharp chill right through me and now I hurried to my car. But then I heard someone yelling my name.

I turned around and saw Rico standing near the building. Apparently I'd walked right past him without paying any attention, but I was glad that he'd stopped me.

"I thought you'd left," I said.

"Not without saying good-bye to you."

His smile was making me crazy.

"So, are you still not interested?" he asked.

"Actually, I never said that."

"No, but you don't wanna go out with me."

"I never said that either."

"Maybe not in those exact words, but that's what you meant."

"You're right. I did. But now I've had some time to think."

"About?"

"Going out with you."

"Then my offer still stands."

"And I would gladly take you up on it except I didn't take a shower."

"Oh," he said, and we both laughed.

"It's not that I'm a filthy person or anything like that, but I knew I was going straight home to do it there."

"That's understandable."

"But what about tomorrow or the next day?"

"That would work, too, but I guess I was still hoping to see you tonight."

"Well, the only thing is, I live in Covington Park, and it'll take me twenty minutes just to get home."

"And I live in Chicago Heights, so that's only one suburb over."

"But by the time I get cleaned up, it'll be almost nine-thirty."

"This is true. So, I'll tell you what, why don't I just follow you home?"

Uh-oh. I'd been hoping he wouldn't ask me that. Partly because I wasn't in the habit of bringing men home the first night I met them, and partly because I didn't trust myself being around Rico—not when there would be a bed in close proximity. As it was, it was nine weeks and counting since the last time I'd been with a man.

"I don't know," I said for lack of a better response.

"I won't stay long. I promise."

"Right."

"I'm serious. I won't stay any longer than you want me to."

I repositioned my duffel bag and grabbed both of my arms. The cold air was causing me to shiver.

"I know I'm going to regret this," I said, "but fine. You can come by. Only for a short while, though."

"Lead the way," he said, and walked over to his Range Rover.

I couldn't believe I was doing this. Allowing a complete stranger to come home with me, knowing that he might be Rico the Ripper. Knowing that I might wind up raped, stabbed to death, and plastered across the front page of the *Tribune*. But for some reason I wasn't afraid. It was true that I didn't know anything about this man, but there was a certain pleasantness that I sensed about him. He was straightforward the way he had explained, and I could tell he was a gentleman.

And I was glad to have someone to spend time with. Someone other than Taylor, Charisse, and my coworkers.

What I hoped was that Rico would still be coming around, at least until my class reunion was over.

Chapter 13

Whitney

"HAVE A SEAT," I said after disarming the security system. Rico and I had just walked into my house and I was glad there wasn't anything lying around. While I was growing up, my mother had always been a stickler for keeping every room in order at all times, and it was the one good trait I had inherited from her.

"You have a very nice home," he said.

"Thank you."

"And the decorating is straight, too. You got skills, girl."

"Thanks," I said, walking into the kitchen. "Can I get you anything to drink? Soda? Juice? La Croix?"

"I never do soda. But I'll take bottled water if you have it."

I opened the cupboard above the sink, pulled out a crystal glass, and grabbed a bottle of water from the refrigerator.

"Can I get you something to eat?" I asked when I came back into the family room.

"No, I'm fine. I'll probably pick up something on the way home."

Rico was sitting on the sofa, so I sat across from him on the love seat.

He took a sip of his water and looked at me. "Why are you sitting all the way over there?"

"No special reason," I said, although I was still thinking about the shower I hadn't taken yet.

And he must have figured the same thing because he didn't force the issue.

"How long have you lived here?" he said, admiring the surroundings.

"Almost ten years."

"That's a long time."

"Yeah, I guess it is."

"I just purchased my first home two years ago and it's a great feeling."

"You said you live in Chicago Heights, right?"

"Yeah. I've lived in a couple of other suburbs, too, but Chicago Heights is where I grew up. Plus, my parents and my sisters are still there."

"It's good when you can live close to family."

"For sure," he agreed, and drank some of his water. "So, what about you?"

"I grew up in Aurora, but when my two best friends bought homes out here, I decided to do the same thing."

"Nothin' wrong with that. So, have the three of you been friends for a long time?"

"Charisse and I have been friends since we were in seventh grade, and we met Taylor while we were in college."

"What school did you go to?"

"Northwestern."

"Man, you were practically right at home then."

"I know, but that's where the partial scholarship and grants came from, so . . ."

"Is that why your friends went there, too?"

"Charisse had a partial like I did, plus her mother refused to pay out-of-state tuition. But Taylor got a free ride all four years."

"Wow. Did she play sports?"

"Nope. It was strictly academic. And then she went to Yale for law school."

"Well, if I ever need an attorney, let her know that I'll definitely be calling her."

We both laughed.

"Yeah, that is my girl of girls. And she's extremely intelligent. She scored in the top five percent nationally on her SAT exam."

"Those are the kinds of stories that make you feel proud."

"I know."

"So, what do you do for a living?" he asked, pouring more water into his glass.

"I'm a manager for Telecom Wireless."

"Then you've done pretty well yourself."

"I can't complain."

Rico leaned back on the sofa, making himself more comfortable. I picked up the selector and switched on the television, but I turned the volume down to a murmur.

"So, what about you?" I said. "Where did you graduate from?"

"Howard."

"Great school. What did you major in?"

"Accounting."

"Oh, okay."

"And I work for AIC Healthcare."

"Is that one of the PPOs?"

"It is. And there's a lot of room for advancement if I can ever pass the CPA exam."

"I'll bet."

"I took it two times right after college and then I sort of gave up on it. But my plan is to start back studying so that I can take it again next year or the following."

"I don't blame you, because I've been thinking about going back for my M.B.A. There's this accelerated program that I've been researching, so at some point I'm definitely wanting to do it."

"It's never too late."

"I turned thirty-eight this year, so a part of me was thinking that it was, but now I'm planning to just go for it."

"And I'm thirty-five, so I do know the feeling."

I'd been hoping that we were at least the same age, because my history with men who were younger than me wasn't good. Either they proved to be immature or they eventually realized that they didn't want to be with an older woman.

I glanced over at the television, unable to look at Rico.

"Does that bother you?" he asked.

"What?"

"Our age difference."

"Somewhat."

"Well, please don't let it, because I date women of all ages."

"And you don't prefer one over the other?"

"No. I don't. As long as a woman is good to me, I don't care if she's twenty or fifty."

"I feel the same way."

"You know," he said. "The more I sit here, I am getting a little hungry. Do you have any fruit?"

"I've got apples, but that's pretty much it. I started this low-carb diet today, so I can't have a lot of fruit in the beginning. Do you want me to grab you one?"

"Please."

"I've got some cheese, too, if you want it. My grandmother used to eat them together, so I kinda picked up on it."

"Get outta here. My parents do the same thing. What kind do you have?"

"A block of cheddar."

"Then I'll take it."

I stood and walked back into the kitchen. When I returned I passed Rico a plate with a sliced Rome apple and a wedge of cheese.

"Can I ask you something?" I said.

"What's that?"

"And please don't be offended. But are you part Puerto Rican?"

He laughed. "It's my name that has you curious, right?"

"Well, actually, yes."

"No. My parents went to Puerto Rico on their honeymoon and my mother swears that I was conceived there, so she named me Rico."

"That's neat."

"From time to time I ask her how she knows for sure and she says because she was a virgin until the day she got married and six weeks later the doctor told her she was six weeks pregnant."

"Then it must be true."

"It is, but I like giving her a hard time."

I thought about sitting back down but I was starting to feel more and more sticky. I didn't think I smelled bad, but I'd learned years ago that women my size needed to shower and bathe more often than everyone else. There were so many creases and crevices that needed to be dealt with, and I made sure to pay careful attention to them.

"If you don't mind, I'm gonna take a shower."

"No problem. Go ahead. I'll just flip through the channels to see what's on."

"I won't be a minute, and if you want anything else to drink, just help yourself."

"I will."

I turned and walked down the hallway to my bedroom. When I closed the door, I leaned the back of my body against it. Just thinking about how fine Rico was made me breathless. The man looked good. And his personality was so in tune with mine. It was already apparent that I could sit and talk with him for hours. He was noticeably outgoing and all I could pray was that he wasn't trying to run any games on me. Such as robbing me blind as soon as he heard the shower running. But if he did, I knew I deserved it because the truth was still staring me in the face—the same as it had been at the health club. I didn't know a single thing about Rico.

I removed all of my clothing, slipped on a silk robe, and went into the bathroom. I started the shower and scanned the top of my vanity, which was filled with body products. The vanilla collection was my favorite, the scrub, shower gel, mist, and lotion.

I lined everything up, preparing to take it into the shower, but when I shed my robe I became depressed. It was the image I saw in the mirror that saddened me. I'd made it through an entire day, monitoring what I ate, but eight weeks was a long time. And then after my reunion, I would have to continue this same process if I wanted to lose the other fifty.

But the advantage I had this time was that my normal manner of thinking was different. In the past, I would diet when I knew there was an upcoming event and then hold a bingefest as soon as it was over. But now I realized that good eating habits would have to become a new way of life for me. And I wouldn't stick to simply eliminating carbohydrates either. I was doing this early on because it was a quick way to lose weight, but I would eventually learn to eat more healthily. No red meat, if any meat at all. More fruits and vegetables. A lot of water and a lot less refined sugar.

I stepped into the shower and closed the glass and chrome door behind me. The water was hotter than most people could stand, but I loved it. I stood there, savoring every moment, turning slowly, making a 360-degree turn. I did this for five to six minutes and then opened the shower gel.

I squirted it into the palm of my hands and rubbed it across my body. I started at my shoulders and moved down to my toes. The smell was most satisfying and I didn't want this to end.

Next, I rinsed off the gel, opened the jar of scrub, scooped out a portion, and massaged every area. My body always felt smooth whenever I used this. When I finished, I rinsed off the residue and turned off the water. Then I dried my body and sprayed mist over it. Afterward, I sealed everything I'd used with lotion. There was nothing like layering any sweet-smelling scent.

As I reentered the bedroom, I tied my robe the rest of the way and jumped when I saw Rico sitting at the foot of my king-size bed.

My first thought was to ask him what he was doing, but when I tried, nothing came out. I wasn't sure if it was because I was terribly in shock or if it was because I didn't mind him being there.

"I hope you don't think I'm trying to use you or disrespect you because I'm not. But the truth of the matter is, I wanna make love to you."

I guess he was a lot more straightforward than I realized. He'd told me that from the start, but I certainly hadn't expected anything like this.

"Aren't you going to say anything?" he asked.

"Like what?"

"I don't know. That you want me just as badly or that you want me to get out. Because I'll understand either way and I won't be upset with you."

"The problem I have with this is that we don't know each other. And I don't want to be in some wham, bam, thank you ma'am situation come tomorrow morning."

"And I promise you, it won't be that way. I'm really and truly attracted to you and I'd like us to keep seeing each other long after tonight is over with," he said, standing and walking toward me.

My nerves went haywire and Rico must have noticed.

"Why are you so uncomfortable? Is it your weight? Because I'm telling you, I don't have any issues with that. If you want to know the truth, I'm fascinated by it. I've always wanted to date someone your size, but you're the first person to catch my eye like this," he confessed, and grabbed both sides of my face. "You really are beautiful, Whitney, and don't ever let anyone tell you different."

Then he kissed me slowly and gently. I kissed him back and after seconds we kissed rough and uncontrollably. We kissed just the way I liked it and I wanted him. I needed him to make love to me immediately.

But Rico had other plans.

He backed away, untied the belt to my robe, and stared at me seductively. I was feeling self-conscious again, but not as much as before. Within seconds he took me into his arms and kissed me again. He wrapped his arms around my waist and I wrapped mine around his neck. He kissed my neck in all the right places, caressed my breasts, and then rubbed his hand back and forth between my legs.

I squirmed and moaned and pleaded with him to take me. But he wouldn't.

Instead, he kneeled to the floor and looked up at me.

I knew what he wanted me to do but I didn't have the heart to tell him: I couldn't spread my legs unless I lay on the bed. It was the only possible way with all the fat surrounding them.

But Rico didn't care about any of that and quickly found his way to my glory. Surprisingly, I opened my legs farther than I'd thought I could.

I rested my hands on his shoulders and whimpered like a child. Real tears actually fell down my face. The feeling was that ridiculously wonderful.

When I felt myself preparing to explode, I held his head with my right hand.

When it happened, I screamed at the top of my lungs and cried even harder.

Rico stood up and smiled at me, but he never said a word. He led me to the bed and I pulled back the rich purple duvet and tossed the matching throw pillows anywhere they wanted to land.

"Still think I'm just here to use you?" he asked.

At this point, I didn't care if he was or not. But I shook my head negatively and lay on my back.

Rico undressed his well-cut body and I learned very quickly why his hands and feet were so big.

I opened my legs, Rico lay on top of me and then slid inside. He moved in and out, slowly at first and then picking up speed. Now, he moaned with me.

"Oh." He sighed.

"Is it good to you, baby?" I asked.

"The best," he answered, groaning.

I bent my knees and Rico plowed into me even farther. He worked fast, rocking back and forth, and I gyrated my pelvis forcefully.

"Oh shoot," he spoke loudly. "Oh . . . my . . . goodness."

He breathed heavily and relaxed his body.

He lay there for a while and then raised his head up and moved to the side of me.

"Are you okay?" he asked.

"I'm fine."

"Was it worth it?"

I chuckled. "Do you really need me to answer that?"

"I guess not. And I meant what I said. You are the best. I don't know if I've ever been with a woman who felt this good."

"Maybe it's the cellulite," I joked.

He couldn't help laughing. "Are you always this critical of yourself?" he said, smoothing down my hair.

"I don't want to be, but sometimes it's better to make fun of myself so that I won't have to wait for other people to do it. Sometimes it's better to beat 'em to the punch."

"You should give yourself a lot more credit. You're a good person, and whether you realize it or not, you have a lot to offer."

"Like what?"

"You're smart, you have a good career, you own this immaculate home, and I can tell you have a big heart."

"But I'm still overweight."

"And?"

"And I don't want to be."

"But you're working on it, though, right?"

"Yeah, but I've got this class reunion coming up in eight weeks and I don't want to look like this."

"So, what's the plan? I know you're watching your carbs, but what else?"

"I ordered this workout program."

"Well, the bottom line is that you have to stay conscious of it every day. You have to wake up thinking about the proper food you're going to eat and what workout you're going to do. It has to become the most important thing in your life."

"I know, but that's still easier said than done."

"You want me to help you?"

I turned to look at him.

"I'm serious," he said. "You want me to?"

"You would do that?"

"Without a doubt. I know you ordered some program, but why don't I just train you at the health club three to four times a week?"

"Okay. And I'll pay you if you want."

"This is payment enough," he said, stroking my breasts.

"Will you stop?" I said, blushing.

"Why don't we start tomorrow?"

"Right after work?"

"Yep. The same time you came this evening, because that way I can get my own workout in before you get there."

"Okay, Rico, when do I wake up and what is it that you really want from me?"

"Why do you say that?"

"Because this is too good to be true."

"Why? Because we met only a few hours ago and we already had sex?"

"No. Because I weigh two hundred and fifty pounds and you can have any skinny woman you want."

"But I don't want just any woman. I'm interested in you."

I sighed deeply.

"You'll see," he said. "Come next year this time, you'll see that I'm still here."

Then he moved on top of me and said, "By the way, what color suit do you want me to wear to this class reunion of yours?"

Now I knew what heaven must have felt like.

Chapter 14

Charisse

"Marvin, what is it going to take?" Charisse asked, holding him around his waist.

"Time."

"How much time?"

"I don't know. I guess we've been through so much that I'm just not attracted to you anymore. I'm sorry if that hurts your feelings, but I need to be honest with you."

"But I love you, Marvin. I've always loved you."

"But you haven't always acted like it. You treated me like I was beneath you, and over a period of time, I started to hate you for it. And then last week when I told you I was going out, you hauled off and slapped me. And pushed me into the wall."

"I know, I know. And I'm sorry. Sometimes I get so angry that I blow things out of proportion."

"Well, it can't ever happen again."

"It won't. I promise."

Marvin moved his wife's arms away from him and walked away.

"Where are you going?"

"To get dressed for work."

"Why don't you stay home so we can talk?"

"I can't. I have a full calendar today."

"What about lunch?"

"I thought you were meeting Taylor and Whitney."

"I'm supposed to but they'll understand if I can't make it."

"No, you go, because I'll be too busy. The most I'll have time for is to get something from the cafeteria."

Marvin closed the bathroom door and Charisse heard him turn on the shower.

Asshole.

Today was Wednesday, only three days since Marvin had revealed what he knew about that policy, and already she was sick of begging and pleading. She was sick of lying, faking, and pretending that she loved him when deep down she wanted him dead.

But her hands were tied. She wasn't sure how this was all going to play out, but she was smart enough to know that she had to feign her affection toward him, otherwise he would tell her mother everything. Even now, Charisse still hadn't accepted what was happening to her. She'd spent hours on Sunday afternoon, again all day Monday and most of yesterday, trying to figure out how she'd lost control of her marriage. And when had she lost it? And when exactly had Marvin wised up? And found the balls to stand up to her? He had always been such a pathetic little wimp, and now he was acting like king of the jungle. He acted as though the entire world was his and he could do whatever he wanted with it.

And she'd even had to force a relationship with Brianna, something she'd never had to do before. Although she had to admit, it wasn't as bad as pretending with Marvin. With him, she had to pretend like she wanted him sexually when she didn't. Once upon a time, she'd wanted him to make love to her every other day and she'd told him exactly how to do it. She'd told him which way to move, at what speed, and when he could finally release himself. Their lovemaking had always been on her terms and her terms only.

But now things were different. Temporary, she reminded herself, but definitely very different. Meaning, she would continue to beg and plead until she arrived at a permanent solution. She would walk the walk and talk the talk but her thinking would not be in agreement. She would play the perfect wife until she found a way to get rid of him. She would do it without serving one day in prison.

Charisse left the bedroom and walked into Brianna's.

"Rise and shine, sleepyhead," she told her daughter.

Brianna pulled the covers closer to her neck but didn't say anything. She looked dumbfounded.

"Do you have anything in your dirty clothes basket?"

"Yes," Brianna said timidly, and looked toward the closet.

Charisse could tell she didn't know what to think or why her mother was treating her so nicely.

It was time Charisse set her mind at ease.

"Look, Brianna," she said, sitting down on the bed. "I know we've never been all that close and that I haven't been the mother I should've been, but those days are no more. What I want is for us to start doing things together and for you to realize that you can come to me about anything."

Brianna didn't move or blink.

"I mean it, honey. I don't want us at each other's throats the way we have been. You're my baby and I love you."

Charisse was so good that she'd almost fooled herself. She deserved an Academy Award for this one.

But Brianna did something she wasn't expecting.

"Mom, I'm so sorry," she said, coming from under the covers, practically leaping across the bed and hugging Charisse. She sobbed and wouldn't let go.

Charisse hugged her back but she wasn't sure what to do next. Charisse's mother had never hugged her and she would never approve of what she and Brianna were doing now. This was such uncommon ground compared to what Charisse had been used to. Compared to what she had been taught when she was growing up.

"Mom, I love you, too. I've always loved you, but I thought you didn't love me. You always act like you hate me."

Charisse didn't know what to say but for whatever reason she squeezed Brianna tighter. She pretended that she was Brianna and that Brianna was her mother. She closed her eyes and imagined her mother holding her in her arms more than thirty years ago. She pretended how happy those times had been. She imagined a life where there had been no beatings, no yelling, and no ridiculing. She pictured a life where her parents had loved each other and had never had an argument.

Charisse smiled and rocked back and forth with her mother but then reality set in. She remembered the extension cord, the back of her hand, and even, once, a baseball bat. She remembered all the horrible things her mother had done to her, and when she opened her eyes and saw Brianna, she burst into tears. She stared at her daughter, shook her head in confusion, and ran into the hallway.

She hurried down the stairs and into the basement so that Marvin wouldn't see her. She sat on the bottom step and wailed hysterically. She wailed as if she were going insane.

But Charisse had experienced bouts like this before and she knew how to handle it.

"Dear God, please give me strength. Please help me to understand why Mother was always so cruel to me. Help me to understand why I am the way I am and why I've done so many terrible things. Lord, please, please, forgive me—especially for the way I treated my brother. I didn't mean it, Lord, but I was so tired of Mother bragging about him and all his money and then saying that I should be more like him. Lord, I was tired of her loving him and not me. Lord, please help me to be a better person."

Charisse sat for a few minutes, wiped her tears away with her hands, and walked back upstairs. She went into the powder room and splashed cold water across her face. She dried it with a napkin and went into the kitchen.

She pulled herself together and did what she did every Wednesday.

She fixed breakfast for her family.

Chapter 15

Whitney

TAYLOR WAS ALREADY sitting at the table when I walked inside Ambrosio's. I still wasn't all that ready to mingle with Charisse, but Taylor wouldn't have it any other way. She'd made it clear that she expected to see me or else. I'm not sure what the "else" actually meant, probably nothing, but I'd still shown up.

I walked over to the table and hugged her.

"Hey, Whit," Taylor said. "I'm glad you decided to come."

"I am, too. Where's Charisse?"

"She called to say she was running a few minutes late, but I'm sure she'll be here soon."

"Then that gives me time to tell you my news. I wanted to tell you yesterday, but you were so busy in court that I decided to wait."

"What is it?"

"I met somebody."

"Really?" As always, Taylor was noticeably excited for me.

"Yes. And he is a dream come true, girl."

"Oh my God. Where did you meet him?"

"At the health club. He was there Monday night and he just started talking to me."

"What's his name?"

"Rico Anderson."

"Is he Puerto Rican?"

"I asked him the same thing, but no."

"So, have you gone out with him, did you see him yesterday, what? And now that I think about it, you're actually glowing."

"And for good reason, too. Girl, the man made love to me so brilliantly that I can barely think straight. He's an absolute master at it. And he did it two nights in a row!"

"Is he from Chicago? What does he do for a living?"

"He's from Chicago Heights and he's an accountant for AIC. And T, he doesn't even care about my weight. At first, I didn't believe him, but after last night I'm really starting to think he means it. And he's even showing me the proper way to work out."

"That's wonderful, Whit. I am so happy for you."'

I could tell Taylor wanted to cry. The woman was my rock. Chronologically, we were the same age, but Taylor had been born with a very old soul and sometimes I looked up to her like a mother.

"I gotta tell you, though, I keep waiting for the bomb to drop. Because I just don't want to believe a man that looks that good could want to be with me."

"Well, I say enjoy the moment. If it lasts forever, then great. But even if it doesn't, you're happy with him now and that's what's important."

"I agree."

"I can't wait to meet him."

"What I'll probably do is invite you, Cameron, Ms. Thing, and Marvin over for dinner one Saturday."

"Just let me know when and we'll be there."

"Just let you know what?" Charisse said, sitting down at the table.

"Whit has a new man," Taylor answered.

"What? That's great, Whitney. I'm really happy for you."

I didn't know whether she was being genuine or not, but I wasn't in the mood for arguing with her, so I assumed she meant what she'd said.

"Thanks."

"When did you meet him?"

"The other night at the health club."

"Oh? When did you start back going there?"

"On Monday."

"Well, good for you. Maybe I'll go with you sometimes."

I knew now that Taylor must have had a talk with Charisse because there was no way she was being this approving and not criticizing my every move.

"That would be nice," I said, and Taylor smiled. She was happy that Charisse and I were making amends with each other.

"And I want to apologize for speaking to you the way I did last week," Charisse continued. "I really was trying to look out for your well-being, but I guess I didn't say it in the right way."

Taylor never ceased to amaze me. She was good. Had to be if she could tame a woman like Charisse. The killing part was, I'd known Charisse longer than Taylor. Six years to be exact. But Taylor knew how to handle her much better than I did. Taylor was a lot more patient.

"Truce?" I said, and reached over to hug Charisse. It was the least I could do since she was being so kind to me.

"Okay, girls, now that we have that all taken care of, let's order some food," Taylor said. "I'm starving."

When the waitress arrived we settled on our usual choices. Grilled chicken Caesar salad and diet colas. Before today, I never would have ordered a diet anything, especially not a soda, but it was this new-way-of-life thing I had going on. It killed me, though, when I heard Taylor and Charisse ordering crème brûlée. It had always been our favorite dessert and we never denied ourselves of having it. But as soon as Taylor saw the disappointment on my face and realized I wasn't ordering, she told the waitress to cancel hers. To my surprise, Charisse did the same, and the three of us never discussed it. They had my back and I loved them for it. Charisse was Charisse, but she was my friend. Maybe in a strange sort of way, but she was as much of a friend as she knew how to be. And Taylor? My friendship with her never required any explanation. It was always the same every day of the week.

"So, how's the family?" Taylor asked Charisse.

"They're fine."

"I was planning to bring Brianna's package, but I forgot about it. I'll bring it over this evening, though."

"I'll be at Bible study but Marvin and the kids'll be there."

"Marvin isn't going to Bible study?" Taylor asked.

I was just as shocked as Taylor was. For as long as I could remember, Marvin had never been given a choice in terms of where he did and didn't want to go. He'd never had a say-so with anything, so I wondered what was up.

"He doesn't go as often as he used to," Charisse said.

"And you're okay with that?" I chimed in, and hoped Charisse hadn't taken my question the wrong way. The more I thought about it, I'd had no right saying anything. It was the kind of comment she would've made, but I wasn't like her.

"I'm fine with it," she said. "I don't agree with him missing church, but he's the one who will have to answer to God for not going."

I knew Charisse was throwing hints at Taylor and me, too. She'd never liked the fact that first of all, we didn't go to her particular church (which was another reason we were going to hell), and secondly, we didn't go every single Sunday like clockwork. There was a time when she'd ministered to both of us on a regular basis and practically begged us to change our denomination. We were Baptist, she was Church of God in Christ, and that was a problem for her. But when she'd realized that we weren't going to change, she'd been satisfied to know that at least we went to somebody's church, even if it wasn't the right one.

"Well, I think you're doing the right thing by letting him make his own decision," Taylor said.

I looked at Charisse and waited for the fireworks to ignite.

But once again, she surprised me.

"You might be right," she said. "After all, he is a grown man."

Taylor and I raised our eyebrows at the same time and I decided that the woman at our table had to be an impostor. There was no way this was the real Charisse Richardson sitting here in front of us.

"That's a good way to look at it," Taylor offered.

"Yeah, it is," I added.

Then we changed the subject. We talked about Cameron and how Taylor was planning to cook dinner for him tomorrow evening and how I'd already lost five pounds in two days. It was water weight for sure, but I was still extremely proud of it. We talked about our jobs and some of the issues we had with them, and then Charisse paid the check and left a tip on the table. It was her turn to take care of it but next week it would be mine.

Taylor rushed out so she could make it to court on time for a small case she was handling, and Charisse said she was going to a few stores before heading back to the suburbs. Charisse didn't work downtown like Taylor and me, and that was the reason we had lunch on her day off. Every now and then, Taylor and I would have lunch with just the two of us, but we never mentioned it to Charisse. We'd told her one time before, but it was obvious that she hadn't been too happy about it. It was almost as if she'd felt completely left out of the equation.

I walked back to my building, which was only three blocks away, and took the elevator up to the twentieth floor. When I walked inside my office I saw two dozen roses sitting on my desk and I quickly grabbed my chest. Then, when I'd settled down from being so excited, I read the card.

Which said: "Hey, beautiful, thank you for a wonderful two days. I promise this is only the beginning. Rico."

I sat down in my chair and wondered what this man was trying to do to me.

Because whatever it was, it was working.

Chapter 16

Charisse

IT WAS ONLY 6:30 P.M., but the parking lot at Mount Calvary Church of God in Christ was already half full. Charisse was getting excited already. There was nothing she loved more than being in church with hundreds of people, worshiping God and studying His written Word. There was nothing like being filled with the Holy Spirit and having the freedom to express yourself. It was a privilege to have such an awesome opportunity and Charisse took advantage of it. She did it every chance she got.

After parking her Mercedes 430, she got out and strutted across the parking lot in three-inch heels. Some of the members didn't feel it was necessary to get all dressed up on a Wednesday night, but Charisse felt obligated. It was her belief that she should do it out of respect for the Lord. Especially since folks got dressed up all the time to go to work, go out dancing, and everywhere else she could think of, but didn't seem to care about looking their best for God. Sure, they were good about doing it every Sunday, but any other time, they wore whatever they wanted.

Charisse walked through the side door and immediately saw a woman she had never been able to stand. Sister Holloway.

Charisse had tried to get along with this woman on more than one occasion but it had never worked. Sister Holloway was a lukewarm Christian, the type of person who looked holy on the outside but had a lot of evilness on the inside. She was one of those women who never missed church under any circumstance but would lie, cheat, and backstab her own mother given the chance. Charisse thanked God that she herself wasn't like that.

"How are you, Sister Holloway?" Charisse said, smiling and walking up the stairway.

"I'm fine, Sister Richardson, how are you?"

"Very well."

"I noticed that you weren't at church on Sunday."

Yeah, and it's none of your nosey-ass business either.

"No, I wasn't," Charisse said. "We had to rush my husband to the emergency room."

"Oh my. Is he okay?"

"He's fine. He had a really high fever, but the doctor said it was just a virus."

"Well, maybe we should put him on the sick list."

"I thought about that, but he's feeling much better already. As a matter of fact, he's planning to go back to work tomorrow."

"Well, that's good to hear. And please give him my best," she said, walking down the hallway.

Charisse wanted to tell her how ridiculous she looked and how she should spend less time monitoring Charisse's church attendance and more time going to the hair salon. Lord knows that weave she was wearing looked a mess. Almost like a hornet's nest. And Charisse didn't even want to get started on the difference in texture. Sister Holloway's hair was off-black and boogeyman nappy, and the weaved hair was jet black and silky straight. Did she think she was fooling somebody?

Father, please forgive me for my wayward thinking.

Charisse continued toward the door to the sanctuary and saw Pastor Damon.

"Hi, Pastor," Charisse said, hugging him.

"It's good to see you, Sister Richardson. We missed you on Sunday."

"I know. I was just telling Sister Holloway about Marvin going to the hospital."

"Is everything okay?"

"Yes. It was just a flu."

"Well, good."

"Pastor, do you think it would be possible for me to speak with you after Bible study?"

"Of course."

"There's something I need to discuss with you."

"Okay. Why don't I meet you in my office when we dismiss."

"I appreciate it."

Pastor Damon walked away and Charisse felt better about her problems already. Marvin hadn't thought Pastor was the person they needed to talk to, but Charisse knew that Pastor could fix anything. He'd done so, time and time again, for so many other people. She hadn't planned on telling him about the problems she and Marvin were having, but now she needed him to help her. She needed someone to understand what she was going through.

Charisse greeted and mingled with a few more members and finally entered the sanctuary. It was seven o'clock on the dot, the organist played quietly, and Pastor Damon stepped to the podium.

"If ye be willing and obedient, ye shall eat the good of the land, but if ye refuse and rebel, ye shall be devoured with the sword, for the mouth of the Lord hath spoken it."

Amens came from every direction.

"It's so good to see all of you here this evening and shame on those who didn't come."

"Amen, preacher," one of the deacons yelled.

"Lord have mercy on their souls," said one of the missionaries.

"You know," Pastor continued, "God doesn't like it when we rebel against His Word. He doesn't like it when Christians rebel against what their pastor has instructed them to do."

"All right, all right," one of the associate ministers offered.

"Now, I've explained to every member in this church how important it is to attend Bible study, and even more so now that we have actual service. But it seems to me that there's a lot of bad talk about that, too."

"My Lord," an older woman said, sighing.

"But what I want all of you to know is that *I* didn't make the decision to have full service on Wednesday night. This whole thing isn't even about me. It's about God and what He wants. I can still remember the night he woke me up out of my sleep and said, 'Terry, sixty minutes of Bible study just isn't enough anymore. There's not nearly enough worshiping going on as there needs to be. So, what I want you to do is teach a full Bible lesson the same as always, but I also want you to add in all the other aspects of morning worship. The choir needs to sing the way they normally do, you need to hold general altar prayer, and you must collect regular tithes and offerings."

Charisse was so glad Pastor was addressing all the negative comments and attitudes she'd been witnessing herself over the last few months. It was almost as if people didn't understand that they needed to be in church as much as possible. For her, three to four times a week would have been acceptable, let alone two.

Charisse was behind Pastor one hundred percent.

"So, what I want all of you to do, you, the loyal members, is to encourage those who are being disobedient. If you have their phone numbers, call them on the phone. If you work with them, talk to them face-to-face. If you only see them on Sunday morning, then pull them aside and tell them what God wants them to do."

Amens resonated throughout the building. Everyone who was present was in agreement with Pastor and that made Charisse happy. She had never understood how anyone could go against any man who had been called to preach. Pastor Damon had always said that he was an instrument of God and that to really reach out to the Lord, members needed to connect to God through him. He'd told his members about the special connection that only pastors could have with the Lord and how it was their job to do whatever Pastor Damon asked of them.

Charisse couldn't wait for service to be over with. Pastor Damon would make her feel better about everything.

"So, Sister Richardson, what can I do for you?" Pastor said, leaning back in the chair behind his desk.

"My marriage is in a lot of trouble."

"I'm truly sorry to hear that."

"Marvin has changed so much and he's so cold toward me."

"And how long has this been going on?"

"I first noticed it a few months back but now it's out of control. He won't listen to anything I say. And as you can see, he won't even come to church anymore."

"Hmmm. Have you talked to him about it?"

"Yes, but mostly all we do is argue."

"Have you suggested that the two of you come in for marriage counseling?"

"Yes, but he refuses to do it."

"Then I'm not sure what to tell you. I mean, if Brother Richardson won't come in to talk with me by his own free will, there's not that much we can do for him."

"But what about me?"

"*You* need to take care of you. Brother Richardson is a grown man, and if he can't appreciate a beautiful Christian woman like yourself, then it's his loss."

"Pastor, I'm so unhappy. And remember last year when I told you how miserable I was starting to feel with Marvin?"

"I do."

"Well, this time it's so much worse. I feel like I'm stuck in a terrible situation and that I'll never be able to get out of it."

Pastor Damon got up, walked around his desk, and stopped directly in front of where Charisse was sitting.

"Stand up," he said.

Charisse obeyed him and waited to see what else he had to say.

He caressed the side of her face. "You do know that this is all the work of Satan, don't you?"

"Yes."

"I mean, only Satan would have you thinking this way and making you believe that there just isn't any hope."

Charisse gazed into Pastor Damon's eyes. "But sometimes I feel like I don't have anyone to turn to, not even my friends or some of the people at the church. And now all Marvin wants is for us to go see some therapist."

"Sister Richardson, look. From what I've learned over the years, most of these so-called therapists are only in the business to rip people off. What they do is charge you a ton of money but they don't really ever help you."

"Then tell me, Pastor, what should I do?"

"Remember last year when you came to me?"

"Yes."

"And I fixed things for you, didn't I?" he said, pulling her body flush against his and holding her around her waist.

"But I can't ask you to do that again, because there are so many other people who need your help."

"Why don't you let me worry about that? Because the thing is, you're the one who really needs me right now. You're one of the most faithful members of our church, and if anyone deserves the special connection that I have with God, it's you."

"I just don't feel worthy."

"Well, you are. And while you don't know this, God had already spoken to me during the service and told me to help you. That's why when you came up to my office at the church like we had originally agreed, I asked you to come over here to my condo. It's because of cases like yours that I have this office, too. God had already authorized me to take care of you and you didn't even know it. He is using me, his instrument, to give you His love."

Charisse stared at him and Pastor Damon kissed her passionately.

Charisse's body was on fire and she was glad she'd made the decision to come see him. She was glad that Pastor was so willing to satisfy her needs, especially since Marvin didn't want to.

Still, she couldn't help wondering if Pastor really thought she was that naïve—that she actually believed he was preparing to do God's work. That he'd actually been doing God's work the last time they'd had buck-wild sex. That time Marvin had spent two full days away from her so he could sit at some hospital with his father.

She could still remember the entire evening, moment by moment, and how Pastor had shown a side of himself that Charisse hadn't been aware of. She remembered how kinky he'd been, how good he'd made her feel, and how he had begged her to see him regularly. But Charisse had decided that once or twice a year was enough. She'd decided to control the situation the same as she had with Marvin. She'd decided to save their meetings for times like this, when she desperately needed him. More so, she hadn't wanted to commit an outlandish number of sins in a twelve-month period. It was a self-made rule she'd come up with during her college years. No one was without sin, but unlike so many others she knew, Charisse only sinned every now and then. She only did it when it was very necessary. When she'd had all she could take from Marvin or when her childhood memories were too vivid.

Pastor Damon moved his lips from Charisse's mouth and kissed her up and down her neck. He breathed heavily and his hands wandered all over her body. Charisse moaned without realizing it. Pastor Damon unzipped her dress and pushed it off of her shoulders. When it dropped to the floor, Charisse stepped out of it and unbuttoned the one-piece garment she was wearing. Then she removed her panty hose. Pastor Damon removed his suit jacket and loosened his tie but never bothered removing his shirt. Then he stripped off his pants and boxers and waited for Charisse to bend over the edge of his desk.

When she did, Pastor Damon entered her aggressively. He acted as though he was punishing her.

He gave her exactly what she wanted and she welcomed it.

Chapter 17

Taylor

HEY, MARVIN," I said, walking into the entryway. "I'm sorry to stop by so late, but I promised Brianna I would bring her package to her."

"No problem. That girl has been waiting for you all night. She's a clothes fanatic."

"Auntie Taylor," Brianna said, rushing down the stairway, smiling.

"Hey, sweetie," I said, hugging her and kissing her on the forehead, and she reached for the UPS box I was holding.

"Let me see," she said. "Will you wait for me to try it on?"

"I won't leave until I see you model it."

Brianna skipped back up the stairs.

"I was in the kitchen looking at the new television I bought today," Marvin said. "Wanna see it?"

"Is it one of those miniature flat-screens?"

"Yep. I've been wanting to get one for a while but I kept waiting for the price to go down."

We walked into the kitchen and I sat my purse down in one of the chairs at the granite-topped island.

"This is nice, Marvin. I'm not sure when I'd be able to watch it, but I'm getting one of these."

"I like it, too. Charisse will probably throw a fit since I didn't consult her. But that's just too damn bad."

Okay, time-out. First, Charisse was acting strange at lunch today, and now Marvin was saying that he didn't care what she thought regarding his TV? And had he actually used the word *damn*?

But I decided not to comment.

"Can I get you anything to drink?" he said, and I sat down in the chair.

"No, actually, I'm fine. I had a vanilla latte on the way over here."

"This late?"

"Unfortunately, yes. I'm planning to leave work kind of early tomorrow, so that means I'll be up to the wee hours tonight working at home."

"The life of a big-time attorney."

We both laughed and he sat across from me.

"Check this out, Auntie Taylor." Brianna appeared, sporting her new jeans outfit.

"You look good, girl. It's definitely you."

"I like it, too, sweetheart," Marvin said.

"Now I'm going to try on the dress," she said, and left the room.

I looked at my watch and saw that it was ten-thirty. "Charisse is at church awfully late, isn't she?"

"To be honest, I really hadn't noticed," he said, popping the top from a bottle of beer.

At that moment, I wanted to run for cover. Why? Because I didn't want to be anywhere near Marvin or this new beverage of his when his wife got home. Liquor? In Charisse's house? Please.

"You know how she is when she goes around her church people," he continued. "Time just flies like the wind. And she doesn't even notice it."

Marvin was being so sarcastic and now I was even more curious about what was going on between them. Usually he was this very reserved, speak-only-when-spoken-to sort of guy, but today he was different. He was acting like, well . . . a real man.

"Is everything okay?" I asked.

"Has it ever been?"

I wasn't sure how to respond to his question. Not when he'd always been such a yes-man and had always allowed Charisse to rule over him. The man was as compassionate and pleasant as can be, but Charisse treated him like he was soft.

"I guess I don't know what you mean," I finally said.

"Now, Taylor. Let's be honest. Charisse and I have been married for years, but things were never okay. Maybe for her it was, but I was miserable."

As much as I litigated cases week in and week out, I was still at a loss for words—again.

"I guess you're shocked to hear me say that, huh?"

"No, not really," I admitted.

"Well then, you understand why my attitude has changed."

"So, how does Charisse feel about all this?"

"Your friend has got some real mental problems and she needs to see a doctor. Don't you think?"

I'd heard that one before, even back in college from some of our dorm mates. Charisse did do and say some strange things, but I'd always overlooked them. Maybe I'd just gotten used to her personality and had accepted her for who she was.

Brianna walked back into the room before I could say anything and I was glad. She twirled around like she was on a fashion runway.

"I love that one, too," I said. "And it fits perfectly."

"What do you think, Daddy?" she asked.

"It looks good. As a matter of fact, I'll probably have to hurt some little boy when you wear it."

"Daddy," she said, whining, and then said, "Thanks, Auntie Taylor. I love you so much."

"I love you, too, sweetie." Brianna held on to me longer than usual. She didn't seem sad or like anything was wrong, but it was almost as if she hadn't wanted to let go. Now I wondered what had gone on today between her and her mother. There was just no telling.

"I've gotta call Ashley to tell her about my stuff. Make sure you come say good-bye, Auntie Taylor, before you leave."

"I will."

Marvin flipped through the channels of his new toy.

"Well, I was planning to wait around until Charisse got home, but if I'm going to get any work done, I need to get going."

"Aren't you going to answer my question?"

"Which is?"

"Don't you think Charisse needs to see a psychiatrist?"

"I don't know. I mean, before tonight, I wouldn't have thought she needed to see anyone."

"But that's only because she acts pretty normal around you and Whitney. She does the same thing at work and at church. But around here, she acts like a raving lunatic. Just this morning, she told Brianna that she loved her and that she wanted them to start doing things together, which is pretty weird in itself because you know how she normally treats Brianna. But when Brianna hugged her, she burst into tears and ran downstairs. And then guess what?"

"What?"

"When the kids and I finally got dressed and came down here to the kitchen, she had already cooked breakfast. It was as if nothing had ever happened. She was acting like June Cleaver or somebody. You would have sworn she was the perfect wife and mother."

"Maybe you should get her to talk to someone after all."

"I already tried. I figured I would wean her into it by getting her to see a marriage counselor with me, but she's not hearing it. She went through the roof when I suggested it."

"Maybe she'll listen to me."

"Maybe. But just so you know, I only want her to get help for Brandon and Brianna's sake. Because as far as our marriage is concerned, that's pretty much over. I'll stay here until the kids graduate from high school, but after that, I'm outta here."

All I could do was stare at him. I wanted to ask him to rethink his position, but I could tell his mind was made up.

"I really hate hearing that, Marvin."

"I know, but it is what it is," he said, and at that moment, Charisse walked inside the house.

"Hey, Taylor," she said. "Marvin."

"Hey," I said.

Marvin just looked at her and turned up his bottle.

Now I wished I had left ten minutes ago.

"Did Brianna like what you bought her?" Charisse asked, and I couldn't believe she was ignoring Marvin's drink. She hadn't said a thing about the television either.

"She loved the jeans outfit and the dress," I said. "She tried them on and then went up to her room to call her girlfriend."

"Good."

"But hey, how was church?"

"Taylor, for the first time in a long while, I felt like God was right in my presence. I don't mean in the usual way, but like He was with me physically. It was an experience that everyone should have before they leave this earth."

Amazing. I was astonished by the way she was acting, and I could tell that Marvin was completely disappointed because he'd been hoping his new drinking activity was going to upset her. I assumed he'd wanted to reimpress upon her his new freedom to do whatever he wanted. But Charisse didn't care. She'd had this massive revelation with God and was sitting on top of the world.

Marvin had said she was crazy, but now I didn't know what to think.

Although I had a feeling I'd learn soon enough.

Chapter 18

TAYLOR

"YOU KNOW WHAT, Jessica? I wouldn't pay attention to a thing your husband says. He knows he's going to have to pay and that's why he's trying to discourage you."

"He told me that his attorney is much bigger than mine and that I won't get a single dime. He says he has information that will keep me from collecting anything."

"Like?"

"Nothing. I haven't done anything but be a good wife to him and a good mother to our children. I've never done anything except what he wanted me to do."

"Then if I were you, I wouldn't worry about it. He's only bluffing because he knows he doesn't have a leg to stand on. The man has a deluge of residential and commercial property situated throughout this entire city, so he can certainly afford to give you child support and alimony. As a matter of fact, he's going to pay you a percentage of everything he owns."

"You really think you can make that happen?" Jessica asked.

"I'm positive."

Jessica was so fearful, yet so innocent. It was the reason I wasn't about to let her husband walk away scottfree. Jessica had somehow found the guts to follow him and his mistress to a hotel and had called me the very same afternoon. That was three weeks ago, but it hadn't been the first time. She had called me six months ago, too, when she'd learned that Thomas was sleeping with yet another woman who lived down the street from them, but Thomas had convinced her to reconcile with him.

Now, though, Jessica had finally had enough, and I could tell she was going all the way to the finish line. She had finally decided that ten different women over the last twelve months were enough. And those were just the ones she knew about personally or those that the private investigator had discovered.

"Well, I sure hope so," she said. "Because I can't make it without money or a place to live."

"Of course you can't, and you're not going to. When I'm finished, your husband will regret the day he slept with anyone."

"Then I can't wait till this is over."

"It won't happen overnight, but you'll be satisfied in the end."

"I appreciate all your help, Taylor. Especially since I can't pay you up front."

"It's no problem at all. Thomas is going to compensate both of us eventually and I certainly don't mind waiting."

"I just hope he doesn't become violent. He never has in the past, but I'm not sure what'll happen once he realizes all the money he has to give up."

"Well, if he does, we'll slap an order of protection against him. We'll do whatever we have to to keep you safe."

"Maybe I'm just being paranoid."

"Cautious is a better word, and there's nothing wrong with being that way."

"Like I said, I'll be glad when this is over."

"Believe me, I understand."

"Oh well, I'll hang up now, but I'll call you if anything develops."

"Please do. And you take care."

It was almost a shame, but for as long as I'd been practicing, I'd always found satisfaction in punishing men who messed around on their wives. There was something so liberating about bringing them to their knees and then making them surrender part of their assets. I was sure it had to do with my college boyfriend proclaiming his love for me and then sneaking around with one of my sorority sisters. I remember how he hadn't even denied my accusation. He'd acted as though he was well within his rights and that I should simply accept and get over it. It was the reason I hadn't truly trusted another man until I'd gotten to know Cameron.

I made a few more phone calls and dictated a few letters for my administrative assistant. It was only two o'clock, but I'd cleared my calendar for the rest of the afternoon. I'd decided yesterday to cook dinner for Cameron. I didn't do it very often, but I was starting to feel like we needed an entire evening with just the two of us. I wanted to have dinner, make love, and then talk about our future plans together. Quite obviously, the making-love part would be special because it had been over a week for us.

As I packed a few items in my briefcase, I heard a knock on my door.

"Come in," I said, and sighed when I saw that it was Skyler.

"Going somewhere?" he said.

"Why?"

"Because your secretary told me that you were leaving early."

"And?"

"You were just gone three days last week."

"So," I said, and looked away from him.

"So? Well, in case you haven't realized, we have responsibilities around here."

"Oh please, Skyler. My work is always done when it needs to be and I work more than enough overtime to make up for taking off the rest of the afternoon. The *real* partners aren't complaining, so why are you?"

"You know, I've just about had it with you snubbing my position of authority."

I looked at him and laughed. "You are such a whiner and the sad part is that I don't even think you realize it."

"What's going on with the Harris case?" he said, ignoring my comment.

"I just got off the phone with her and everything is fine. With the PI report, we're home free."

"I hear her husband just retained John Wilcox."

"And?"

Now Skyler was laughing. There was no doubt that he wanted us to win the case, but there was a part of him that wanted John to clobber me. He had seen me lose a few small cases, but never any major ones, and he longed for it. He needed it to happen so he could feel better about himself.

"You don't have a chance in hell," he said.

"Whatever you say."

"I'll be happy to take over the case if you want."

"No, that's okay. I'll take my chances."

"And it's a mistake, too."

"Oh well."

"First, you conveniently get out of handling the case against your father's employer, then you take on a case you can't win, and now you're leaving early."

"And I won't be here in the morning either," I said matter-of-factly.

"And why is that?"

"Not that it's any of your business, but I have a doctor's appointment."

"Yeah, right."

"Are you saying that I'm lying?"

"I don't know if you are or not."

"Okay, Skyler, I've had enough and I'd like you to leave."

"You know what your problem is, don't you?" he said, heading toward the door and then looking back at me. "You need a man."

"I already have one, remember?"

"I'm talking about a real one."

"He is real. As a matter of fact, he's more of a man than you'll ever be."

"Then why are you always so uptight?"

"Because you bring out the worst in me. You're always trying to question my ability."

"I do it because you don't respect me."

"I respect those who deserve to be respected."

"See, that's what I'm talking about. You think you're so much, and I get sick of you walking around here all high and mighty."

"Skyler, please go. And for the record, the next time you come into my office trying to hassle me, I'm going to the senior partners."

"Oh, so now you're planning to tattle. I knew you weren't as strong as you pretend to be."

"If you keep pushing me, I'll go see them now."

"I've got a better idea. Why don't you go work at another firm?"

"I wouldn't give you the satisfaction—not personally or professionally."

"You know what, Taylor . . . I'm sure you wouldn't. Especially not personally."

Skyler stared at me in a strange way and then walked out. And I couldn't even say he was angry because that's not what I was sensing. If I hadn't known better, I would have sworn his feelings were hurt. But I knew my thinking was ludicrous. I knew I'd read his facial expression incorrectly and that I'd taken his words out of context—specifically the word *personally*.

I knew that Skyler and I detested each other and that's all that really mattered.

I couldn't believe it was already five and I was just now walking through the doorway. I'd stopped at the grocery store on the way home and picked up four salmon fillets, two bunches of spinach, and a bag of red potatoes. This was Cameron's favorite meal and he loved when I made it for him. I had to admit that I loved salmon, too, and I usually had it at least four times a month.

I unpacked everything I'd purchased, put it away, and then went into my bedroom. It wouldn't take long to bake the salmon, sauté the spinach or boil the potatoes, so I decided to take my shower beforehand. I thought about calling Whitney to see how her dieting had gone this afternoon, but since I'd already spoken to her this morning and she'd seemed fine, I didn't. She was still very much into her new man and I could tell he was helping her motivation.

I also considered calling Charisse. After chatting with Marvin last evening, I was sort of concerned about her well-being. It was true that I didn't see anything wrong with her, but I couldn't dismiss the claims Marvin was making. Not when he had lived in the same house with her for all these years. But I decided that maybe I would call her tomorrow instead.

After giving myself a mini-facial, taking a long, hot, steamy shower, and drying my body, I smoothed oil across my skin. Then I pulled a black pants set from my walk-in closet and laid it across my bed. It wasn't overly dressy, but it was nice enough to wear for dinner and it was always comfortable.

I slipped on a velour sweat suit and went back into the kitchen. First, I poured water into a medium-sized pot for the potatoes and then ignited one of the eyes on top of the stove. Then I preheated the oven, took out an oblong glass dish, and brushed the inside with a touch of olive oil. I took the salmon back out of the refrigerator, rinsed it, seasoned it, placed it in the dish, and then covered it with aluminum foil. Next, I removed the potatoes from the bag, washed them thoroughly, and set them in a bowl.

I waited for the oven to register at the proper temperature and the water to come to a boil. In the meantime, I opened a few pieces of mail and flipped through a magazine.

About an hour later, everything was ready, so I went back into the bedroom, reapplied my makeup and got dressed. Just as I finished, the doorbell rang. I was glad Cameron was on time.

I walked through the living room and opened the door.

"Hi, baby," he said, kissing me.

"Hey," I said.

"The food smells good."

"Thanks. So, how was your day?"

"Busy."

"Did you have a lot of meetings?"

"Yeah. We met with the City again and then two of our other clients," he said, removing his shoes and laying his pinstriped blazer across the sofa. His tie came off next. Cameron always made himself at home and that gave me a warm feeling. The only thing was, I wished we could make our home together.

"But that's a good thing, though, isn't it?" I said.

"Actually, it is. I can't say for sure, but I have a feeling we're going to get the contract."

"That's really good news."

"So, my dear," he said, walking toward the dining room, "what are we having?"

"Guess."

"My favorite?"

"Yep."

"Well, I'm ready for it."

I had already set the table with silver-trimmed china, cloth napkins, and crystal flutes, so now I brought over the food.

Cameron poured us each a glass of Chardonnay and I sat down to join him. Neither of us wasted any time digging in.

"Everything is great," he said after sampling all that I had prepared for him.

"Thanks."

"So, how are your parents doing?" he asked.

"They're fine. I spoke to them yesterday. Daddy is still unhappy with his job, but other than that, they're good."

"You'll have to tell them I asked about them."

I wanted to ask Cameron about his folks, too, but lately he hadn't spoken to them all that much, not after they'd loaned his brother twenty thousand dollars to start a business. Cameron was angry because they hadn't done the same for him when he'd called on them two years ago. I wasn't sure what the reason had been exactly, but it was something about his brother's deli franchise being more of a sure thing than Cameron's architectural firm. I tended to side with Cameron, though, because I knew he was going to be successful and because I believed his parents should have supported both of their sons equally. Especially since Cameron was already in a position to pay them back and his brother clearly wasn't. But I didn't dare bring it up.

We made small talk, and when we finished eating, Cameron asked me to come over to him. I did and he pulled me onto his lap in a straddling position.

"Thank you," he said.

"For what?"

"Fixing me dinner."

"I'm glad you enjoyed it and there's dessert in the fridge."

"Really? What kind?"

"Strawberry cheesecake."

"I guess that sounds pretty good, but I was thinking of having something else."

"Is that right?"

"Yeah, and you know what, too."

"Maybe we should let our food digest," I teased him.

"I don't think so," he said, pulling my face toward his.

We kissed and chills spiraled through my veins. After all this time, Cameron still had this effect on me. I loved him so much that it was scary. I was so afraid that one day I would wake up and our relationship would be over. I worried that he might decide I wasn't the woman for him.

Cameron unbuttoned my top, I caressed his face, and we never took our eyes off of each other. He kissed my chest and then my lips again. We kissed for a while and then he unsnapped the front closure of my bra. He took both my breasts in his hands and I dropped my head backward. Then he took them into his mouth, one by one. He alternated between them, almost as if he couldn't decide which one he enjoyed more, and I wanted to scream. I wanted to tell him to stop what he was doing before I disturbed my neighbors.

"Tell me you love me," he said.

"I love you, baby."

We kissed again and Cameron asked me to stand up. We kissed like wild animals and then we removed all of our clothing. We dropped every stitch to the floor and he led me into the bedroom. He lay on his back and I knew what he wanted.

He moaned agreeably and I was glad I knew how to satisfy him. We'd known how to satisfy each other since the very beginning.

I continued to pleasure him and then he returned the favor tenfold. He was so good at what he did that I thought maybe I was dreaming. It was hard to believe that any man could make a woman feel so extraordinary. But that's what Cameron always did for me. He always raised me to new levels of ecstasy and I couldn't get enough of him.

When I reached my orgasmic peak, I yelled out and Cameron smiled at me.

Then he eased inside. He moved slowly and gently, and I

moved with him. We made sounds that we would never want our colleagues to hear. We made love like our lives depended on it. Our bodies forcefully became one and shared such beautiful rhythm. I could literally feel the love wedged between us.

Cameron started to move a bit more briskly, and I swerved my hips at the same velocity. In the end, Cameron yelled louder than I had.

We lay their recovering from our experience and all I could think was how good we were together. I wondered if Cameron was thinking the same thing, but I couldn't see how he wasn't.

"Girl, don't you ever make me wait this long again," he said, still lying on top of me with his head slightly buried into the pillow.

I laughed. "Well, I can't help it that Mother Nature calls on me every month."

"Yeah, but for you, Mother Nature calls way too often and for much too long."

At that moment, I wanted to tell him everything. I wanted to tell him that I knew something was wrong and that I was seeing Dr. Green tomorrow morning. But for some reason I still couldn't. I decided it was better to wait until I knew the actual diagnosis. I decided there was no sense alarming him until I knew what was what.

"Every woman is different," I tried to explain. "Some women have long cycles, some have shorter ones. It just depends."

"I guess. But yours is definitely more often than when I met you."

"Well, it's not like I'm getting any younger."

"True, but maybe you need to get checked out. Maybe you're having some sort of female problem."

"Maybe."

Cameron breathed deeply and I could tell he was falling asleep. But I interrupted him. We needed to have a very important discussion.

"Cameron?"

"What is it, baby?" he said, kissing me on the cheek.

"How long are we going to do this?"

"Do what?"

"Sleep together and live in separate households."

"Taylor, please. Not tonight," he said, rolling to the side of me. "Not now. Not after enjoying each other the way we just did."

"I need to know, Cameron. I love you and I'm committed to you and I need to know why you aren't as committed to me."

"But I am," he said, frowning, clearly defensive. "You know I'm not seeing anyone else."

"Then what's the problem?"

"I don't want to marry you until my business is solid. It's doing well, but I need at least another year to see how it continues."

"But why? I mean, it's not like I don't earn decent money myself."

"I understand that, but this is something I need to do for me. I won't be happy until I know that my finances are in order."

"But Cameron, when two people love each other, none of that matters. Even if your business doesn't work out the way you want, that won't change the way we feel."

"I know that, but Taylor, I'm not ready to get married. I will be eventually, but for now you're going to have to be patient."

"Patient for how long? Because I've been *patient* for two years."

"Look. I love you and I certainly don't want anyone else, so why isn't that enough for you?"

"Because it's not."

"Well, I'm sorry."

"Not as sorry as I am," I said, sliding out of bed. I went into the bathroom and slammed the door behind me.

For the first time since I'd met Cameron, I wanted him to leave.

I wanted him out so I would no longer have to look at him.

Chapter 19

Taylor

IT WAS FRIDAY MORNING and I was at the medical building for my appointment. I wasn't sure what the outcome would be, but I was glad to finally be getting this over with. Good or bad, the news would be a major relief because there would be no more wondering. I was even planning to tell Cameron, although I'm not sure he would actually care. He'd left rather abruptly shortly after our blowup, and I still hadn't spoken to him. Honestly, I really wasn't in the mood for any more arguing.

Inside the office, the receptionist gave me a few forms to fill out. They were attached to a clipboard and the first document asked questions relating to my medical history. The other two talked about financial responsibility in case my insurance carrier didn't pay, and the other concerned my right to privacy. I completed each of them and then walked back up to the desk.

The receptionist reviewed my information, made a copy of my insurance card, and told me to have a seat. When I sat back down, I picked up an old issue of *Good Housekeeping* and flipped through the pages pretty quickly. Normally, I would have found an article to read while waiting, but my nerves were already racing. There was no denying that I was prepared to hear the worst. Just a few hours ago, my mother had prayed by phone, but now my faith was waning. My mind was consumed with thoughts of cancer, surgery, and everything else imaginable. I was now a nervous wreck.

I swallowed hard and dropped the magazine back on the table. I scanned the room, looking at the two other ladies who were sitting across from me, and crossed my legs. Then I uncrossed them and pulled out my Palm Pilot. I searched through my schedule for the coming week and then I turned it off and pushed it back into my purse. I couldn't believe I was getting myself so worked up before any tests had actually been done.

I sat for another half hour and finally the nurse called my name and held the door open for me.

"How are you?" I asked, walking past her.

"I'm fine. And you?"

"I'm good."

"I'll just have you get on the scale before we continue down the hallway," she said.

I kicked off my three-inch mules, dropped my handbag on the floor, and stepped onto the platform. The digital readout registered at 160 and I smiled. I was definitely not overweight, not at five foot nine, but it was sometimes a struggle to keep it that way. Well, not a struggle exactly, but I did have to work at it. I made sure I watched my calories and fat intake, although not on Saturday or Sunday, and I worked out at least two to three times per week.

When we arrived in the examination room, the nurse asked me to sit on a padded table that was covered with a white liner. She asked me a few additional questions, took my pulse, checked my blood pressure, and all was normal. Then she passed me that infamous cotton gown, the one that showed the crack of your butt, and I was starting to feel even more uncomfortable. It was one thing to bare all to my primary physician, who was a woman and who I'd gone to for many years, but showing everything to a man that I didn't even know would take some getting used to.

"You'll need to remove all of your clothing, including your underwear and the doctor should be in shortly."

"Thank you," I said, and she left the room.

As instructed, I removed everything and sat up on the table. I gazed out the window, but since I was on the fifth floor, the only thing I saw was the clear blue sky. I scanned the room, looking at the various charts nailed on each wall, and then I noticed Dr. Green's degree from the University of Chicago. I also saw a certificate outlining his teaching credentials and I was impressed.

Just when I realized how chilly the room was starting to feel, Dr. Green walked in.

"Good morning," he said.

"Good morning, Doctor."

The man was as handsome as they came, and while I didn't want to admit it, he reminded me of Skyler—a man with deep caramel flawless skin and broad shoulders.

"So, how was your trip?"

"Not as good as I wanted it to be, but what can I say?"

"That's understandable. Especially since you weren't feeling well."

"Thanks again for speaking to me long-distance."

"No problem," he said, sitting down on a stool. "So, did Dr. Cilletti prescribe you the iron?"

"Yes, and it seems like it's been helping. I definitely feel a lot stronger."

"Good," he said, reviewing my chart and jotting down notes. "Because the last thing you want is to end up having a heart attack or needing a blood transfusion."

I looked at him but didn't bother telling him that sometimes when I awakened in the middle of the night, my heart did feel as though it was going to beat straight through my chest. I just didn't have the nerve to admit how lightly I'd been taking my anemia.

So instead, I watched him, checking to see if he was wearing a wedding band, but he wasn't. I knew it was wrong of me, considering I was already spoken for, but I guess I was just curious. So curious that now I wondered why a man that looked this good wasn't married.

"And how about your bleeding, has it stopped?" he asked.

"Yes."

"Good," he said, writing a few additional words and then putting down his pen. "Well, overall, it looks like you're a pretty healthy young woman."

"Healthy maybe, but I don't know about the young part."

"Oh, c'mon now. Thirty-eight? When you turn forty like me, then you can complain."

We both laughed and I realized that Dr. Green was as pleasant as Charisse had told me.

"Well, what I'd like to do is start with a breast exam and Pap smear, and then if we need an ultrasound, we'll do that, too."

"Okay."

Dr. Green stood, walked closer to where I was sitting, and let down the back of the table.

"You can lie all the way down and I'll get my nurse in here."

When she came in, she stood near the wall with her arms folded, and I knew she was only there as a witness. She was there to combat any false claims of sexual misconduct, and I didn't blame him for protecting himself.

"Do you perform breast exams on a regular basis?" he asked, starting with my right one.

"Not really."

"I know it's easy to forget, but you really should get in the habit of doing it. You'd be amazed at the number of my patients who have discovered lumps on their own."

My former gynecologist had told me the same thing year after year, but for some reason I never did it. But now I would make a more conscious effort.

"Everything feels normal," he said when he finished checking the left side. "Now what I want you to do is place both feet in the stirrups and scoot your bottom all the way down to the edge of the table."

When I did, I took a deep breath. I was starting to feel nervous all over again, wondering what he was going to discover.

He slipped on a pair of latex gloves, inserted the cold metal instrument, snapped it open, and took samples of my fluids with a cotton swab. Next, he removed the instrument and pressed down on my stomach with his hand.

"Ouch," I said, flinching.

"Does that hurt?"

"Yes. A little."

"What about here?" he said, pressing in another area.

"No."

"And here?"

"Yes."

"And here?" he said, moving back to the original spot.

I frowned and said, "Yes."

Dr. Green removed his gloves.

"Are you sexually active?" he asked.

This of course made me feel awkward, but I knew he was asking for a reason.

"Yes."

"Do you experience pain?"

"Sometimes."

"Is it minor or excruciating?"

"Mostly minor."

"Marie, let's get set up for an ultrasound."

"What do you think it is?" I couldn't help asking.

"I'm not sure just yet, but you might have a uterine fibroid."

I'd read about those months ago, and the one good thing I knew was that while they were tumors, they weren't cancerous. If only that could be it.

When Marie returned with the machine, Dr. Green performed the ultrasound and I watched on-screen.

"That's exactly what it looks like," he said, moving the probe from side to side. "And it appears to be pretty large."

"Is there only one of them?"

"From what I can see," he said, pausing. Then he asked, "When was the last time you had a Pap done?"

If there had been some way I could ignore his question, I would have. Marie had already asked me about that but maybe Dr. Green hadn't seen her notation. Either that or this was his subtle way of making me talk about it.

"It was maybe two or three years ago."

"And you said you've been bleeding heavily for how long?"

"Six months, maybe longer," I confessed.

"You can sit up," he said, raising the table back to an upright position.

Then he continued, "What I'd like to do is run a few more tests, including some blood work. Then we'll see exactly where we are and how we should proceed."

"Can you treat it with medication?"

"I was hoping that I might be able to embolize it, which would stop the blood flow and cause the fibroid to die. But because it's so large, a myomectomy may be our only option. Meaning, we may need to remove it surgically."

"Is that an outpatient procedure?"

"If I do it by laparoscopy, which is less invasive, you'll probably only spend one or two nights in the hospital. But full recovery will take about two to four weeks."

"But you definitely don't think I have cancer."

"Well, if for some reason you have cancerous cells in your cervical area, the Pap result will show it. But in terms of the uterus, I won't know if there's any malignancy until we do the surgery."

"And what would happen then?" I asked.

"You'll have to decide beforehand how you would want me to

proceed. Meaning whether you would want me to go ahead and remove your entire uterus."

Dear God, not a hysterectomy? Not when I wanted to have children.

Dr. Green was scaring me and I guess he noticed it because he said, "But don't be alarmed. I'm only telling you this as a cautionary measure, but in reality, only one in two hundred women with fibroids are found to have uterine cancer."

That calmed my thinking to a low simmer, but I wouldn't be satisfied until I was completely in the clear. I wouldn't be happy until this tumor was out of me and my life was back to normal.

"Marie will get the rest of the testing scheduled and will be in touch with you," Dr. Green said. "Then we'll concentrate on the surgery."

"Thank you, Doctor."

"We'll get you taken care of," he said, smiling.

I smiled back, but to be honest, I wasn't so sure.

Still, I hoped for the best.

I did this because hope was all I really had.

During the drive over to Cameron's office, my nerves had started to settle, but now they were in an uproar. I'd purposely shown up unannounced and he didn't seem too happy about it. Imagine that. The love of my life acting as though I was an intrusion. And sadly enough, my feelings were very hurt by it.

"Cameron, I know you're working, but there's something I really need to talk to you about."

He closed his office door so his secretary couldn't hear us.

"What is it?" he spoke coldly.

"Well, first of all, I'm sorry for getting so upset with you last night."

"You came all the way over here to tell me that?"

"Why are you being so cruel?"

"Because, Taylor, you ruined our evening for no reason. You

know how I feel about getting married, so it was senseless for you to bring it up."

"Senseless? Is that what marrying me would mean to you?"

"No," he said. "You're putting words into my mouth. What I meant was that you know how I feel, so it was unnecessary for us to have that discussion."

"But it's important to me, Cameron, and you know it."

"Look, I can't do this right now. I have a meeting that I'm trying to prepare for, so maybe we can talk about this later."

"Why are you so irritated with me? And why have you been acting so different lately?"

"I'm not. I'm under a lot of stress here at the office, and if I've been taking it out on you, I'm sorry."

All I could do was sit there. I'd wanted to tell him about my doctor's appointment, but now I didn't know if I should.

"Maybe I could call you before I leave work and we can get together," he finally said, hinting that I should leave.

"That's fine, but first I need to talk to you about something else. I went to the doctor this morning."

"Why? You're not pregnant, are you?"

"No. But what if I was? Because it's not like we've been abstinent."

"I know, but you're on the pill, right?"

I sighed rather loudly. I was so frustrated.

"Well, what did you go to the doctor for?"

"I've been bleeding a lot more than usual and he thinks I have a fibroid tumor."

His face softened almost immediately and he pulled me out of the chair I was sitting in and held me. I still wasn't happy about the way he was treating me, but I was happy to have someone embrace me. I'd needed someone to hold me more than I realized.

"Baby, I'm so sorry," he said. "I didn't know. Is it cancerous?"

"Fibroids are benign, but he won't know if I have cancer until he does the actual surgery."

"Why didn't you tell me you were having problems?" he said, leading me over to his office sofa, where we sat down.

"I don't know," I said.

"Because just last night I brought up the fact that you bleed an awful lot and still you didn't say anything."

"I guess I was afraid of how you might react. Especially if you knew there was a chance I might need a hysterectomy."

"Did the doctor tell you that?"

"Not exactly, but there's a one-in-two-hundred chance."

"Then there's nothing to worry about."

"But what if there is? I mean, what if I do need a hysterectomy and we can't ever have children?"

"Well, to be honest, I don't have a problem with that."

What was he talking about? Not once had he ever mentioned the idea of not having children, so I wondered where this was coming from.

"So, what are you saying?" I asked.

"That having children is not that important to me. Once upon a time it was, but now with me almost turning forty, it's not."

"Well, don't you think you should have informed me about that?"

"Well, it's not like I'd given it a lot of thought. I mean, if we got married and had a child, I would be fine with it, but if we didn't I would be fine with that, too."

I listened but didn't say anything and he continued.

"I will say this, though. I've heard that the sex is different after women have hysterectomies."

"What?" I said loudly.

"I heard that it doesn't feel the same."

"Please. That's just some stupid myth that some stupid man came up with," I said, getting to my feet.

"I'm just telling you what I've heard."

"Well, Cameron, if I have cancer, there's nothing I can do about it," I said and snatched my handbag. "And I'm sorry I even bothered you about this."

"No, baby, wait," he said, stepping toward me and then grabbing both my hands. "I didn't mean it like that. I'll be here for you no matter what."

"I need to get back to work," I said.

"Then why don't I come by tonight when you get home?"

"Fine. Whatever."

"Taylor," he said, placing his finger under my chin. "Look at me. I'm sorry, okay?"

"I'll see you later," I said, and walked out.

I'd gone to see Cameron in hopes that he would make me feel better, but now I wished I hadn't told him anything. Because the fact of the matter was, I felt worse. I was terribly wounded by his not wanting to have children, and I was appalled by his idiot philosophy: Sex was horrible without a uterus.

I'd wanted him to show me some much-needed compassion, but what I'd gotten was a high-pitched wake-up call.

I'd learned that after two long years I really didn't know the man.

Chapter 20

Whitney

“YOU’RE GOING TO BE just fine,” I said. Taylor had just phoned me at work, informing me about the outcome of her doctor’s visit, and I could tell she was upset.

“I hope so, Whit, because if I need a hysterectomy—”

“You won’t. So don’t even talk like that. You have a fibroid, the doctor is going to remove it, and that will be that.”

“I hope you’re right.”

“I am. You’ll see.”

“And then there’s this situation with Cameron. He’s acting so different and like he doesn’t even care about me.”

“So you told him?”

“Yeah, I went by his office an hour ago, but he wasn’t happy to see me. Although a lot of it had to do with the fact that we had an argument last night.”

“About what?”

“Marriage, of course. I told him that I was tired of dating him and that I wanted to know when he was going to fully commit. And that’s when he got mad and said he wasn’t ready to get married. He claims that first he wants his business to be on track.”

Wow. I liked Cameron a lot, but I was sort of shocked by what I was hearing. I'd known that he wasn't in a hurry to get married and that Taylor wasn't happy about it, but now I wondered myself why he was so hesitant. Especially since Taylor was such a good person and she was truly in love with him.

"I'm sorry to hear that," I said. "But maybe he's just being cautious."

"Cautious about what? Because it's not like I've ever given him a reason to be."

"I know. But you know how some men are. Some men are simply afraid to sign on the dotted line and that's all there is to it."

I heard Taylor sighing. "Well, as much as I love him, I won't keep seeing him if he's not planning to marry me. Life is way too short for that."

"I hear you, but maybe you need to give him the benefit of the doubt. Maybe you should have another talk with him and let him know how serious you are."

"Maybe. But if he doesn't change the way he feels, then I'm going to end things between us. I don't want to, but I really don't see where I have a choice. I won't live the way my Aunt Hilda has for the last thirty years, shacking up with a man who isn't her husband and who probably hasn't provided for her."

"Geez. That's a long time," I said, but deep down I wondered if I would end up having to accept something similar. I mean, over the last four days, things had gone wonderfully between Rico and me, but what if he only wanted to go out with me or eventually live with me? What if he never wanted to make everything legal? Would I complain? Would I be okay with it? Would I have enough strength to send him packing? I wanted to believe that I would do what was right, but I couldn't be sure of it. Not when the alternative would mean being alone. I was too ashamed to admit this to Taylor, but a part of me understood Aunt Hilda's decision. I understood because if I remembered correctly, Aunt Hilda was heavier than

I was. Like me, she probably assumed there wouldn't be many more offers.

"I just won't do it," Taylor said, sounding as though she was thinking out loud.

"Look, T. Just talk to him."

"I will, but I'm telling you, if he still has the same attitude, we're over."

"I have a feeling he'll come around once he realizes he's about to lose you."

"But there's also something else he said that I can't stop thinking about. The man actually had the nerve to say that he's heard that sex is different with women who've had hysterectomies."

"Different? Different how?"

"I don't know, but that's what he said."

"That's just crazy."

"I agree, but I could tell he was serious about it."

"Well, if he is, he's been completely misinformed."

"I know, but hey, hold on a minute," Taylor said, I assumed answering another call.

I signed a stack of service orders and pushed them to the side of my desk. Then I opened a file and saw a name I didn't think I'd have to see again. At least not for a while. It was Tacquinisha Bell's. Apparently she'd finagled her way through to my boss's boss and gotten those free minutes that I'd told her she couldn't have. The same minutes we'd basically told her to forget about. Some people just didn't know when to quit.

"Girl, this is Mom calling me back, so let me talk to you later, okay?" Taylor said.

"Okay, but T, remember what I said. Everything is going to be fine with your surgery, and please talk to Cameron."

"Thanks, Whit. I'll see what I can do."

"I'll call you tonight."

"Sounds good."

When I hung up the phone I prayed for Taylor and what she

was going through, both medically and personally. I really did believe she was going to be all right, but I wouldn't be satisfied until the doctor confirmed it. I wouldn't be satisfied until he confirmed that my best friend in this whole wide world wasn't going to leave me. Until he told her that she didn't have cancer and that she would eventually have children. Lord knows I didn't want to think the worst about any of this because I just couldn't bear it.

After realizing it was right at two o'clock, I called Rico to make sure we were still on for this evening. He'd been working out with me every day as promised, but this morning he hadn't been sure if he'd be able to make it tonight. Something about a business meeting after work.

"Rico Anderson," he said.

Whitney Todd Anderson was all I could think because it had a nice ring to it.

"Hi," I said when I finished daydreaming.

"What's up?"

"Just checking to see if you're going to make it to the health club."

"Actually, I am. The meeting I told you about was postponed until next week."

I grinned from ear to ear and I was glad he couldn't see how silly I must have looked. I couldn't wait to see him.

"Good," I said. "Then I'll meet you at the same time?"

"That works for me, and plan on working a lot harder than you did last night."

"I will," I affirmed, but I wasn't sure how I could do any more than he was already making me. My muscles were ridiculously sore, and while I would never let on, I didn't want to work out tonight at all. I had decided yesterday that it would be okay to take a break on Fridays and Sundays, but I knew Rico wasn't going for it. He was so serious about all of this. He was more serious than I wanted him to be but I didn't want to seem ungrateful. I didn't want him thinking I was a quitter, not when I was making so much progress. I'd already lost ten whole pounds in four days.

"So, I guess I'll see you then?" he said after pausing for a few seconds.

"Yep. See ya."

When I arrived at the health club, there weren't as many cars in the parking lot and I was happy. Apparently a lot of the members were thinking like me, that Friday should be a rest day, and I didn't blame them. If anything, I envied them.

I walked inside, went into the locker room, and put on my brand-new T-shirt. Next, I pulled on my stretch pants. Normally, I wouldn't have cared too much about my workout clothing, but I guess I was trying to impress Rico. I knew I still had a long way to go, but I wanted to look as good as possible.

After pulling my hair into a ponytail, I went up to the weight training area. My heart dropped into my stomach when I looked across the room. Rico was laughing with some woman who was standing too close to him. Not to mention, she looked like a supermodel, the kind that any agency would fight to represent.

My first thought was to walk back out, but my feet wouldn't move. So I stood there, wishing this woman would go away. I wanted her to go find her own man to mingle with.

Finally, Rico saw me and beckoned for me to come over.

I ambled slowly, trying to give Ms. Thing enough time to vacate,, but she just stood there, waiting. For all I knew, she was laughing her insides out because of how fat I was.

"Bethany," Rico said to her, "this is Whitney, a very good friend of mine who I've been training on weights."

"Whitney, this is Bethany. Bethany just joined here last week."

A good friend of his who he's been training with? Was that what he saw me as? Not after sending me flowers only two days after meeting me and having sex with me four nights out of four. I didn't know whether to feel used or offended.

"It's nice to meet you," she said.

"Nice to meet you, too," I muttered, looking away from both of them, and I guess she took the hint.

"Well, I'd better get going," she said. "But I'm sure I'll see you around."

When she left I stared at Rico disapprovingly.

"Hey, you," he said, smiling.

But I walked toward one of the Life Cycle machines, ignoring him.

"What's the matter with you?"

"Nothing, and if you don't mind, I'd like to get started so I can get out of here."

"Whoaaa. What's this all about?"

"I told you, nothing."

"Then why are you acting like this?"

"I'm not. I'm tired and I want to get this over with."

"Fine, but instead of doing two reps on each machine, I want you to do three."

"Why?"

"Because you won't be exercising this weekend and this will make up for it."

"I don't think I can do any more than what I've *been* doing."

"Yes you can."

I realized he wasn't taking no for an answer, so I climbed on the biceps curler, set the resistance, and started working.

"Slower and more controlled," he said immediately.

I did as he instructed but I never looked at him. Which was interesting, because until now I hadn't been able to take my eyes off of him, not privately or publicly.

I finished up the first set and started the second and I was already feeling my biceps burn. But I kept curling.

"That's it," he said, standing with his arms folded. He was acting like a well-paid naval commander who'd been hired to whip me in shape.

When I completed the second set, I tried to continue but I couldn't. Just as I had imagined, three sets were too much.

"Keep going," he said.

"I can't, Rico. Maybe next week, but not tonight."

"Yes you can," he said matter-of-factly. "You've got to push yourself."

"And what exactly do you think I've been doing?" I said, staring at him.

"Not as much as you should be."

"What do you mean? I've done everything you told me to do every single night."

"I know, Whitney, but if you want to lose fifty pounds by the end of November, then you're going to have to up your game a little bit."

I got off of the machine and moved on to the next one. When I sat down, I started working my triceps.

"Then suit yourself," he said. "It's your body."

"Why are you speaking to me this way?"

"No reason," he said, scanning the room.

I had a feeling my greatest fear was being realized. Rico really was too good to be true. The man was showing his true colors and he was doing it rather quickly. Much too quickly for someone who'd been treating me like a queen all week. I knew that wasn't a long time, but I was still surprised by the way he was acting.

I finished two sets and moved on to the chest press.

Rico was walking alongside me and some short guy came up to him.

"Long time no see, man," Rico said.

"I know, man," the short guy said. "My work schedule has been outrageous, so I haven't been here in a while."

"So, how's everything been?" Rico asked.

"Can't complain. The job is good. My girl is good. Everything's lovely."

"Glad to hear it."

Rico glanced over at me, making sure my form was correct.

"So, who's this?" the short guy asked.

"This is Whitney, a good friend of mine. I'm training her on the machines."

"Oh, okay. How are you?" he said to me. "I'm Terrance."

"It's nice to meet you," I said, trying to be polite, but I was furious with Rico. This was the second time he'd referred to me as his *good friend* and insinuated that we were nothing special. I felt like such a fool.

I finished the third machine, moved on to the fourth, fifth, and sixth, and then I nixed the final two. And there was no way I was getting on any treadmill. I was exhausted and I wasn't up to it mentally either, not after Rico had humiliated me in front of that Tyra Banks–looking chick and the guy he was still chatting with.

So, I left the area and went into the locker room. As soon as I walked in, I sat down on the bench and burst into tears. Thankfully, no one was around to see me, because I looked pretty pitiful. I shed one tear after another, feeling sorry for myself, and then it dawned on me. I didn't have to feel this way if I didn't want to. I had always been a master at fixing my pain, and I could do it again fairly easy. There was certainly still time for my evening to end on a happy note, and why shouldn't it?

I smiled at my solution, gathered my personal belongings, and went out to my car.

"Mm, mm, mm," I moaned. "It doesn't get much better than this."

I was stretched out like a Cheshire cat on the sofa, all by myself, relishing every moment.

I'd already inhaled seven Krispy Kremes and was still counting.

I'd purchased one full dozen, six chocolate-iced and six originals, and they were better than I remembered. It had only been five days since I'd consumed any, but I was a fiend needing a fix and these doughnuts were taking care of it. I was sure they were better than any drug available.

I finished the final five and debated whether I should remove the box from the coffee table and take it into the kitchen, but I didn't feel like it. Pieces of frosting had dropped onto my shirt and onto the carpet and were probably strewn in a few other places, but I wouldn't worry about it until morning.

I lay there quietly and contentedly. I thought about Rico and how he'd treated me, but the pain wasn't as noticeable. And while I could hear some movie on Lifetime beginning to fade, I batted my eyes, trying to stay awake. I batted them until I couldn't fight it any longer but then I heard the doorbell ringing.

I sat up and looked around and then it rang again. I had a feeling it was Rico and I debated whether to let him in.

But I did.

I opened the door and walked away from it and he came in and followed me into the family room. I wanted to die when I realized the Krispy Kreme box was still hanging wide open.

"Please don't tell me you just ate a bunch of those," he said, taking a seat.

But I didn't respond.

"Whitney? Tell me you didn't. Not after all the progress you've made."

I still didn't say anything.

"Oh, so now you're not going to answer me?"

"Why are you here, Rico?"

"No, the question is why did you walk away from me without saying anything and then just leave the health club?"

"Because I was tired of you talking to me the way you were."

"And how was that?"

"Like you were irritated because I couldn't lift those weights the way you wanted me to."

"I was only irritated because I want you to meet your goal and it seems to me you're not trying very hard. And on top of that, I come here and find an empty doughnut box?"

"My feelings were hurt, Rico. Can you understand that?"

"Hurt why?"

"Because you kept introducing me as your friend."

"Well, we are friends," he said with a confused expression on his face.

"When two people sleep together on a regular basis, they shouldn't be categorized as just friends."

"Look, Whitney, I like you a lot, but we've only known each other for four days. I mean, it's not like we're in love or anything like that."

I knew he was right, but I didn't have the nerve to tell him that I was already heading in that direction. I hadn't wanted to feel this way, but I couldn't help myself.

"Then why did you send me flowers with a note saying 'This is only the beginning'?"

"Because to me this is the beginning . . . of a wonderful friendship."

"So, are you saying you sleep with all your friends?"

"No, I'm saying that I want us to take things slow."

"Are you sleeping with other women now?"

"No."

"Don't lie, Rico."

"I'm not, and let me make something clear. I'd have no problem letting you know if I was. I told you on Monday that I'm a straightforward kind of guy and that means I don't hide anything."

"So, are you planning on sleeping with anyone else while you're still seeing me?"

"No. My plan is for us to get to know each other a lot better."

Now I didn't know what to think. He was being on the up-and-up but I still didn't like what I was hearing. I didn't like the fact that he could sleep with someone else at any time and he might expect me to be okay with it. I didn't like the fact that I'd made the decision to sleep with him myself so quickly.

Rico gazed at the empty box and shook his head disappointedly.

"I still can't believe you ate those."

"I was desperate. And on top of that, the only thing I had today was a grilled chicken breast with no bread."

"That's bad. Because even if you're going to watch your carbs, you have to eat at least five times a day. I told you that on Tuesday. Three small meals and at least two snacks. If you don't, you'll keep bingeing the way you just did."

"I'll start over tomorrow," I said.

"Well, I hope that's true, because if you don't, you'll never be ready for that reunion."

I averted my eyes toward the TV and Rico relaxed farther into the sofa. When he'd first offered to train me, I'd thought this would be a good thing, but now I wasn't so sure. I was starting to wonder if it might be better for us to keep this *friendship* of ours separate from my weight loss program. Because I could see it was going to cause conflict.

But for now I would keep things as is.

I would do it for the same reason Aunt Hilda had shacked up with her man all these years. I would do it so I didn't have to be alone.

Chapter 21

Charisse

TODAY WAS definitely not the norm. It was a beautiful autumn morning and Charisse and Brianna were headed to the hair salon for back-to-back appointments. Not once since Brianna had become old enough to get her hair done professionally had she and Charisse gone to the salon on the same day. As a matter of fact, Charisse had even made sure that Marvin was the one who took Brianna so she didn't have to.

But since three days ago, when Charisse had been pretending to show Brianna this newfound affection and Brianna had told her how much she loved her, Charisse had begun feeling somewhat differently about her daughter. Even though she'd misconstrued the entire event by hallucinating about her own mother, it was almost as if her feelings for Brianna had changed. It was as if Charisse had awakened from a bad dream and actually wanted to spend time with her. She couldn't explain it exactly, but a part of her wanted to love her daughter. Of course, she had always loved her son, but now there was something special about Brianna. There was something special about the way her daughter had hugged her and spoken to her on Wednesday and the way she truly seemed to need her.

"So, who's this Halston person your brother was teasing you about last week?" Charisse said, turning the corner and driving out of their subdivision.

Brianna blushed and Charisse could tell Brianna didn't know how to answer.

"You can tell me," Charisse said. "Who is he?"

"Just some boy," she said, gazing out of the window.

"Some boy that you really like, apparently."

Brianna smiled but kept looking out of the window.

Charisse had wanted to talk about boys with her own mother, but her mother hadn't wanted to hear about them. She hadn't wanted to hear about anything or anyone Charisse was interested in. Their relationship had forever been such a sad state of affairs and now Charisse was sorry that she'd treated Brianna almost worse. She was sorry that she'd actually despised an innocent child, her own flesh and blood, since the day she had been born.

"Mom?" Brianna said after a couple of minutes passed by. "Can I ask you something?"

"Of course. What is it?"

"Why did you start crying the way you did when I hugged you the other day?"

Charisse paused because she didn't know how to answer the question. In all honesty, she'd wanted to forget altogether about that spell she'd had.

"I guess I was just emotional," she finally said.

"But you looked really upset and then you ran down the stairs."

"I know. And I'm sorry. I guess I got upset because you and I have never hugged that way before."

"Not even when I was a little baby?"

"Well, yeah, I always hugged you that way back then," Charisse lied with a straight face. She didn't have the heart to tell her the truth.

"Well, why did you stop?"

"I don't know," Charisse said, starting to feel uncomfortable with all of these questions.

"Well, I'm glad you like me now. And I'm glad we're going to get our hair done together just like Ashley and her mom do."

Charisse wanted to break into tears again. She wasn't sure what was happening to her but this whole scenario with Brianna was baffling her. For the first time in her life, she felt guilty. She'd never regretted or felt guilty about anything she'd ever done or said, but she was definitely feeling that way about Brianna. At this very moment, she wished she could start life all over again and do things a lot differently.

As Charisse continued driving, she wondered how Taylor was doing. Taylor had called her yesterday to tell Charisse about her doctor's visit, and Charisse could tell that Taylor was worried. Charisse did sympathize with her, but she still didn't understand why Taylor had waited two years to have another Pap exam. It just didn't make any sense, not when a woman knew she needed to have them annually and had medical insurance to cover it.

"Dial your Aunt Taylor for me," Charisse said to Brianna.

Brianna waited for Taylor to answer.

"Hi, Auntie Taylor. How are you?"

Charisse watched Brianna's face light up, and for the first time, it didn't bother Charisse. In the past, Brianna's love for Taylor had tended to irritate Charisse, but not today. Today, she had the utmost respect for it, and surprisingly, it gave her a warm feeling.

"Okay, Auntie Taylor, I'll talk to you later," Brianna said, passing her mother the phone.

"So, how are you?" Charisse asked Taylor.

"I guess I'm hanging in there. And I'm trying my hardest to stay positive."

"Which is good because chances are you won't need to have a hysterectomy."

"I hope you're right."

"I am. You'll be just fine and this will be over before you know it."

"So, where are you and Brianna on your way to so early in the morning?"

"The hair salon."

"On a Saturday!"

"I know. Normally, I'm her first client of the day because I hate waiting. But I made this appointment at the last minute and this is what we got stuck with."

"Well, good luck."

"Tell me about it. But hey, how's Whitney doing with her diet?"

"I just spoke to her a few minutes ago and she's fine. She fell off the wagon a little bit last night, but now she's back on track."

"Why'd she do that?"

"I guess she just wanted something sweet."

"She needs to pray for determination. Pray for a lot more willpower."

"Sometimes it's just not that easy."

"I believe we can do whatever we set our minds to, so if Whitney really wants to lose weight and lose it for good, she's going to have to want it bad enough."

"Well, I think she does want it bad enough. I mean, no one would be overweight if they could help it. And the fact that we're in our late thirties and our metabolisms have slowed down makes it that much harder."

"Which is why both you and I work out at least three times a week."

"But not everyone is the same, Charisse."

"To a certain extent we are. Especially when it comes to issues like this."

"Okay, Charisse. I think we should just agree to disagree on this one."

"Fine," Charisse said, pulling in front of Lisa's Hair Unlimited. "I just wanted to see how you were, but I'll probably give you a call later. If not, I'll talk to you tomorrow."

"Have fun," Taylor said, laughing.

"Yeah, right."

When Charisse and Brianna walked inside, Charisse looked around and got angry. There was some middle-aged woman sitting in Lisa's chair, another client sitting under the dryer, and another on the other side of the room, waiting. This was the very reason Charisse demanded to be the first client of the day or she preferred not to come at all. She'd never understood why beauticians did this because it wasn't like they could do any more than one head at one time. It wasn't like they could work some amazingly awesome miracle with just two hands.

"Hi, Charisse," Lisa said. "Hi, Brianna. Please have a seat and I'll be with both of you as soon as I can."

Was she serious? The woman had five people in her shop and she was acting like it was no problem.

Charisse wanted to tell Lisa to go purchase some foundation to cover up all those blemishes on her face, but Charisse calmed down and took a deep breath instead. She settled herself before she lost it. When it came to Marvin and Whitney, she was only pretending to be more compassionate, but for Brianna she truly did want to be a better person. She didn't know why exactly, but she definitely wasn't faking when it came to her and she didn't want to act indignant in front of her now.

"Why don't you read one of those magazines?" Charisse said.

"I brought one of my novels," Brianna said, pulling out *The Princess Diaries.*

"When did you get that?" Charisse asked.

"Daddy bought it for me last week."

"Wasn't there a movie with that title?"

"Yep. Daddy took Ashley and me to see it when it came out three years ago, and he took us to see *The Princess Diaries 2* last month."

Charisse saw the woman sitting a few seats down looking over at them and Charisse felt embarrassed. She knew the woman was wondering why she didn't know what movies her own daughter had gone to. Worse, she probably wondered why Brianna's father had been the one taking her to see movies when it clearly should have been her.

But Charisse's mother had never taken her to the movies or anywhere else that would be considered entertaining. She hadn't even taken her to church all that much or to visit many of their relatives.

"We should rent the DVD," Brianna said. "I think you would like it."

"Then maybe we will," Charisse said, pulling out a book by Joyce Meyer.

After about forty minutes or so, Lisa finished curling the middle-aged woman, a.k.a. client number 1, and removed her smock. Then, she called over client number 3, the woman sitting not too far from Brianna. But the killing part was that the woman that had been sitting under the dryer, client number 2, who'd obviously just gotten a deep conditioner, was now waiting to be rinsed. Still, Lisa took client number 3 back to the shampoo bowl like she didn't see her. Charisse could tell that client number 2 was teed off but just wasn't saying anything.

When Lisa finished shampooing client number 3, she saturated her hair with deep conditioner and stuck her under the dryer. Then she called over client number 2 and rinsed out hers. After that, she led the woman back over to her styling chair and prepared to create some finger-wave concoction.

Charisse shook her head and then looked toward the door when she heard it open. It was Dominique the ghetto-boo who rented a chair from Lisa.

"Hey, everybody," she said, strolling in, drinking something from a Styrofoam cup and carrying a white paper bag.

"Hey, girl," Lisa said. "One of your clients was here about an hour ago, but she left when I told her you weren't in yet."

"Skip her. I told her I would be here between nine and ten, and if she couldn't wait, then that's just too bad. She be trippin' anyway."

"Well, she said to tell you she wasn't coming back."

"Good. Because I'm about to eat my food and that means she won't be disturbing me."

Lisa looked over at Charisse but Charisse didn't crack a smile. As far as Charisse was concerned, Lisa didn't have any room to criticize, not when she had five clients stacked one on top of the other herself. And now that Charisse was thinking about it, why didn't Lisa have a shampoo girl? Or better, why couldn't Dominique help Lisa out since she didn't have any of her own clients to service at the moment? This whole lack of customer service was starting to piss Charisse off.

But she decided to keep her mouth shut because she really needed her hair done. She wanted it to be fresh for church tomorrow morning.

"I brought you something to eat," Dominique said to Lisa.

"Thanks. I'll have it a little later."

"How come y'all sittin' in here watching some corny movie?" Dominique said, frowning and picking up the TV selector.

When she changed the channel to BET, Nelly's voice blasted through the speaker. Dominique bobbed her big head like she was silly and Charisse wanted to slap her. She wanted to slap Lisa for allowing such craziness in her place of business.

Now Charisse wondered why she was putting up with this. But she knew it was because Lisa really did do a good job with her hair. It was true that she was famous for certain styles that Charisse wouldn't be caught dead with, but still, she kept Charisse's hair healthy and silky and she styled it exactly the way Charisse told her to.

Charisse glanced over at Brianna, but Brianna was engrossed in her book and wasn't paying Dominique or Nelly any attention.

As soon as Lisa finished smoothing the freezing gel on client number 2, she put her back under the dryer. Charisse was sure Lisa was going to shampoo her or Brianna next and then rinse the conditioner from client number 3. But how wrong Charisse was.

"Charisse, you're next. Right after I eat my food."

"Right after you do what?" Charisse said loudly.

"Eat my food. Dominique brought it in for me but I won't be a minute."

"No, I don't think so. Brianna and I have been sitting here for over an hour and I'm not waiting any longer."

Lisa pursed her lips together. "So what do you expect me to do, Charisse, starve myself?"

"To be honest, I really don't care. We came here to get our hair done and we've waited long enough."

"Well, I'm hungry," Lisa said, walking over to Dominique's station.

Dominique stared at Charisse and then looked back toward the television.

"I'm telling you right now, Lisa, if you can't start one of us right now, then we're leaving."

Lisa pulled out what looked to be some sort of sandwich and said, "You do whatever you have to, Charisse."

Charisse couldn't believe what she was hearing. The woman was actually willing to forgo at least a hundred dollars for her and Brianna together, because Brianna needed a relaxer.

"Come on, Brianna," Charisse said. "Let's go."

Brianna followed her mother to the door, and while Charisse had tried to remember that Christians just didn't say certain things, she turned around and stared directly at Lisa.

"Bitch," Charisse said, and walked out.

Brianna followed behind her.

Chapter 22

Charisse

"Wow, Mom, you're back already?" Brandon said when Charisse and Brianna walked inside the house. He and Marvin were sitting in the family room watching college football. It was just after twelve and Charisse knew they'd be glued for the rest of the afternoon. If Brandon could have things his way, he'd watch game after game well into the evening.

"We never even got our hair done. Lisa had a ton of people in there, so we left."

"Oh," Brandon said, his eyes still focused on the game.

"Let's go, Illinois," Marvin screamed at the television, but never acknowledged his wife.

"Mom, can I go over to Ashley's?" Brianna said.

"Go ahead."

"Bye," she said, rushing out.

"Marvin, can I speak to you for a minute?" Charisse said.

"About what?" he answered, still gazing at the television.

"It's important."

This time he looked at her. "Can't you see I'm watching the game?"

"It won't take that long."

"We can talk when this is over."

Charisse stood behind the sofa for a few seconds and then went upstairs.

Marvin was really worrying her. They hadn't spoken more than a couple of words to each other since that night Taylor had come over, and now Charisse was starting to get nervous. It wasn't that she really cared whether Marvin had anything to say to her or not, but she wondered what he was thinking. She wondered what he was planning to do with the information he had on her. Especially since he was treating her more coldly than he had just a few days ago. She'd noticed it the night she'd come home from church after Taylor had left. Which she hadn't understood because he'd purchased a new television without her consent and she hadn't complained one bit. He'd even brought alcohol into their home but she'd acted as though she was happy about it. She pretended to love everything he'd been doing, trying to make sure he didn't blab anything. She did it so he wouldn't be tempted to have any conversations with her mother.

In her bedroom, she picked up the phone and called Taylor again.

"Hello?" Taylor answered.

"Hey."

"What are you doing calling me from home?"

"Because Brianna and I got up and walked out of Lisa's. Can you believe she had the nerve to have three people in there when we got there?"

Taylor laughed. "That's ridiculous."

"I know, and on top of that, she had the audacity to tell me she was taking a break to eat before she started on me. And that's when I'd had enough."

"My last stylist used to pull that same crap and that's why Whitney and I started going to Sheena. Sheena does a great job and she never has more than two people in her shop at one time. And in most cases, she only has one client in by themselves."

"And that's why I'm calling to get her number. You know I don't like that she's a Jehovah's Witness, but I'm willing to tolerate anything if I can get in and out without waiting."

"You're a trip," Taylor said. "And I'll be honest with you, Charisse. If you can't accept Sheena for the decent person she is and respect her right to believe what she wants to, then I think you should go somewhere else."

"Taylor, please. Just give me the number."

"No, I'm serious, Charisse. You do this all the time and I don't think it's fair for you to judge people and their religion."

"I won't even bring it up. I admit that I don't agree with what they teach, but as long as she doesn't try to discuss it with me, I'll be fine."

Taylor recited the number and Charisse wrote it down.

"So, what are you and Cameron doing today?" Charisse asked.

"I don't know yet. Haven't figured anything out."

"Oh well, I guess I should go so I can give Sheena a call."

"Remember what I said, Charisse."

"Good-bye, Taylor."

Charisse pressed the flash button and dialed the number. Sheena told her that she couldn't get her and Brianna in until next Wednesday, but of course Charisse wasn't missing evening church service for anybody. So instead, she took a Thursday appointment.

As soon as Charisse jotted down the information in her Blackberry, the phone rang. She cringed when she saw that it was her mother calling.

She allowed it to ring three additional times and then picked it up. Marvin answered at the same time and Charisse held her breath.

"How are you, Mattie Lee?" he said.

"I'm fine, Marvin. You?"

"Couldn't be better. How's Roy?"

"He's fine."

"Good." Marvin said. "You tell him I said hello and that maybe he and I can go hunting together before it gets too cold."

"I doubt it," Mattie Lee said. "Roy has a lot of remodeling work that needs to be done around here, so until that's finished, he won't be goin' nowhere."

"Well, I think Charisse is on the other extension," he said. "You take care now."

"Hi, Mama," Charisse said when Marvin hung up.

"What is he doin' answerin' the phone?"

"I guess because I took so long to get to it."

"Well, since I hadn't heard from you or seen you, I figured I'd better find out what was going on."

"I'm sorry, Mama, but I've been working a lot of overtime."

"Well, is that right?" Mattie Lee's tone was sarcastic.

"Yes."

"Unh-huh. And which do you think is more important, some job or your mother?"

"You are."

"Then you'd better start acting like it."

Charisse didn't say a word because she didn't want to say the wrong thing. She didn't want her mother to have anything else to scream about.

"So, what's going on with that Marvin?" Mattie Lee continued.

"Nothing. Everything is back to normal."

"Meaning what?"

"That I have him back under control."

"And did he apologize for acting a fool like he did?"

"Yes. He's been apologizing to me almost every day ever since."

"Well, I suggest you keep it that way . . . wait, Charisse, hold on a minute. Roy, what are you standing there for, lookin' all stupid? Don't you see me on this phone? Now get back in there and wait until I tell you to come out . . . Just sickening," Mattie Lee said.

Charisse felt so sorry for her father and sorry that there was nothing she could do to help him. As it was, she couldn't stand up to her mother about her own issues, so she certainly would never confront her about her father. Her mother ruled over both of them and it was the reason Charisse tried not to go around her. She knew the time would come, though, when her mother wouldn't hear any more excuses and Charisse would have no choice but to go visit them.

"So, when should I expect to see you again?" Mattie Lee wanted to know. She spoke as if she'd been reading Charisse's mind.

"Maybe tomorrow. And if not, I'll come by next week."

"No, next week won't work. I'll see you tomorrow after you leave that church of yours. Because I know you don't miss a Sunday going to see that Reverend Demon."

"His name is Reverend Damon," Charisse reminded her.

"No, I said it right. The man is a demon. So, I'll call him whatever I feel like calling him. And don't you ever correct me."

"I'm sorry."

"Yeah you're sorry all right. A sorry-ass excuse for a woman."

Charisse opened her mouth, preparing to apologize again, but Mattie Lee hung up on her. Charisse would just have to make it up to her tomorrow. She wasn't sure how, but she would think of something.

After washing and drying a load of clothing, Charisse read a few more chapters of Joyce Meyer's book and then ordered food from the Italian restaurant down the street. Brianna had come back from Ashley's and she and Brandon both wanted lasagna. Marvin claimed he would eat anything, but Charisse knew he was only saying that so he wouldn't have to talk to her. His attitude was worse than ever and she was still trying to figure out what the reason was.

When they'd finished eating, Brandon went up to his bedroom to get ready for the movies and Brianna got her stuff together so she could sleep over at Ashley's. Ashley's mother was picking her up and one of the parents of Brandon's teammates was stopping by to get him.

In the meantime, Charisse cleared the table and Marvin left and went upstairs. She'd been hoping he would stay in the kitchen so she could talk to him, not because she wanted to be in his company but because she really needed to get on his good side. She needed to make things right until she figured out how to muzzle him.

She loaded one plate after another into the stainless steel dishwasher, then the utensils and drinking glasses. But suddenly she thought about Pastor Damon. She thought about the way he'd seduced her and how she'd allowed him to do it. She couldn't help thinking about the way he'd kissed her or the way he'd forced himself inside her so anxiously. She thought about how good he'd made her feel and how she'd been considering the idea of being with him again and soon. He'd made her feel so wonderful that she was prepared to forget about her rule—that she could only be with him once or twice per year. She knew it was wrong, but she had already prayed about their sexual relations and God had forgiven her. She believed that God understood the strain she was under at home and that He would forgive her as many times as she needed Him to. And of course, He would forgive Pastor Damon, because he'd chosen him to lead His people.

When the kitchen was spotless, Brianna was gone and Brandon was on his way out the door, Charisse wasted no time, heading upstairs to see Marvin. When she walked in, though, she saw a large plush towel wrapped around his body, his back covered with beads of water.

She didn't want him the way she wanted Pastor Damon, but she was willing to do what she had to.

"Marvin, why won't you talk to me?" she said, walking over to him.

"Talk to you about what?"

"Us. Life. Anything."

"Because I don't have *anything* to say."

"But why?"

"I just don't."

"Well, what am I supposed to do?"

"Whatever you want, Charisse. Hell, you've always done whatever you wanted anyhow, so what's the problem now?"

"I want us to work this out, Marvin. I don't want you hating me the way you do."

"But you're only saying this because I know some of your secrets. The kind that could ruin you if anyone found out about them."

You dirty bastard.

"That's not it at all," she said. "I know you're unhappy with the way I've treated you, but I promise I'm ready to change. I want to change because I love you, Marvin."

"No you don't. The only person you love is Charisse."

"That's not true. And to prove it, I've really been trying with Brianna, too. I've really been trying to be a good mother to her."

"Maybe. But how long will that last?"

"Forever."

"Well, if that's true, then I'm happy for Brianna, because she deserves that. She's a good girl, and while I'll never understand why, she really does love you."

"Just tell me what to do and I'll do it. I'll do whatever you think will help us. I'll even go to counseling like you wanted. We can set it up first thing Monday."

"We are so beyond that now. I mean, at first, I thought it might help, but then something started happening."

"Like what?"

"I started thinking about every terrible thing you've said to me, every horrible thing you did to me and how I've wasted all these years of my life for nothing. And that's when I realized I no longer want to be married to you."

"So, what are you saying?"

"That I'm willing to stay until Brandon and Brianna have both enrolled in college, but after that I'm out of here."

"You don't mean that. You're just upset."

"I've never been more serious about anything."

"So, what's going to happen until then? Between now and the time the kids finish high school?"

"I'm moving into the guest bedroom and you and I will be going our separate ways. You'll do whatever you want and I'll be doing the same."

"Have you lost your mind?"

"No."

"I won't live like this. I won't allow you to treat me this way," she said, almost in tears. She felt so frustrated when she couldn't control him.

"You can take this deal or leave it. Either we do it my way or there are going to be real problems. Either you dance to my music or I'm telling your mother about that insurance policy. And after that, I'm telling her how you used to call your brother in the middle of the night, telling him how much you hated him. The man was on his deathbed, dying of cancer, Charisse. And still you would ask him, over and over, why he wouldn't just hurry up and die. And interestingly enough, the last time you did that, he died the next morning."

Charisse was stunned.

"Yeah, you always thought you were so clever. But what you didn't know was that I wasn't always being the good little boy you wanted me to be. You didn't know that I wasn't always asleep every time you slipped downstairs. There were many nights that I eased out of the bedroom and stood at the top of the staircase and I would hear you saying the meanest stuff to your brother on the phone. There were times when I felt so sorry for him but I never said a word. But I'll bet if your mother found out what you did, she would make your life a living hell. She does a pretty good job of that now, but knowing her, she would probably kill you over something like this."

Charisse stared at Marvin in a daze. She wanted to beg him to change his mind but she didn't have the strength. She couldn't find the words to convince him if she wanted to.

Just this morning, she'd been thinking that all she had to do was find a way to silence him, but now he had something else on her. And she wondered if he knew more than what he was admitting. She wondered if maybe he would reveal some of her other secrets, but only when he thought it was necessary. He would do it as a way to control her.

But Charisse would die before she would allow him to expose her. Either that or she would kill Marvin and put an end to all of this for good.

Chapter 23

Whitney

NORMALLY, I didn't weigh myself in the evening, but I stepped onto my chrome-trimmed scale and waited for the digital readout. I'd done exceptionally well all day long, only eating what was allowed, but I was still concerned about that pound I had gained. I'd discovered it first thing this morning and I knew this was a result of all those doughnuts I had eaten. Of course, I was wishing I hadn't purchased them, but last night had been a depressing time for me. It had been a time when I wasn't feeling all that great about myself and I was worried that Rico didn't want me. I worried that he was losing interest in what we had together and that my latest attempt at trying to lose weight was hopeless. Then, subconsciously, I worried about Taylor and what she was going through medically.

I stepped off the scale, and thankfully, I still weighed the same as I had this morning. This was a good thing because chances were I could lose that extra pound with no problem.

Next, I walked over to my vanity and started applying my makeup. I'd already finished my hair, and while Rico wasn't planning to pick me up for another hour, I didn't want to wait until the last minute to get ready. We'd made plans to see a movie and then have dinner afterward.

I pulled out six cosmetic brushes, one to apply foundation, one to set it with powder, one to apply blush, two to apply eye shadow, and one for my lip color. Once upon a time, the only brushes I had ever used were those that came with each product. But then one day, one of the Lancôme reps had insisted that brushes were a necessity. She explained that if I used them, my makeup would go on so much more smoothly and a lot more evenly. At first, I'd decided that she was simply trying to make a sale and that I didn't really need what she was suggesting, but the more she spoke the more I understood what she was saying. So, before I knew it, I had spent well over a hundred dollars and was on my way out to the parking lot.

But I had to admit that it was a good decision because I'd soon started receiving a ton of compliments on how perfect my makeup looked. It became so noticeable that Taylor and even Charisse, the woman who never took advice from anyone, had rushed out to buy the same thing. And best of all, a Mary Kay consultant had asked if I wanted to become one of her models and attend some of her parties. Which I still couldn't fathom because who in their right mind would want to see a two-hundred-plus woman modeling anything? It didn't make much sense to me, and while the woman had called me periodically for two straight months, I'd never agreed to do it. I'd chickened out the same as always. Still it was nice to know that someone had actually been interested.

When I finished the final touches, I walked out into my bedroom and picked up the outfit I'd purchased earlier. I'd been trying hard not to buy anything expensive, not with me still losing weight, but when I'd seen this periwinkle V-necked sweater, I hadn't been able to bypass it. Plus, I couldn't imagine not buying it when I was now able to wear it one size smaller. This, for some, would have been a tiny feat, but for me it was something to be very proud of.

I sprayed on Sicily, my favorite cologne, and slipped on my new sweater and a pair of black pants. Actually, I didn't look half bad, and I was hoping Rico felt the same way. I wanted him to be content because it still bothered me that he had never gone out with someone my size. There was still a part of me that wondered when he was going to inform me that he couldn't take it anymore. But hopefully, it wouldn't be tonight—and definitely not before my reunion.

I still had maybe another half hour so I went into the family room and turned on the CD player. Anthony Hamilton belted out strong, endearing lyrics the way I wanted him to. I'd loved this man's work from the moment I'd first heard it.

I sat down on the sofa, flipping through the latest issue of *Essence*, but my doorbell rang. Rico was early, but I was fine with that because I was completely ready.

However, when I opened the door, my heart sank. I wasn't sure why they were here, but my mother and sister just stared at me. I stared right back and then finally my mother spoke up.

"Bet you didn't expect to see us, did you?" she said, walking in without being asked.

"I hope we didn't interrupt anything," Tina said, following behind her.

I was still speechless, but I closed the door and joined those two skinny witches in the family room. I would never mention it, but with both of them having the same shoulder-length weave, the same mocha complexion, and being about the same height, they actually looked like sisters. Not to mention they both had that same irritating voice I hated hearing.

"Are you expecting someone?" Mother said.

"Actually, I am," I said, already wishing they would leave.

"Who?" Tina asked.

"A friend."

"Oh. Well, Mother and I were just in the area and we figured we'd stop by."

I didn't say anything.

"You are okay with this, aren't you?" Mother asked.

"I'm fine. I won't be able to visit with you for very long, but this is fine."

"I guess we could have called, but since you're my daughter, I didn't think it was necessary," Mother said.

Well, it was necessary and I wish you wouldn't just drop in like this. That's what I wanted to say, but I held my tongue.

"This is fine," I said again. "So, how have you been?"

"Fine," she said, and I wondered how many more "fines" we were going to exchange. It was a sad day in America when this was the only thing a mother and daughter could think to say to each other.

"Good," I said.

"We went shopping all day today," Tina boasted. "And we bought a lot of nice stuff. There were so many sales at the mall."

"Really?" I said. I already knew about the sales because I'd gone to the mall myself, but I acted as though I was surprised by it.

"I bought two pairs of shoes, a pair of fitted boots, two cashmere sweaters, a pair of riding pants, and a leather jacket," Tina continued.

"What did you buy, Mother?" I asked, hoping Tina would shut her trap.

"Oh, not a lot. Just a new fur coat."

"I'll bet that's nice," I said. "I know you love those."

"It's beautiful," Mother said. "I've been wanting a full-length sable for quite some time. It's sort of an early birthday present to myself."

Tina cut her eyes at me but I ignored her.

"So, who are you expecting?" Mother asked.

"He's just a friend," I said.

"He?" Tina said.

"Yes."

"So, you're going out on a date?" Mother said.

"Yes."

"And who is this person?" Mother asked, and I knew right then that the conversation was about to head downhill.

"I met him at the health club."

"Health club?" Tina asked. "Since when did you start going there?"

"Last week."

"Well, is it helping?" she said, smirking.

"As a matter of fact, it is, Tina. As a matter of fact, I've lost ten pounds," I said, proudly.

"Ten pounds? Where? Because to me, you don't look any different."

"Well, maybe it's because you haven't seen me in a while," I explained.

"I guess," Tina said, raising her eyebrows.

"Are you watching what you eat?" Mother asked.

"Yes. I'm watching my carbohydrates."

"So, are you saying you're not eating any bread, sweets, or anything with sugar?" Mother said, clearly not believing me.

"Yes. That's exactly what I'm saying."

"Hmmph," Mother grunted. "Well, I sure hope you can keep it up this time."

And I sure hope I never have to see you again.

I wanted so desperately to tell Mother just that but I didn't want to disrespect her. Mostly, I didn't want to work myself into a frenzy before Rico got here.

"What did you have to eat today?" Tina asked.

"Why?"

"I'm just asking because I just can't believe you're not eating any sweets. And what about soda? Because I remember a time when you would drink whole six-packs in one afternoon. Especially, when we were in high school."

"Well, I wouldn't worry about it, Tina. I'm doing what I need to do for me and it's really none of your business."

"Your sister is only trying to encourage you," Mother said, and

I wanted to punch her. Sadly enough, I wanted to assault my own mother, and I hated when she forced me to feel like this.

"Mother, why do you always take Tina's side with everything?"

"I don't. I only stand up for what's right, and right now, you're wrong for speaking to your sister like this."

"What?" She's the one who's being rude to me. And in my own house for that matter."

"Mother, let's go," Tina said, standing up.

"This is such a shame," Mother said, still sitting. "It's such a shame, Whitney, that you can't get along with your only sister. Especially since I raised you so much better than that."

"No, Tina is the one who can't get along with me. She's always picked with me and I refuse to put up with it anymore."

Mother finally stood up and then said, "I hate saying this, but the reason you act this way is because of how you look. All that weight has you miserable and it has you taking out your frustrations on your sister. Sometimes you even take it out on me, but I don't let it bother me because I know you can't help it."

I could feel my heart beating rapidly and my hands felt sweaty, but this was not uncommon. Not when I had to physically see and deal with these two tramps standing before me. I hadn't planned on attacking them, but if they didn't leave soon, they would leave me no choice.

"Mother, I'm really sorry to hear that you feel that way, and maybe it'll be best if the two of you just leave."

"This is so typical," Tina said, snickering.

"Meaning what?" I asked.

"You getting upset because I look better than you. You getting upset because you can't get a man. You getting upset because Mom and I are best friends. Shall I go on?"

"No, that's quite enough. But for the record, I don't care about any of what you just said. And if you think I'm jealous of you in any way, you need to think again. I mean, why would I envy any woman who slept with a married man for three years, was stupid enough to get pregnant by him and then think he was going to leave his wife?"

I felt redeemed when I saw the shock on my mother's face.

"Yeah, Mother," I continued. "I'll bet you didn't know about your precious little girl stalking one of the vice presidents where she used to work and him getting a restraining order against her. I'll bet you didn't know he gave her money to get rid of that baby she was carrying and then made her resign from the company. And I'm positive you don't know that Ms. Thing here started having sex when she was only eleven."

"You're a liar," Tina yelled. "Mother, she's lying on me and she knows it."

"I know," Mother said, caressing my sister's back, both of them walking to the front door.

"Whitney, you should be ashamed of yourself," Mother said. "I mean, I knew you were jealous of Tina, but this is insane. You've really gone too far this time."

I shook my head, trying to understand how my mother could disregard what I was saying. Because the thing was, I would never lie on my sister. I wondered why Mother didn't want to hear how sneaky Tina was, because she had always been that way since we were children.

"I am so disappointed in you," Mother said, looking back at me when they both stepped outside.

"Well, you know what, Mother, not as disappointed as I am in you."

"Disappointed why, Whitney?"

"Because you've always treated me so terribly. And the more I think about it, Tina is only being the person you taught her to be."

"You're talking crazy, girl," Mother said.

"No I'm not. When we were children, you slept with more married men than I can count. So, my guess is that you're not all that shocked about Tina doing the same thing. You're just shocked that she never told you about it."

"I won't listen to this," she said, and they started walking.

I watched and waited until they were ready to get into the car.

"Oh, and Mother," I said, "one last thing . . . have a great time at your *surprise* birthday party on November twentieth."

She stared at me in a dejected sort of fashion, and next I saw Rico parking his SUV. My sister slammed her door and jammed on the accelerator and I was happy they were gone. I was even happy that I'd finally stood up to both of them and told them what I thought.

"Who was that?" Rico said, coming up the sidewalk.

"My mother and sister."

"Really? I wish they had stayed so I could meet them."

"Maybe some other time," I said, knowing it wouldn't be anytime soon. Rico scanned me from head to toe.

"You look good," he said, kissing me on the lips.

"Thanks. You do, too."

"I know," he said, and we both laughed.

"So, are you ready?" he asked.

"Actually, I am. Just let me turn off the stereo and get my purse," I said, heading toward my bedroom and leaving him in the entryway.

"Hey," he said and, I turned to look at him.

"Yeah?"

"I meant what I said."

"About what?"

"You really, really look good. You look beautiful."

I smiled and wondered if he knew how much I'd needed to hear that.

I was sure he didn't have a clue.

Chapter 24

Taylor

IT HAD BEEN THREE WEEKS since I'd first seen Dr. Green, and while I'd also gotten a second opinion, the diagnosis had remained unchanged. The tumor in my uterus needed to be removed and there were no other options to be considered. Still, a part of me had been hoping I wouldn't have to go through with this. Deep down, I'd been hoping that there was some other procedure, something a lot less aggressive, that could be performed on me. I'd been praying that there was a better way to go about handling this but there wasn't.

And now here I was packing the last of my overnight bag and preparing to head to the hospital. My parents had driven into town last night, but they were now at a restaurant having breakfast. I, of course, had been fasting since just before midnight and wouldn't be able to eat until well after surgery. Which actually wasn't as much of a problem as I had thought it would be. I'd been sure that I was going to be completely famished but maybe my nerves were preventing it. I was nervous because I'd agreed to sign a consent form authorizing Dr. Green to perform a hysterectomy in the event that he did find cancer. I'd had to think long and hard about it, but in the end, I knew that staying alive was more important to me than having a child. Still, the thought of it all had me uneasy.

And then there was my relationship with Cameron. He'd been extremely attentive ever since that day I'd gone to his office and told him about my illness, but I couldn't get past what his first reaction had been. I couldn't ignore what I knew he still had to be thinking and it had even affected our normal level of intimacy. I'd gotten my period again last week, only twenty days after returning from Los Angeles, but this week Cameron had wanted sex with me every evening. He'd acted as though we might never be able to make love again, and that truly bothered me. It made me wonder just how long we would continue being a couple.

But I couldn't worry about such issues at the moment. What I needed to do was try to calm myself down and prepare for whatever was going to be. I'd prayed more than I had in my life, my church members had done the same, and my mother had already claimed a positive recovery. She'd told me first thing this morning that God's will would be done and that I was going to be fine. Of course, I was hoping that His will would be for me to marry and have children one day, and I tried not to focus on anything different.

I stuffed a comb, brush, some body lotion, and a few other needed items into my bag and zipped it closed. Thankfully, I wouldn't be there more than a day or two and I would be wearing a hospital gown for the duration. I smiled when I remembered the days when patients could count on being in the hospital at least a week and it didn't matter how minor their illness was—days when insurance carriers didn't force medical facilities to kick you out as soon as possible. I remembered the time my mother had gone to the hospital to have something similar to what I was having today and she'd packed the most beautiful lingerie. It had been almost like she'd been planning what clothing to take on a vacation, but the real reason was that she wanted to look good for any visitors. It was so amazing how times had changed so radically.

When I started to walk into the bathroom, my phone rang. I was sure it was Cameron, wanting to know if we were ready, but instead someone from my firm was calling.

"Hello?"

"Taylor, I'm sorry to bother you at home, but I just need to ask you a quick question." Strangely enough, it was Skyler, and I couldn't believe he was calling me personally and hadn't asked his secretary to.

"Okay," I said.

"You remember that malpractice case you tried with Jim and Morgan last year? The one where the woman's daughter died because the emergency room physician misdiagnosed her?"

"Yeah."

"Well, we've got a similar situation again. Except this time we're dealing with a man's wife who died because the hospital told her she wasn't having a heart attack. But when they sent her home, she died an hour later from exactly that."

"Unbelievable."

"It is, and while I know you're going to be out for a couple of weeks or so, I wanted to ask you now if we can conference you in on our initial meetings. And if you will, I want you to second-chair this with me."

This was definitely a first, and I was stunned to say the least. Skyler was, in a very roundabout way, acknowledging my expertise.

"You know I love huge cases like this, but I guess I'm not sure why you're asking me."

"I'm asking because right after the husband left here yesterday, Jim immediately thought about all the research you did last year and the way you closed at the other trial."

"I don't doubt that Jim feels that way, but if this is mainly going to be your case, I guess I'm surprised that you would even want me involved with it. I mean, have you forgotten that you can't stand the sight of me?"

"That's just not true. And ever since I heard about you needing to have surgery, I've wanted to come and talk to you. I know you won't believe me but I'm sorry for always pestering you the way I have."

"Skyler, please. If you want me to help you with the case, then I will, but you don't have to exaggerate."

"I'm not."

"Okay, look. You and I both know that people don't change overnight, and this is definitely an overnight situation because just yesterday you were ragging on me for no reason."

"But after you left in the afternoon, I overheard your secretary telling mine that you have a tumor and you might not be able to have any children."

"And?" I was fuming because I wished people would mind their own business and that the clerical staff would stop gossiping so much.

Skyler didn't say anything.

"And?" I repeated, and I wasn't cordial about it.

"My mother had uterine cancer and she died when I was ten years old."

Now I felt bad because of how nasty my attitude had been.

"I'm really sorry to hear that," I said. "I didn't know."

"You didn't know because I never talk about it. Still, when I hear about any woman going through the same thing, my heart goes out to her."

"Well, I appreciate that, but the doctor doesn't know if I have cancer or not. He won't find out until he goes in."

"That's good to hear and I'll keep hoping for the best."

"Thanks."

"And Taylor there's something else I need to say."

"Wow. I'm almost afraid to hear it."

He laughed in a cheerful way and that shocked me even more.

"I can imagine," he said. "But what I want you to know is that things are going to be different when you come back. I promise I won't criticize you or your work ever again."

"And why is that?"

"Because it's not necessary. I only did it because you really are good at what you do and I didn't want to accept that. I didn't want to accept that you've won certain cases I'm not sure I would have been successful with."

"Well, I gotta tell you, I can't believe what I'm hearing, but I do respect you for saying it. It takes a real man to give a woman that kind of credit. Especially when they're in the same line of work."

"You have no idea," he said, chuckling. "And when you're well, I'd like to take you to lunch. You know, sort of as a peace offering."

"I can handle that."

"Well, I'd better let you go, but please get well soon."

"Thanks, Skyler. You have no idea how much that means."

"Take care."

I hung up and breathed deeply. I knew I'd heard Skyler correctly, but I still needed time to register everything. The man was actually being nice to me and he had apologized for all of our previous run-ins. Not to mention this was all because of what his mother had died from. Although now his news did have me wondering if I would end up just like her. I couldn't help wondering if maybe Skyler was thinking the same thing and was simply trying to clear his conscience. But I guess I would see soon enough. I would learn what my fate was in a matter of hours and I would just have to deal with it.

"I think that's everything," the admittance representative said when I'd signed the last document. They'd phoned me a couple of days before to preregister me, so most everything was pretty much in order.

"So, where do we go from here?" I asked.

"You're going to head out this door," she said, pointing. "Down the long corridor to your right, and then you'll take a left when you see the surgical area. There will be signs that will direct you to the pre-op nursing station."

"Thanks," I said, and my mother and I walked out. When we did, I saw Whitney and Charisse sitting near Cameron and my father. I think I was happier seeing them now than ever before. I was comforted in knowing that everyone who cared about me was there to support me.

"So, you ready?" Whitney said.

"As ready as I'll ever be," I said, hugging her. "Thanks for coming."

"You know we would never let you go through this without us," Charisse said, and I embraced her also. Then we followed the directions I had been given, and when we arrived I signed in and a nurse escorted me back to a room. I removed all of my clothing and slipped on one of those backless gowns again, but this time they gave me a robe and light blue ankle socks to cover my feet.

When I was ready, the nurse informed me that they'd be coming in to check on me and that just before they took me to the OR, Dr. Green and the anesthesiologist would be in to speak with me. When she left everyone came into my room. I'd seen a sign that said there was a limit of two, but at least I could see them all together for a few minutes.

"You know, Whit," I said, "you've really lost a lot of weight, girl."

"We were just complimenting her on that before we came in here," my mother said.

"I've lost twenty-five pounds and I can actually feel it in all of my clothing."

"Well, you look good," I said.

"Thanks. I feel good, too."

"Didn't I tell you it would make a difference?" Charisse chimed in, and Whitney and I looked at each other.

"That you did, Charisse," Whitney answered, and I knew Whitney was trying to be cordial because of my parents.

"Next thing you know we won't be able to see you," Cameron teased her.

"I doubt that," she said, and we all laughed.

"The hospital is pretty strict about having so many people in the room, so why don't Whitney and I step out so you can visit with your parents," Charisse said.

"Yeah, we'll come back just before they take you," Whitney agreed.

"I'll come back, too," Cameron said, kissing me on the forehead, and the three of them left.

"You're not scared, are you?" Daddy said.

"Probably not as scared as you are," I said, smiling because I could tell how restless he was. I could tell he was worried about his only child.

"She's going to be just fine," my mother added. "God is running all of this so there's no need to fret about it."

"That's right," I said, trying to convince my father—and me.

"Is there anything we can get for you?" he asked.

"No, Daddy, I'm fine. Why don't you sit down and relax."

When he did, Mom joined him.

"Don't forget that I have copies of my will and power-of-attorney documents in my file cabinet at home and there are also copies at my firm."

"I'm glad you have things in order the way you do, but we won't be needing any of that this weekend," Mom said.

"I'm sure you won't, but just to be on the safe side."

We sat and chatted for a while and then Mom suggested that she and Daddy go out so that Cameron could come in.

"Are you comfortable?" Cameron asked when we were alone.

"Very."

"I'll be glad when this is over."

"Me, too."

"But at least we got to see the Prince concert the other night."

"I know because after today it'll be a while before I can go out in crowds like that again," I said, remembering every lyric Prince had sung. The man definitely still had it and I was glad Cameron had gone out of his way to get good seats, regardless of what he'd had to pay for them.

"Taylor, I'm really sorry for the way I acted that day you came to my office," Cameron said without warning. "I had no right speaking to you that way and I should have shown you a lot more compassion."

All I could think was how apologetic everyone seemed to be today—specifically Cameron and Skyler. It was amazing the way people treated you when they thought you might die.

"You've already apologized for that more than once," I said, "and I forgive you. But I still think we have some issues to work out. I want to be married but you don't, and that's a major problem for us."

"And I've tried to explain why."

"I realize that, but I'm still not happy about it."

"Let's just get you well first and then we can talk more about this later. What I want is for us to focus on the love we have for each other and not our differences."

I looked at him silently.

We sat there not saying much else and soon the nurse appeared. Shortly after, Dr. Green and the anesthesiologist came in as planned and explained what would happen over the next few hours. When Cameron and I were alone again, my parents, Whitney and Charisse came back in and Mom prayed one final time.

I closed my eyes and squeezed both her and Daddy's hand like my life depended on it.

Chapter 25

Whitney

As soon as the OR staff person pushed Taylor's bed down the hallway, Charisse and I decided to get something to eat. Mr. and Mrs. Hunt weren't hungry, and believe it or not, Cameron had gone back to the office. He'd mentioned something about some meeting he couldn't miss but his words had sounded sort of bogus. Although, maybe I was just being paranoid because of everything Taylor had shared with me. Still, I didn't think it was right for him to leave until she was in recovery. It just seemed to me that he would want to know she was all right.

"So, what are you going to have?" Charisse said as soon as we entered the cafeteria.

"Not much, so maybe just a ham and cheese omelet."

"I am really shocked at you," she said.

"Well, you shouldn't be, because I'm really serious about my weight this time."

"I know, but Whitney you know how many times you've said that before."

"Why do you always do this?" I said, walking past her and picking up a tray and silverware.

"I'm only trying to keep you on top of things. I know it might seem harsh, but the more I remind you of all the times you've failed, the more you'll want to prove me wrong."

No, what I *wanted* was to put out a contract on her. I wanted someone to silence Charisse once and for all. And for the life of me, I don't know why I kept tolerating her. Although only a few weeks ago, she'd seemed to have changed. She'd appeared to be a much better person and I'd been happy about that. But now the true monster in her was back and I didn't like it. I was afraid she was going to make me tell her something I might later regret.

I told the cook what I wanted and Charisse ordered the same thing, only she added wheat toast and orange juice to hers. Then we paid for our meals and found a table near the window. The day was sort of gloomy and the forecast called for rain, but I was still hoping the sun would shine instead. Days like this sometimes depressed me, and right now I didn't want to feel that way. I wanted to remain in good spirits for Taylor.

"No matter how I try to understand this, I just don't get it," Charisse started, and I just looked at her.

I could tell she wanted me to respond to whatever it was she was talking about, but I ignored her.

"You know what I'm saying?" she continued. "I mean, can you believe Taylor waited all this time before going to the doctor?"

I ate a forkful of my omelet and scanned the room. There were quite a few people coming in and I wished I could go sit with any one of them. What I wanted was to separate myself from Charisse because the woman was clearly on a mission.

"Whitney, do you hear me?"

"I hear you, but what do you want me to say?"

"I don't know, maybe that you feel the same as I do."

"But the truth is I don't."

"Well, I don't know how you couldn't," she said, drinking some juice.

"Because unlike you, Charisse, I care about Taylor."

"I care about her, too, and that's why I feel so strongly about this. I'm angry because she could have caught that tumor before it got so big."

"Yeah, but what's done is done and now we have to move on."

"You just don't get it," she said, buttering her toast. "You really don't."

"Oh, I get it all right. I understand perfectly."

"No, I don't think you do."

"You know, it's not even worth arguing about, so let's just end this."

Charisse glanced away from me and I could tell she was hot. But I didn't care. As a matter of fact, I was planning to leave her sitting here just as soon as I finished my meal.

"So, what's going on with your new man, Rico?" she said.

"Everything's fine."

"So, is he serious about you?"

"From what I can tell," I said, and I was glad I hadn't introduced him to Charisse. I'd invited Taylor and Cameron over last weekend and the four of us had had dinner and then gone out to a jazz club. I'd purposely not told Charisse about it because I hadn't wanted to be bothered with her.

Still, I decided it was time for me to ask her a few questions. "And what about you and Marvin? I mean, is he still not going to church with you?"

"No," she said, and I could tell she was irritated. She never liked when the loaded gun aimed in her direction.

"Well, that's really strange. Especially since Marvin has always done whatever you instructed him to do."

"You make it sound like he can't even think for himself," she said.

And I cracked up laughing.

"Well, that's how it always seemed. Because ever since I can remember, you've been bossing Marvin like some play toy. And interestingly enough, I've never heard him complain about it."

She stared at me and I wanted so desperately to tell her what Taylor had told me. That Marvin thought she was unstable and wanted to leave her. But I knew I couldn't let on that I knew anything and I kept quiet.

"He never complained because he's content with our relationship. Marvin knows what it takes to make me happy and he knows how to be a good husband . . . oh, but I'm sorry, you wouldn't know anything about that, now would you? Because the truth is you've never had one."

She was cutting me in two but I tried to hold my peace.

"I don't know why I ever became friends with you," she said, and even though no category of rudeness was beyond Charisse Richardson, I was still a bit surprised by what I was hearing. I don't think I'd ever heard her go this far before. But I wouldn't let her speak to me like this and get away with it. Not when I'd finally stood up to my mother and sister just three weekends ago.

"And the feeling is mutual, Charisse. Once upon a time I thought you were a good person and a great friend, but I stopped thinking that a long time ago. And to be honest, the only reason I didn't cut you off is because of Taylor. She's the one who kept defending you and insisting that I shouldn't."

"Well, Taylor shouldn't have done me any favors, because I outgrew you right after college. And the only reason I didn't end our friendship then was because I felt sorry for you."

"Sorry?"

"Yes, sorry, Whitney. You're a truly pitiful person so I've always sympathized with you. I tried to be there for you because I knew no one else would be. That is, with the exception of Taylor, who I'm sure feels sorry for you, too. I mean, what in the world would Taylor and I have to gain by being friends with someone like you? You eat everything you see, you can't keep a man, and the only reason you have such a good job is because of affirmative action. Because who on earth would choose to put a two-hundred-fifty-pound black woman or any fat woman for that matter in a management position? I mean, it's not like that can be all that great for business. If anything, someone like you could turn people away just from disgust."

"You know what, Charisse, you're nothing but a two-faced, conniving little hypocrite. Here you run around claiming to be saved, claiming to know Jesus, but yet you've hated your own daughter since the day she was born. And don't get me started on the way you've treated Marvin like he was some animal on the street or how your own son is afraid to bring home his friends because he never knows when you might humiliate his father. Just about every parent in our neighborhood knows about that, but you've been too stuck on yourself to see it. Although maybe the reason you act like this is because your own mother can't stand you. She never loved you when we were kids, she doesn't care anything about you now, and I finally, finally understand why. You're just not a likable person and I'm sure you deserved every ass-whipping she gave you."

"You are one miserable fat bitch, Whitney, and nothing you do will ever change that," she said, standing up. "And in case you haven't figured it out, this Rico character is only temporary, too. Because if the man looks as good as you claim he does, he couldn't possibly be serious about you. I mean, please, he might be using you for sex, but that's where it ends. That's where it's always ended with every man you've been with," she said, lifting her tray from the table.

Her words had trampled me but I wouldn't let her leave without having the last say.

"After this, I just might tell Marvin everything. As a matter of fact, I should call him at his office right now."

"And when you do, you'd better start watching your back every second," she said, and stormed away.

By now, heads were turned in our direction and I couldn't help feeling embarrassed. I also couldn't believe Charisse and I had argued so loudly and so severely. We'd spat a ton of venom at each other and it was obvious that the animosity between us had been building for years. It was as if we couldn't wait to toss criticisms back and forth, hoping to hurt each other at the core of our being. Still, I felt a sense of relief and like a major weight had been lifted from my soul. I was glad that I no longer had to stomach Charisse and her idiocy.

I sat for a while longer and then I pulled out my phone so I could call Rico. I was glad to have Charisse out of my life forever, but her words were still stabbing me slowly yet surely down the center of my back. I couldn't erase the mental tape of her insisting that Rico couldn't be serious about me or that she'd been so quick to call me a "miserable fat bitch." I think it bothered me because I was afraid she'd been right on both counts.

When I dialed the number, Rico picked up on the first ring.

"How are you?" I asked.

"I'm good. And you?"

"I'm okay."

"Is Taylor all right?"

"She's in surgery but Charisse and I came down to get something to eat. But I'm going back up there when I hang up with you."

"Are you sure you're okay, because you don't sound like it."

"Charisse and I had a huge argument and our friendship is over."

"Why? And when did this happen?"

"Just a few minutes ago. We both said some terrible things, but nothing we can ever take back or would want to."

"That's too bad, because you guys were friends for how long?"

"Twenty-six years."

"Man."

"It's unfortunate but actually we should have stopped being friends years ago. I hadn't paid much attention to it before, but now I know we haven't liked each other for a while."

"But twenty-six years is a long time. A long time to be friends and then just say forget it."

"Maybe, but I know for a fact that this is a good thing. Life will be so much better now that I won't have to deal with her. I won't ever have to listen to her madness or try to figure out what her problem is. I realize now that Taylor is my only real friend."

"Honestly, I don't know what to say."

"Nothing, because I'm fine with this."

"Then I guess that's all that matters."

"So, what are you doing this evening?" I asked, wanting to change the subject.

"Since you're planning to be at the hospital, I'll probably hang out with a couple of my boys. Other than that, I'm not doing much of anything."

"But we're still on for tomorrow, though, right?"

"Yep."

We paused for a few seconds and then I spoke. "Oh well, I'll let you get back to work so I can go check on Taylor. I want to be sitting there when the doctor comes out to talk to us."

"No problem. But call me when you hear how she's doing."

"I will. Speak to you later."

I dropped my phone in my purse, took my tray over and sat it on the belt leading into the kitchen, and walked toward the exit. On my way out, I spied a cluster of desserts. German chocolate, which was my favorite, strawberry shortcake, pecan pie, coconut pie, and a few others. After that ugly fiasco that had evolved between Charisse and me, I was tempted to stop and purchase one or two of them. But I decided it was time I doubled my determination. I decided that my emotional ups and downs were not good reasons to eat what I knew I shouldn't.

I was proud of myself for finally doing the right thing when it came to food.

Chapter 26

Taylor

I HEARD NURSES CHATTERING with each other and monitoring their patients but my eyes were too heavy to open. It had taken me a minute to remember where I was, but now I knew I was in the recovery room. My body felt like lead and I was already experiencing a bit of throbbing in my abdomen. But still I lay there quietly. That is, until I began crying uncontrollably. My chest heaved up and down, tears rolled down my face, and I sniffled repeatedly. I hadn't thought much about it before, but I remembered doing the same thing when I'd had my tonsils and appendix removed.

"Taylor, are you okay?" one of the nurses asked.

"Yes," I said between breaths, still trying to open my eyes.

"Are you having a lot of pain?" Dr. Green said.

"No . . . I . . . always . . . cry . . . after . . . I'm . . . put . . . under."

"Oh," he said, slightly chuckling. "You're having an allergic reaction. You should have told us."

"I'm . . . sorry," I said, now crying more intensely.

"There's nothing to be sorry about," he said. "We just want to make sure you're okay."

The nurse held my hand and Dr. Green continued talking to me.

"Are you sure you don't have any pain, because if you do, we would prefer to give you something before it escalates."

"I'm throbbing a little, but it's not that bad," I said, finally settling down and speaking more clearly.

"Then I'll get it for you now," the nurse said.

When she walked away I turned toward Dr. Green, who looked to be writing something down on a chart.

"So, did everything turn out okay?" I asked him.

"Everything turned out wonderfully," he said, smiling, and I thought my heart had stopped beating. "The fibroid was a big one but there was no malignancy and we didn't have to take your uterus."

"Thank God," I said with tears pouring down my face again. This time, though, it wasn't because of the anesthesia, and instead I was thrilled about what he was telling me.

"So, as I mentioned in my office, it'll take you two to four weeks before you're completely healed, but other than that you should be fine. You should start seeing a major difference with your menstrual cycle."

"Thank you so much, Doctor."

"You're quite welcome. I'm glad we were able to get this taken care of so quickly for you."

"I am, too. I'm so relieved."

"I've already spoken to your family and you should be heading up to a room in a couple of hours. Also, I'll be by first thing tomorrow morning to see how you're doing."

"Will I be able to go home?"

"We'll see. But chances are you'll be here until Sunday."

I knew he'd mentioned that I might have to spend two nights, but I'd still been hoping it would just be one. It was true that it had only been a few hours, but I was already missing my own bed.

"I'm going to get out of here," he said. "But be sure to tell your nurse if you need anything."

"I will, and thanks again, Doctor."

"We'll see you tomorrow," he said with that same enchanting smile of his, and I was sorry that he was seeing me without makeup.

Although I wondered why another man's perception of me even mattered when I was completely committed to Cameron. But maybe it was because only hours ago Cameron had reconfirmed his position on getting married. He'd made it clear that he didn't want to do it.

However, I was at the point where I didn't want to live like this anymore. I didn't want to continue dating a man I might never have a future with. It just wouldn't be beneficial to me in the long run, and while I didn't want to do it, it was time I gave him an ultimatum. He could either propose or find someone else to be with.

As planned, I'd been moved to a room on the third floor and two nurses were getting me situated. An IV was still in my arm so they could administer pain medication, but they were no longer monitoring my heart rate or blood pressure. The aching, unbelievably, was still under control and I was hoping that it stayed that way.

"Here's a fresh container of ice water," a male nurse said, pointing toward the bed tray. "But let us know if you need anything else."

"If I could, I'd like to have a Sprite or something later on," I said.

"I can get it for you now if you'd like."

"That would be good. Thank you."

"I'll let your family know they can come in now."

I flipped on the television and was glad I'd remembered to request a private room. My insurance, of course, wouldn't cover it, but I had no problem paying the difference. It was so well worth it when it came to having visitors, not to mention when it was time to get some rest.

"Hey, sweetie," Mom said, walking in and kissing me on the cheek. "How are you?"

"A little tired, but I'm fine."

"Hey, little girl." Daddy beamed and I smiled at him. I knew he was just as relieved as I was.

"Hey, T," Whitney said, rubbing my arm. "Didn't I tell you everything was going to work out?"

"That you did."

"Your mom and I prayed almost the whole time," Charisse said. "We knew God would take care of you."

"I'm really glad you did," I said, but saw Whitney rolling her eyes. I knew immediately that she and Charisse were into it again.

"So, did Cameron call while I was in recovery?" I asked no one in particular.

But Charisse quickly answered, "No, we haven't heard from him."

"He said he had an important meeting," Mom added, probably trying to defend him. Either that or she was trying to keep me cheerful. Since I'd been a child I'd shared just about everything with Mom, but for some reason I hadn't told her about Cameron and how rocky our relationship was. I hadn't wanted to admit that at thirty-eight, I still hadn't found my soul mate.

"I'll call him in a little bit to give him my room number," I said, trying to seem okay with the fact that he hadn't bothered to wait with the rest of them. But deep down, my feelings were hurt, because there was no meeting I could think of that should have been more important than me.

We all chatted for maybe ten minutes and then Whitney told me she would come back in a couple of hours and Charisse said she would see me in the morning. Mom and Daddy left the hospital to go have a late lunch, but they were coming back to check on me before heading over to my place to spend the night.

One of my nurses came in to see how I was doing and I asked if I could have some medication. The ache in my lower stomach was starting to heat up and I wanted to numb it before it got worse. Afterward, I lay there for a while, debating whether I should even call Cameron. In my heart, I truly wanted to, but my brain was telling me I shouldn't. My brain insisted that if he really cared about me, he would be here. At the very least, he would have called to see what was going on. Which actually shocked me because this wasn't like him. The Cameron I had always known was extremely attentive and considerate, that is, until the last few weeks, so the idea of him having another woman was starting to eat at me. I'd thought about the possibility a lot as of late, but mostly I pushed it out of my mind without taking it seriously.

I lay there continuing my debate and then my male nurse walked back in.

"Well, aren't you the special one," he said, sitting down two bouquets of flowers on the ledge in front of me.

"They're beautiful," I said.

"Here're the cards," he said, first passing me the one from the huge arrangement and then the one from the smaller vase.

"Thanks for bringing them," I said.

"I was happy to do it."

I started to open the first envelope and wondered if Cameron thought paying a florist was actually going to justify his absence. If he did, he was dead wrong, because if anything I was more upset.

But when I pulled out the card, I was speechless.

It read, "Know that I meant every word I said this morning and please get well soon. Skyler."

This just didn't seem real and I could barely comprehend Skyler's new attitude. I reread his message and then opened the second card. This one was from the entire office. I smiled when I thought about how nice it was for them to think of me, but then a cloud of sadness drooped over me. I'd been sure that at least one of these was from Cameron.

Nevertheless, I picked up the phone and dialed my firm.

"Martin, Sable and Wesson," one of the receptionists answered.

"Hi, Naomi, it's Taylor."

"Oh hi, Taylor. How are you?"

"I'm doing fine. The surgery was successful and I should be home in a couple of days."

"Well, that's good to hear. Did you get the flowers we sent you?"

"I did and that's why I'm calling. They're beautiful."

"I'm glad you liked them."

"If you don't mind, please let the partners know that I called."

"I will."

"Also, can you transfer me to Sharon?"

"Actually, she took the afternoon off since you weren't going to be here," she said, referring to my assistant.

"Oh, that's right. She told me yesterday that she was going to, so just leave her a message asking her to call me at home on Monday."

"Will do."

"Also, is Skyler around?"

"Sure, hold on a minute. And you take it easy, okay?"

"I will."

I listened to office music until Skyler answered his phone.

"Skyler Young," he said.

"Hey. It's Taylor."

"How are you?"

"Well, they didn't find cancer, so I guess I'll live."

"That's great news. You must be so relieved."

"I am. But the reason I'm calling is to thank you for the flowers. You certainly didn't have to do that."

"I know, but I wanted to."

"Well, I appreciate it. They're gorgeous."

"Do you need anything?"

"No. I'm fine.

"Are you sure?"

"Positive," I told him, and neither of us said anything after that. It was an awkward conversation and it was obvious that we were both slipping into unfamiliar territory.

"Well, I guess I should go, but thanks again, Skyler," I finally said.

"No problem. I was glad to do it."

"I'm sure we'll speak next week."

"I look forward to it."

I hung up the phone and wondered what the heck was going on. Was Skyler being real or was he up to something dirty? Because the truth was, the man had never liked me and there was no way I could simply forget about that. There was no way I could forget that he'd always made things difficult for me. But on the flip side, I couldn't deny that people did sometimes change for the better. Not usually as quickly as Skyler had, but they changed nonetheless.

I lay there once again, thinking about Skyler and the fact that Cameron hadn't sent me anything. Worse, he hadn't even tried to contact me. And what was I supposed to do about it?

Finally my curiosity got the best of me.

I dialed his cell number and he answered right away.

"Did you forget that I had surgery or is it that you simply just don't care?" I began.

"Taylor? Baby, I was just about to call you. Did everything go okay? Did the doctor do the biopsy?"

"Everything went well, and no, they didn't find any cancer."

"What a relief." He sighed.

"I can't believe you," I said, and at that moment I wanted to hang up on him.

"Why?"

"We've been together for a long time, Cameron, and even though you knew how worried I was, you couldn't even be here for me."

"Baby, you know I had a meeting. And I explained to you why I couldn't miss it."

"Yeah, but it could have been rescheduled."

"It was important, Taylor."

"More important than me?"

"No, but you know I'm trying to take my business to the next level, and I don't have the luxury of putting off clients. Especially not the City of Chicago."

"Okay, but why didn't you come straight here when the meeting was over?"

"We met for three hours this afternoon and I'm just now leaving there."

"I'll bet."

"Are you saying you don't believe me?"

"I'm not saying anything."

"Look, let's not do this."

"Why don't I just talk to you later?"

"Can I bring you anything?"

"No."

"Are your parents still there?"

"No."

"They're coming back, though, aren't they?"

"Of course they are."

"Well, I'll see you in about an hour."

"Whatever."

"Taylor, I know you're mad, but I really am sorry."

"Good-bye, Cameron," I said, and hung up.

I was so livid with him, and while I wanted to feel nothing except anger, my heart was crumbling into pieces. As much as I didn't want to, I still loved him. If only he'd do what my grandmother used to say, 'straighten up and fly right,' we wouldn't have to have these pointless arguments. I wouldn't have to wonder if he was losing interest in me or whether he was sleeping with someone else.

I lay there for a few minutes, my mind in a whirl, then finally my eyes began to close. I could tell I was going to drop off to sleep, and this was a good thing.

It was good because at least for a while, I wouldn't have to think about anything.

Chapter 27

Whitney

"Girl, I didn't want to tell you this yesterday, but Charisse and I had it out while you were in surgery."

It was just past seven and I had purposely come to the hospital bright and early, hoping Taylor's parents wouldn't be here yet, and they weren't.

"I knew something was up yesterday when I saw you rolling your eyes like you couldn't stand her," Taylor said, repositioning herself in the bed and slightly frowning.

"Charisse has always been a trip, but after this one, I'm through with her."

"What happened?"

"You know how she is with her usual criticizing. First she started on you and how you hadn't had an exam in two years and then she started on me. Then she had the nerve to say I eat everything I see and that I can't keep a man. But when she called me a miserable fat bitch, I knew that was it. I knew our friendship was over for good."

"She actually called you that?"

"Yeah, and she went on to say how Rico was only using me for sex and that my relationship with him was only temporary. She even said she'd outgrown me right after college but she felt sorry for me."

"That's too bad. I knew you guys haven't been on the best terms, but I never thought it would come to this. Not after all these years."

"Well, if you ask me, this has been a long time coming and it's long overdue. Charisse has despised me for years and I've pretty much felt the same way about her."

"I still don't believe it."

"Well, you might as well get used to it, T, because I'm never speaking to Charisse again. Not after the way she spoke to me."

"I'm surprised Mom didn't say anything about this after you left."

"She didn't know about it because it happened down in the cafeteria."

"With all those people around?"

"Unfortunately, yes. We were sitting toward the back, but once we got going, I know everyone heard what we were saying."

Taylor shook her head and I felt more ashamed than I had yesterday. It was so unlike me to act so indignant, especially in public. But Charisse had pushed me too far and I hadn't been able to contain myself.

"So, now what?" Taylor asked.

"Meaning?"

"Meaning, am I going to have to be friends with both of you on a separate basis?"

"I guess so, because when I say I'm never speaking to Charisse again, I mean it. And to be honest, I don't know how you can still put up with her either. She talks about both of us like it's nothing, and I can only imagine what she says when we're not around."

"But it's like I've told you before, Charisse is just Charisse and she's always been that way."

"Well, I couldn't care less and I'm just glad I don't have to deal with that lunatic anymore."

"But maybe that's it. Maybe there really is something wrong with Charisse like Marvin was saying."

"Maybe, but that's not my problem. And if Marvin knew what was good for him, he'd take those children and leave there running."

"I hope you didn't say anything like that to Charisse, did you?"

"What do you think? After she started yelling at me the way she was, I said whatever I felt like saying. I brought up everything from the way she controls Marvin to the way she hates Brianna. And I even mentioned how two-faced she was. I called her a two-faced hypocrite to be exact."

"This is bad."

"I told you it was. But it's like I said to Rico yesterday, I'm relieved."

"But still, you have to feel some hurt behind this. I mean, you guys grew up together. You've been friends since junior high school."

"Well, none of that matters any longer. The relationship was ridiculously toxic and I'm glad to be rid of it."

Taylor sipped water from a straw but didn't comment. And I changed the subject.

"So, what's up with Cameron? I know he was here when I called you last night, but I could tell by the way you were talking that you weren't happy."

"I don't know. He apologized a thousand times but I just didn't want to hear it. I guess I'm just tired of the same ole-same ole, and I really don't know what's going to happen with us."

"I was shocked, too, that he didn't stay until your surgery was over, but maybe he really couldn't miss that meeting."

"Couldn't or just wouldn't?"

Now, I didn't comment.

"He came in here acting as though everything was kosher between us."

"How long did he stay?"

"Until midnight."

"Then maybe he really is sorry."

"But whether he is or not, I still want him to make a solemn commitment to me. Because if he doesn't, that's going to be it."

"Are you sure?"

"I'm positive, because I realize now that if I want to have children I need to do it sooner rather than later. Especially since I'm now at risk for more fibroids."

"When are you going to tell him?"

"Today when he comes to see me."

"Well, maybe he'll have a different attitude when he realizes he's about to lose you."

"He might. And then again he might not. But either way, I'm doing what I have to do."

I crossed my legs and looked up when Dr. Green walked in.

"So, how's my number one patient this morning?"

"I'm good. I'm a little sore, but other than that I'm fine."

"Glad to hear it."

"So that means I can go home, right?"

The three of us laughed.

"Not exactly. But you can tomorrow, though."

"Well, I'm definitely ready."

"Have they gotten you up to walk yet?"

"Yes, I went to the restroom early this morning and then the nurse said she would come back for me before noon."

"Good, because the last thing we want is for stiffness to set in."

"That's for sure."

"Well, I guess I should get going, but I'll see you in the morning."

"Thanks, Doctor."

"You ladies have a good day," he said, smiling at both of us and leaving the room.

"T, I gotta be straight with you, girl. I don't know how you can stand it."

"Stand what?"

"Being around a man that looks that good and who doesn't have a ring on his finger."

"So, you noticed that, too, huh?"

"It's the first thing I look for," I said, laughing. "And it seems like to me there's some thick chemistry floating between the two of you."

"Whit, please. The man is just being nice. Charisse told me that he's one of the nicest doctors around, so I'm sure he acts the same with all his patients."

"Yeah, right."

"Just stop it."

"Are you saying you aren't attracted to him? And especially since you're getting ready to dump Cameron."

"I don't know if *dump* is the right word to be using."

"Well, I do. As a matter of fact, I think it's very fitting given the fact that Cameron isn't the one who wants to break things off. And when both parties don't agree to end a relationship, one of them ends up getting dumped."

"You're too much."

"Hey, I'm just calling things the way I see them."

"Well, that's not how they are."

"Tell me anything."

"I'm ignoring you," she said, folding her arms.

"Are you ignoring that gigantic flower arrangement that Skyler sent you?"

I couldn't help teasing Taylor because she'd told me about the flowers as soon as I'd walked in.

"Some people need to mind their own business," she said playfully.

"And when have you ever known me to do that when it comes to you?"

"Unfortunately, never."

"Exactly. So, why not make it easy on yourself and just answer the question."

"About what?"

"Whether you're trying to pretend that those flowers don't mean anything."

"Now, Whit, you know the history between Skyler and me, and the only reason he sent flowers is because we work together."

"Girl, who do you think you're fooling? Your law firm sent their own bouquet, and whether you realize it or not, your face lit up like a Christmas tree when I mentioned his name."

"You're dreaming."

"And so are you if you're trying to tell yourself that Skyler's peace offering doesn't matter to you."

"Do I need to call security so they can drag your butt out of here?"

"Call anybody you want to but you know I'm telling the truth. Plus, what security guard do you know of that will even be strong enough to drag me anywhere?"

We both laughed and Taylor held on to her stomach. It was good being able to spend this time with her, but my spirits dropped instantly when I saw Charisse. She was walking through the doorway.

She looked at me and then turned her attention to Taylor.

"So, how are you?" she said.

"I'm good. Better than I was expecting to be. What about you?"

"Very blessed."

Gosh, how I hated when she said that. I hated when the devil herself went out of her way putting on this Christian facade, trying to deceive everyone. Charisse was a pill that no one should have to swallow. Not even in a life-or-death situation.

"And how's the family?" Taylor asked.

"They're doing well," Charisse said, shifting her weight from one foot to the other. But when she did I remembered what she'd called me yesterday. I heard the words *miserable fat bitch* over and over again and it was making me angrier by the second.

"Well, why don't you sit down?" Taylor told her.

"No, this is fine."

"Okay, you guys, look. This thing that happened between you yesterday is really bothering me and I really think you should talk about it."

"There's really nothing to say," Charisse said. "And let me be clear on something else. What happened is in the past and I suggest we leave it there before somebody gets hurt."

Was Charisse threatening me? Because that's exactly what this was sounding like. And she was doing it right in my face, too.

Miserable fat bitch, I heard once again.

I had insisted that I would never speak to her, but before I knew it, I said, "I know you're not talking to me."

"Taylor, I think it would be best if I came back later," she said, totally ignoring me.

"Why don't both of you just stop this," Taylor pleaded.

"I'll call you first, though," Charisse said, already heading out of the room.

Miserable fat bitch.

No matter what I did, those words wouldn't stop taunting me.

"Yeah, you do that," I said, standing up. "You make sure I'm not anywhere near this hospital the next time you bring your ignorant ass over here."

Charisse turned to look at me and I could tell she was steaming. But she didn't say a word. Instead, she walked out and I sat back down in my chair.

"I can't believe you said that," Taylor commented.

"Well, I'm sorry, T, but I'm sick of Charisse. I'm sick of her waltzing around here like she's God Almighty and then acting like she's so much better than us. And I will never forget what she called me yesterday. I won't ever forget it for as long as I live."

"This is so uncalled for."

"No, not really. Because let's just say for instance that you were overweight and someone called you a miserable fat bitch. Would you overlook that person or would you say something back to her?"

"I understand why you're upset, Whit, but it still wasn't right."

"Well, I'm telling you now, if she threatens me again, my reaction will be the same as it was today. I admit that I was wrong for doing this in your hospital room, but Charisse brings out the worst in me. I kept hearing what she said yesterday and I just lost it."

Taylor looked at me, and while it was obvious that she didn't agree with what I was saying, I knew deep down that she understood how I felt. I also knew that Charisse sometimes rubbed Taylor the wrong way, too, but that Taylor didn't feel comfortable taking sides. She was still hoping that somehow the three of us would remain friends, but I was sorry to say that it would never happen.

So, we sat there not really knowing what to say to each other until, finally, I broke the ice with my next piece of news. I told Taylor how Rico had ended up coming over last night after all and how he'd made love to me like never before. I told her everything that had been said and *almost* everything that had happened and Taylor smiled like she was on a cloud. She smiled like my good news had actually happened for her. I knew Taylor hadn't forgotten about my confrontation with Charisse, but at least we didn't have to focus on it for the rest of my visit.

I was glad there was no longer any tension between us.

Chapter 28

Charisse

CHARISSE SAT INSIDE her car and threw her purse onto the seat like she was at war with it. She was as incensed as anyone could be and she wanted to do bad things to Whitney. She'd wanted so terribly to ask Whitney to step outside to the parking lot so they could settle their differences physically. And she would have done exactly that had this not been the hospital she worked for. It was bad enough that some of her coworkers had witnessed the argument yesterday.

This whole situation was all so infuriating and she wished that she'd ended her connection to Whitney years ago. Come to think of it, Whitney had always been in the way of Charisse and Taylor's friendship anyway, but Charisse had quietly tolerated it. What Charisse had wanted was the opportunity to be friends with just Taylor and for Taylor to be friends with just her. She'd wanted it to be just the two of them because threesomes required too much maintenance. Charisse had wanted Whitney out of the way because Whitney wasn't like the two of them. She was outlandishly overweight, even though she was struggling to slim down, and she simply wasn't on the same level. And she didn't have the necessary intellect to hang out with them. Of course, she tried to speak intelligently, but she was basically in a different category. It was the reason Charisse had never understood why Taylor was so loyal to her.

But maybe it was the fact that Taylor didn't really know what was best for her and she needed someone to tell her. Maybe what Charisse needed to do was have a talk with Taylor, letting her know what was what. Charisse would explain to her that Whitney needed to find another set of friends, people she could relate to. She would tell her that Whitney needed to find a few overweight buddies who understood where she was coming from.

Charisse started the ignition and tore out of the parking lot like a NASCAR competitor. She headed down the street, trying to calm down, but her rage never ceased. If anything, her fury was escalating because she was now thinking about Marvin and the way he had treated her this morning. The bastard had casually dismissed her and had bragged about his move into the guest bedroom. He'd, against her wishes, done it three weeks ago. She hadn't known how to explain any of what was happening to the children, and while once upon a time she wouldn't have cared one way or the other how Brianna felt, she hated seeing her upset. Brianna had cried like a baby the moment she had discovered that her parents might be splitting up. Charisse had tried getting her to see that this whole scenario was only temporary, but Brianna hadn't believed her. And then Brandon had told them the story about how the parents of one of his classmates had started out sleeping in separate rooms and how one of them had eventually moved into an apartment and then ultimately gotten a divorce. Brandon had continued by saying that he knew their lives would not end any differently and that he wanted to know who Brianna and he were going to live with.

So, at first, Marvin had tried to downplay Brandon's analysis of the situation, but before long Marvin had told both Brandon and Brianna the truth—that they would all remain in the same household until the two of them were in college.

Charisse could still remember the looks on her children's faces, and this was another slight she would never forgive Marvin for.

Charisse drove for maybe twenty minutes and then turned into her parents' driveway. Her mother had phoned her last night, practically demanding that she come over there, and she'd even asked her to bring Brandon and Brianna. But Charisse had decided right away that it wasn't going to happen. She'd decided that having them around her mother maybe once every couple of months was certainly more than adequate. Truthfully, even that was too much. But if she didn't bring them with her every now and then, her mother would soon become spiteful. She would make a huge deal out of nothing and it was much easier to simply yield to her requests. At least to a certain extent, anyway.

Charisse stepped out onto the driveway, closed the car door, and headed toward the brick steps. She rang the doorbell and turned to look back across the street. Interestingly enough, the neighborhood still looked almost the same as when they'd first moved in more than thirty-five years ago. Charisse had barely been three, if she remembered correctly, but every homeowner on the street had always taken pride in caring for their property.

She turned back around and raised her hand to ring the bell again, but just then her mother opened the door.

"Where are my grandchildren?" she said, grumbling.

Mattie Lee was a plain-looking woman who was at least six feet tall and Charisse hated when she had to stand next to her.

"I went to see Taylor at the hospital and Marvin took Brandon and Brianna to some open house at the gas company," Charisse lied, not wanting to say that they were all probably sitting around watching television.

"Then why didn't you just wait and come over here this afternoon?"

"Because Marvin was planning to have them out most of the day and I didn't know when they'd be back."

"Then why didn't you just wait until tomorrow after church the way you did a few weeks ago?"

"Because you said you didn't want another day to go by without me coming over here."

"But you knew I wanted to see my grandbabies."

"I'm sorry."

Mattie Lee scanned her daughter from head to toe and Charisse could tell her mother wasn't happy.

"Come on in here and sit down. There's some things I need to talk to you about."

"What is it, Mama?"

"What's goin' on with you and that jerk Marvin?"

"Nothing. Everything is fine."

"You sure about that? Because somethin' just didn't seem right the last time you was over here. I can always tell when there's a dead cat on the line because people like you start acting all nervous."

"I swear, Mama, everything is fine. Marvin and I are doing better than ever and—"

"Hi, baby doll," Roy said, walking in and hugging his daughter.

Mattie Lee looked as though her skin was starting to crawl. She couldn't stand seeing her husband or anyone else show gestures of affection, and Charisse moved away from him quicker than she wanted to.

"Roy, I need some ice water," Mattie Lee said, and Charisse watched her father move on demand, acquiescent yet cowardly.

"So, why are you lying, Charisse? If Marvin is still giving you problems, you may as well just go ahead and tell me."

"He's not."

Charisse wondered why her mother kept questioning her about the same thing every week. She wondered why her marriage to Marvin was so important to Mattie Lee and why her mother just wouldn't mind her own business. But she didn't dare consider saying what she was thinking to her face.

Roy brought his wife a glass of ice water and prepared to sit down on the sofa.

"Did you take those clothes out of the washer and put them in the dryer?" Mattie Lee asked him without even looking in his direction, and Roy stood back up and headed toward the laundry room.

"Now, what was I saying?" Mattie Lee continued.

"We were talking about Marvin."

"Well, all I know is that Negro sounded awfully cocky that day I called and both of you answered the phone. I don't even 'low Roy to answer the phone around here unless there's no way I can get to it. Men are like children and if you 'low them to dip into grown folks' business they'll start getting beside themselves."

Charisse sat at attention, because while there was no way she could relax, she tried to appear dignified. She tried to convince her mother that there wasn't a thing to worry about.

"So, how's Taylor doing?"

"She's still sore but she's good."

"Now, that's one smart girl. She's got a good head on her shoulders and any mother would be proud to claim her. Which is why I never understood how she became friends with the likes of you," Mattie Lee said, laughing. "And the same goes for big Whitney. She might be a little thick, but she's got a lotta personality. And she's got that pretty face, too. Even prettier than yours, Charisse."

By now, Charisse wanted to dash out of there. She wanted to leave and never come back, not for as long as she lived. But instead, she smiled like she agreed with her mother and then smiled at her father when he came back into the room—a third time.

"So, baby doll, what you got up for today?" Roy said, preparing to sit down again.

"Not much, Daddy."

"Fool, don't you see me and Charisse sittin' here havin' a conversation?" Mattie Lee barked. "And last I checked, there weren't any men in here whatsoever."

"Mattie Lee, I just wanted to talk to the child for a few minutes."

"Well, not right now. Because right now, *I'm* talking to her."

Roy stood and walked out in a deflated manner and Charisse wanted to cry her eyes out. She wanted to cry because her father looked eighty and not the sixty years old that he was and because her mother was downright abusing him. She was treating him no better than a slave and her father just took it.

"What I think I need to do is pay you and ole Marvin a family visit. Either that or I need to call and invite him over here to see me."

"That's really not necessary, Mama," Charisse said, remembering all that Marvin had been threatening to tell Mattie Lee. "You know that you and Marvin have never really gotten along all that well, so please don't do that."

"What did you say?"

"I'm just sayin', Mama."

"Girl, don't you ever tell me what to do. Not as long as my name is Mattie Lee Freeman. You hear me?"

"Yes, Mama. I'm sorry."

Mattie Lee shook her head and drank some of her water. "Sometimes I don't know why I ever had you. What I should've done was had me one of them abortions, because it's not like you've done any good on this earth anyhow. And while I know this ain't probably natural, I've never really loved you. Now, don't get me wrong, I loved your brother more than my own life, so it's not that I didn't want children, but when you came along I never got used to it. But then, your brother was the kind of baby everyone fell in love with."

Charisse felt her eyes filling up. "Mama, how can you say that to me? I mean, what did I ever do to make you hate me so much?"

"I only wanted one child and then you came along and messed things up."

Charisse stared at Mattie Lee in a daze. She hadn't heard her mother speak these words before, at least she didn't think she had, but they were the same words she'd been thinking about Brianna for years. It was the same reason she'd given all of her love and attention to Brandon but barely a kind word to her daughter.

A tear dropped down Charisse's cheek and she couldn't have been more sorry than she was now. She was sorry that she'd treated Brianna so cruelly. More than anything, she was sorry for all the times she'd left her in her crib, screaming for more than an hour. She'd done it whenever Marvin hadn't been home to witness it, and there had been way too many times to count.

"The problem with you, Charisse, is that you're weak like your daddy. And I can't stand me a weak woman. Now, your brother, Johnny, on the other hand, he knew how to stand up for himself. He knew how to get people to do things, and that's why that company he worked for made him vice president when he was only thirty-two. But you . . . you'll never have a job like that because you far too simple-minded."

"Mama . . . why?" Charisse pleaded, her face flooded.

"See, that's what I'm talkin' about. Sittin' here cryin' about nothin'."

"What do you want me to do?" Charisse asked, kneeling down in front of her mother. "What can I do to make things right?"

"Ole stupid girl! There ain't nothin' in this world you can do. I just tried to explain things to you as best as I could but I guess you too silly to get it. I don't love you, I've never loved you and it's as simple as that."

"But why are you telling me this now?" she said, sobbing. "Huh, Mama? Why are you doing this?"

Mattie Lee looked at her viciously and said, "Because I wish *you* had been the one who died and not my sweet Johnny."

Charisse gazed at her mother but she knew there was nothing to respond with. She knew, like every other time, it wasn't even worth trying.

Chapter 29

Whitney

I'D BEEN HOME FOR MORE THAN FIVE HOURS, but it was still taking everything in me not to call Marvin. I wanted so badly to call him up and tell him what type of woman he was married to. I wanted to tattle on Charisse the same way I had tattled on my sister to my mother, and I didn't know how I was going to stop myself. In a word, I was consumed. I wanted more than anything to get revenge on the woman who had ridiculed me. And why shouldn't I give Charisse exactly what she had coming to her? Because it wasn't like she didn't deserve it. It wasn't like she had ever spoken favorably about anyone I could think of. Not to mention some of the wicked things she had done that no one except me was aware of.

So, yes, Charisse deserved whatever I did to her and then some. And if those words she'd called me didn't stop playing in my head sometime soon, I was going to take action. I was going to snatch away Charisse's lifelong disguise once and for all. Taylor, of course, wouldn't be happy about it, but I couldn't concern myself with that right now. I did care what Taylor thought, but my priority rested with paying back the person who had hurt me.

I sat down on the sofa and picked up a fitness magazine that I had purchased earlier at the pharmacy. There was an article about a new weight loss program that I'd already started reading, and I definitely wanted to finish it. The program did sound strenuous, but the results that hundreds of women had already experienced were out of this world. The idea was that you needed to drink at least one low-carb protein drink for breakfast and then mainly healthy protein choices such as chicken or fish and vegetables for lunch and dinner. But the killer part of the regimen was that you had to work out a minimum of ninety minutes every other day, doing both cardio and resistance training. Not to mention you had to walk for at least a half hour on the days in between. Still, I was starting to believe I could do this, and now I knew why Rico had wanted me to increase my repetitions and number of minutes on the treadmill. I hadn't wanted to hear what he was saying because working out was such a struggle for me, but now I agreed that it was necessary. I now realized that I would begin to shed a lot more pounds and certainly more inches if I followed his instructions.

And why shouldn't I listen to what he had to say anyway? Because the man was still showering me with attention and giving me the best sex I'd ever had. And I could tell he wasn't being phony. He was really into me and he truly cared about the way I felt, and well, he cared about me as a person. I'd been so afraid that my weight issues would eventually diminish his interest in me, but after last night I'd decided immediately that he was being real. I'd decided that it was time I let my guard down and that I should finally go ahead and trust him.

But the entire evening had sort of evolved without any planning, because when I'd called him from the hospital yesterday morning, he'd said that since I was going to be at the hospital most of the day, he was going to hang out with some of his friends. But as it had turned out, Cameron had come to see Taylor around seven and I had decided to leave. And when I'd arrived home, Rico had left me a message telling me he hadn't wanted to interrupt my time with Taylor, but if I ended up coming home earlier than I'd expected, he wanted me to call him. Which I did, and he'd jumped in his car and driven right over.

And oh, how it had been the night of my life! It had been so amazing that I could still picture everything in its entirety.

"What made you change your mind about going out with the fellas?" I asked.

"You," he said, walking in and leading me straight to my bedroom.

"Then I guess I should feel flattered."

"Why? Because no man has ever treated you like this before?"

"If you want to know the truth, yes."

"Well, I really enjoy being with you. More than I was planning on. I mean, you know how it is when you meet someone. You start dating them so you can get to know them and usually it just doesn't work out. But with you it's different. With you, I feel really content."

"I feel the same way," I said, and Rico started undressing me.

I looked at him shamefully, because I still didn't feel good about him seeing me this way. It was true that I'd lost twenty-five pounds, but I longed to have him see me when I'd dropped so much more.

But Rico kept insisting that he didn't care about that, and to prove it, he sometimes asked me to lie across my satin sheets on my back with nothing on, just so he could admire me. Of course, I didn't like that either, but I did what he told me.

Rico slid my underwear, the last thing I had on, down to the floor and then undressed himself. I sat on the edge of the bed, but all the while he was removing piece after piece, he never took his eyes off of me. When he leaned me back, he kissed me and caressed my body in every place imaginable. For some reason, we were both extremely turned on. More so than usual, and we both realized that foreplay just wasn't necessary. It was almost as if we'd been waiting all day to pleasure each other, and when he entered me I knew we were in love. Not just me with him but I could tell the feeling was mutual. And for the first time since I'd started dating him, I knew he was being genuine.

When we came, Rico rested on top of me, both of us breathing like sprinters. But then, out of the clear blue, tears streamed down both sides of my face and I couldn't hide them.

"Baby, what's wrong?" he asked.

"I've never felt like this before," I said, sniffling.

Rico kissed me on the lips. "Believe it or not, I feel the same way."

"No, I don't think you understand," I said, sighing. "I've been in love before but never like this."

Rico raised his head and looked at me.

"I'm sorry," I said. "But I can't pretend anymore. I've loved you since the first week we started dating, but I never said anything because of what you said."

"Which is what?"

"That we needed to get to know each other, and that if you decided to sleep with anyone else, you would have no problem telling me."

"And I guess I did mean that in the beginning, but that was before I started feeling the way I do now."

"So, how do you feel?" I took a chance on asking him.

"Like I haven't felt in a long time and it's really caught me off guard."

I smiled at him.

"The thing is, Whitney," he continued, "I love you, too. I didn't know it at first, but when I started thinking about you day and night, I knew what was happening."

I tried to say something, but now I was weeping again and couldn't.

So, Rico wiped my tears away and kissed me passionately. And then we made love a second time.

When the doorbell rang, I snapped out of my daydream and hurried over to answer it. I wasn't expecting anyone, but I got excited when I looked out and saw Rico. He wasn't supposed to be here for another couple of hours, but I was glad he'd stopped by beforehand.

"Hey," I said, opening the door. "I was just thinking about you."

"Really?"

"Yep," I said, and we walked over to the family room and sat down next to each other.

"So what were you doing?" he said, but his tone sounded sad.

"Just reading an article and that was pretty much it."

"Is it a good one?" he said, seemingly a lot less enthusiastic than usual.

"Yeah, it is."

Next, we just stared at each other until Rico dropped his head into the palms of his hands. And I knew that whatever he had to say wasn't going to be good. I could see it in his facial expression as well as in his body language.

"You don't know how hard it was for me to come over here," he said, and my stomach started tussling. "But there was no way I could go on without being honest with you. Not after last night."

"Rico . . ."

"No, let me finish before I lose my nerve." He sighed. "God, I can't believe I did something like this."

"Like what?" I said, becoming more flustered by the second.

"Remember the time we were at the health club and this guy Terrance came up and I introduced him to you?"

"Yeah?"

"Well, it wasn't really his first time seeing you. He was there that first night I met you, but he'd left before you came over to the water fountain."

"Okay."

"Well, when you first came in and got on one of the bikes, Terrance asked me if I had ever been with a woman as large as you and I told him no. So, then he said, 'You should try it sometime, man . . . you know, just as an experiment.' But I told him that big women just weren't my type. And then he said, 'I'm tellin' you, big women sometimes give the best sex in the world, so you really ought to try it. I got me a couple of 'em on the side right now, and when my main girl won't give me what I want, I have no problem calling either one of them with the quickness.' Then he told me about some of the things these women had done to him, and when he kept going on and on about how good they made him feel, I guess I just got caught up. And then the next thing I knew, he left the health club, you came over to where I was, and I decided to go for it."

I heard what Rico was saying, but no matter how bad this got, I wasn't going to cry over it. I wasn't going to let him see how much he was ripping me apart—how he was tearing me to shreds with one word after another.

"And Whit, that's not even the worst part," he continued, and I scooted a few inches away but didn't take my eyes off of him. "My divorce won't be final for at least another two months."

"No," I said, shaking my head and trying to register this catastrophic news flash of his. "Please don't tell me that you've been sleeping with me, knowing that you have a wife."

"I know. And I'm sorry, baby. I'm sorry for doing this to you."

"Rico, just go, okay," I said, with tears flowing because I could no longer prevent it.

"Whit, please don't do this. I'm sorry for what I did, but when I told you last night that I was in love with you, I meant it. Yes, this thing started out as some stupid experiment, but as time went on I really started to care about you. I mean, you have to know that from the way I've spent all my time with you."

"And that's supposed to make everything okay?"

"No. But what I'm saying is that I really want us to be together and that's why I decided to come clean about my original intentions. I didn't want what we have to be based on a lie."

"But it is based on a lie, Rico. Can't you see that? I mean, how can I ever trust you again, knowing that you deceived me like this? And to think you actually came on to me just to see what it was like to be with a fat person. I mean, how could you do that? How could you get me into bed the first night I met you and now lie about being in love with me?"

"But that's just it, I'm not lying about that. I really am in love with you. I know you don't believe it, but I'm very serious about that."

"Well, at least now I know why you told that chick at the health club that you and I were just friends. You were ashamed to be seen with me just like I had already imagined."

"But I'm not anymore."

"Oh, so you admit it?"

"Yes, but the only reason I felt like that was because I allowed my ego to get the best of me. But I'm telling you, I've enjoyed every single day that I've spent with you. And then over this last week, I realized I was in love with you. I realized how empty I feel when we're not together."

"You are such a freakin' liar," I yelled, standing up and walking over to the entryway. "And I want you out of here."

"Baby, I'm begging you, don't do this. Let's do whatever we can to work this out," he said, coming toward me with open arms.

"Don't you even think about touching me," I said between clenched teeth. "Now, for the last time, get the hell out of my house."

"Look, I know you're upset, but if I wasn't being on the up-and-up, would I be telling you any of this? Because even though you would have eventually found out that I was married, there's no way you would have found out why I started seeing you. I told you that because I didn't want any secrets between us and because I told you from the beginning that I like to be straightforward about everything."

"If I have to ask you again, I'm calling the police."

"I don't believe this," he said, and I almost laughed at him.

"*You* don't believe this? Then how on earth do you think I feel? Huh? I mean, what if the script was flipped and I'd come over to your place telling you how I'd been laughing about the way you look behind your back and then I planned and plotted to take advantage of you?"

"But the thing is, I decided to tell you everything before it went too far. We've only been dating for barely a month but I didn't feel comfortable with what I was doing."

"Oh yeah? Well, I won't feel comfortable until you leave here."

"Fine," he said, stepping outside. "Now, I wish I hadn't told you anything."

I slammed the door, closed my eyes, and whispered out loud, "I wish you hadn't either. Even more, I wish I'd never met you."

Chapter 30

Taylor

"Good morning," Dr. Green said, strolling into my room.

"Good morning."

"So how's it going?"

"Just fine, but I'm really ready to get out of here," I said, laughing. "I'm starting to feel like I'm claustrophobic."

"I can imagine. Well, for whatever it's worth, you look good. Almost like you haven't even had surgery."

"Why, thank you. I really appreciate hearing that. Especially when I know I'm looking a mess."

He smiled at me like he knew I was being modest and he was right. Because the truth was, I'd already taken a shower, slipped on a fresh gown, and put on my makeup. Of course, I hadn't given myself some full-fledged glamour job, but I'd made sure that I, at least, was presentable.

"No, you definitely don't look a mess," he said, reading through my chart. "But I seriously doubt if you ever could."

"Thanks," I said.

We conversed about the weather, how stressful our careers were, and how neither of us had had a vacation in a long while.

After that, he gave me a mini-examination and explained that he wanted to see me in a week.

"I want to thank you again for taking me on as a patient and for getting me in so quickly," I said.

"You're quite welcome."

We both paused awkwardly and then Dr. Green said, "Well, I guess I should get going. One of my patients is in labor, so it looks like I'll have to be here for a while."

"No rest for the weary, huh?"

"No, I guess not. But anyway, you take care and I'll see you in my office."

"Thanks," I said, and he winked at me on the way out.

Okay, now I knew that Whitney had been right. Because whether I wanted to admit it or not, there was certainly chemistry between Dr. Green and me. But at the same time, I couldn't dismiss the long talk that Cameron and I had had either. He'd come up to see me in the afternoon and then he'd come back just before my parents had left to drive back home. My mom had wanted to stay here until sometime this afternoon, but since their church was celebrating its fiftieth anniversary and Daddy was chairman of the program committee, they needed to be there.

And while I hated to see them go, their leaving had given Cameron and me an opportunity to talk about everything. I'd told him that I couldn't continue being his girlfriend and that I would understand if he still didn't want to be married. He'd responded by saying that he still thought we needed to wait but at the same time he didn't want to lose me. He'd told me that he loved me, that I was the best thing that had ever happened to him, and that as soon as I was well enough, we could start looking at rings. He'd said that we could schedule a wedding date for next year sometime.

So, regardless of what vibe I was feeling toward Dr. Green, it just wasn't that important. Not when I was finally going to marry the man I loved and whom I wanted to have babies with.

After a while, Cameron and Whitney walked into my room at the same time.

"So, what's this?" I teased. "You guys hanging out together behind my back or something?"

We all laughed, but there was a sadness about Whitney that concerned me. I wasn't sure what could be wrong, but I was willing to bet it had something to do with Charisse. All I could hope was that the two of them hadn't had another blowup.

"Are you ready?" Cameron said.

"Yep. All we have to do is ring the nurse so she can order a wheelchair," I said, pressing the call button.

"Geez," Whitney said. "Last I checked, I was supposed to be helping you get dressed and then packing some of your things."

"I know, but I guess I was so anxious I couldn't wait."

"Apparently not," she said, trying to look cheerful, but she wasn't fooling me in the least.

"You and all these flowers," Cameron said. "Whit, you might have to take a couple of them with you."

"That's fine," she said, and to be honest I hadn't thought much about it or how they were going to fit. Because there were now actually five vases. Those from the firm and Skyler, one from my parents, one from Cameron, and one from my next-door neighbor.

It didn't take very long for the elderly volunteer to arrive with the wheelchair, and now I was sitting at the entrance waiting for Cameron and Whitney to pull their cars around. When they did, Cameron helped me inside and Whitney took care of the flowers, splitting them between both vehicles. After that, we headed out of the parking lot.

"You're not hurting, are you?" Cameron asked.

"Not really. I still feel a little soreness, but it's nothing to complain about."

Cameron pulled out into traffic and turned on the radio.

"Hey, did Whit seem upset to you?" I said.

"Sort of. Why? What's wrong with her?"

"I don't know, but she and Charisse really had it out on Friday and it wasn't good."

"I'm sorry to hear that."

"I just hope something worse hasn't happened."

"You should just ask her."

"I will when we get home."

"Did you want something to eat?" he asked.

"Maybe later."

"Well, the thing is, I have to go into the office for a few hours."

"For what?"

"It's that city proposal crap again."

"On a Sunday?"

"They want to meet with us again tomorrow and I promised that I would have a revised version prepared for them."

I sighed and looked out of the passenger window.

"Look, Taylor, it can't be helped. I spent most of yesterday and most of last night with you, so it's not like I had time to work on it."

I still didn't say anything and continued looking at the buildings we were now speeding past. It was obvious that Cameron was in a hurry.

"This is just great," he said, changing the radio station to 106.3. "You try to do the right thing but it's still not enough for some people."

I finally turned and looked at him.

"Well, excuse the hell out of me, Cameron, for wanting to spend more time with you."

"And that's what I want, too, but what do you expect me to do? I mean, it's not like I've ever asked you to leave work early or forget about working on weekends when I know you have a big case coming up."

"But how many times have I put my work before you when it

was important? I have always tried to be there for you whenever you needed me, and in case you haven't realized it yet, I just had surgery."

"I *do* realize that. And as soon as I'm finished at the office, I'll be back to see you this evening."

"You know, I was so happy last night when you left, and now I'm feeling strange about us again."

"Well, you shouldn't. Because I meant everything I said. About the ring and about marrying you next year. But right now, I need you to bear with me until this contract is sealed."

No matter what he'd said, I still wasn't happy about what he was telling me. But I also knew that arguing with him wasn't going to change anything, so I left it alone. I decided that it just wasn't worth dealing with at the moment.

"Okay, Whit," I said. "My things are put away and Cameron is gone, so tell me what's going on with you?"

"Rico . . ." she said, and burst into tears.

"Oh my goodness. What's wrong?"

We were sitting at the breakfast table and I rested my hand on top of hers.

"Whit? Tell me what happened."

But she couldn't. At least not at first, but finally she settled herself down and told me everything.

"I am so sorry," I said for lack of anything better to say.

"Not as sorry as I am. I fell in love with him, T. I fell in love with a man who did nothing except make a fool out of me."

"Well, I don't know if I would say that."

"And why not?"

"Because if nothing else, he had the decency to confess everything. I mean, he could have just as well not told you anything. Not about his so-called experiment or his marriage."

"I don't care. Just the fact that he used me the way he did was enough for me, and I don't ever want to hear from him again."

"And I respect the way you feel, but Whit, I have a good feeling about Rico. I know he messed up, but he seemed so into you that day Cameron and I went out with you guys. And while I know you won't want to hear this, how many men have treated you as well as Rico has? I mean, I know what he did may seem unforgivable, but outside of that, he's basically been really good to you."

"Why are you defending him like this?" she asked, and for the first time since Whitney and I had become friends, she was yelling at me. I knew she was lashing out in pain and that she didn't mean any harm by it, but it still hurt just the same.

"I'm not defending him, Whit. You know I would never go against you to protect someone else, but I really wish you would reconsider your position on this. Because the fact is, we all have flaws, we all make mistakes, and that won't ever change. And what you have to do is weigh the bad against the good and then figure out what's really important."

"But he hurt me so badly. I've been hurt by a ton of no-goods in the past, but I wasn't expecting this from Rico. Although I guess that's what I get for trusting him so quickly. I do this all the time and you would think that I'd eventually learn from it."

"As far as I'm concerned, love can't be defined or given a time frame. You pretty much go with the flow and then hope for the best."

"Maybe. But Rico had his chance and he blew it. I could never trust him again if I wanted to."

I started to prepare my next rebuttal but I could tell Whitney wasn't having it. The disapproving look on her face spoke a thousand words and I certainly got the message.

Still, I thought she was making a big mistake. What Rico had done was the worst, but he had so many other great qualities. For example, he'd come clean about everything and the man looked *good.* And he didn't care about her weight. Maybe he had in the beginning, but it was very clear that he couldn't care less about it now. Not to mention he'd been helping her work out and spending all his time with her. I guess I just didn't get it. I just didn't know how much more a woman could ask for.

But in the end, it wasn't my decision. It was all up to Whit and it wasn't my place to keep talking about it. Of course, I would pray that she came to her senses and that everything worked out for her and Rico, but I would keep my opinion to myself. Obviously, that was going to be hard to do, since I so wanted her to be happy. But this was the best way to handle things. It was the best way whether I liked it or not.

Over the next hour, we talked about everything we could think of, which was mostly nothing important, and then Whitney mentioned that she was hungry.

"What do you want to get?" I asked.

"Anything that'll digest."

Now, why oh why did Whit keep putting me in this position? You know, the kind of position where you had to keep telling people what they should or shouldn't be doing? Whit had lost over twenty pounds and all I could hope was that she wasn't about to overindulge.

"But like what?" I finally said. "I know you can have meat and salad, but no bread or pasta, right?"

"I can have anything I want today. I'm depressed and I need something to help me with that."

"I just hate to see you mess up after losing so much weight."

"I know, and that's why when tomorrow comes, I'll be back on my diet."

"Whit?"

"I promise. I know I've said this before, but Rico or no other man is going to hinder me this time. My goal is to lose fifty pounds by my reunion and that's what I'm still going to do."

"Okay, it's your call."

"I'm serious. I'm going to eat whatever I want today, but that's where it ends."

"So, what do you want?" I asked her again.

"What about ribs?"

"From where?"

"Smokehouse, of course."

"Let's go."

"No, now wait a minute," she said, and I knew why. "You're supposed to be taking it easy and lying down."

"I know, but I've been cooped up for almost three whole days and I need some fresh air."

"I don't think you should, because what if you start bleeding or somethin'?"

"All I'm going to do is get in the car and stay there until we get back here. I won't even go into the restaurant with you."

"I still don't feel comfortable letting you do this."

"Then I guess we're even. Because I'm not comfortable with you saying that you're only going off your diet for one day."

"You're a trip," she said, laughing.

"I know."

"And T?"

"Yeah?"

"I'm sorry for yelling at you. I didn't mean anything by it, but I'm feeling so much pain right now."

"Don't worry about it. You know I understand."

When we stood up, we hugged each other and went outside to the car.

We drove out of the driveway and zigzagged out of the subdivision. There weren't a ton of houses in total, but it was clear that the developer had been fascinated with adding lots of turns in the road. Some streets seemed like two when they were actually part of one, but I had to admit that it did give the subdivision more character. Something that wasn't the norm anymore for newly built houses. Specifically, houses like mine that were only five years old.

Whitney drove out of the main entrance and we continued on

our way. The barbecue joint was maybe five miles ahead and I was glad it wouldn't take us long to get there. I was glad because I was starting to feel a little more discomfort than I had been. I would never tell Whitney because she would probably go ballistic, but I couldn't wait to get back home to take some Vicodin. I remembered what Dr. Green had told me about catching the pain early and I was certainly going to take his advice.

"Whit? Wait a minute," I said when I thought I saw a black Danali.

"Is that Cameron?" she asked.

"It sure looks like it."

"And he's not by himself either."

"Oh no, girl. What do you want me to do?"

"Follow his ass," I said, and Whitney did what she was told. I could feel the adrenaline pumping through my body and it was interesting how my pain was disappearing.

"Do you want me to pull in behind him?" Whitney asked when we were in front of his house.

"Absolutely," I said, and then opened the car door as soon as she stopped.

My future husband stepped out of his vehicle and I could tell he wanted to die.

"What's going on, Cameron?" I asked immediately, and then saw a gorgeous white woman and two handsome little biracial boys getting out on the passenger side.

Cameron dropped his head and didn't answer me.

"Cameron? Did you hear what I asked you? What the hell is going on here?"

"Cindy, please take the boys in the house," he said.

"Why?" the woman asked. "And who is this person?"

"This *person* is the woman Cameron has been dating for the last two years and who he has finally decided to marry," I said.

"Cindy, please," he said. "Take the boys in the house and I'll be in there in a minute."

The woman clearly wasn't happy about this whole scenario but she closed the car door and led her children into the house the way Cameron had asked her to.

"Taylor, why don't you sit back in the car so I can talk to you," he said. "I don't want you to hurt yourself."

"Excuse me? No, Cameron. I want to know who that woman is and I want to know right now."

Whitney came up behind me and rested her hand across my back, I assumed supporting any weakness I might experience.

"Tell me, Cameron!" I screamed.

"She's my wife, Taylor. Okay? She's my wife and those two boys are my sons."

"What?" Whitney and I both mouthed the word in unison.

"It's true. We separated over two years ago but we never got divorced. And then on Thursday she brought the boys here to see me."

"She brought them from where, Cameron?"

"Seattle."

"You know what?" I said, raising my hand. "This is way too much for me to deal with. This is crazy," I said, laughing like a lunatic because it just seemed like the only plausible thing for me to do.

Then I turned toward Whitney's vehicle and told her I wanted to leave.

"Taylor, I'm really sorry, but I have to think about my boys," he said, trailing behind me. "They're eight and nine and they've gotten to an age where they really need me."

I was so close to using the F word that I could hardly stand the temptation. But instead, Whitney helped me into the car and then went around to the driver's side. Cameron was still yapping, trying to make me understand, but Whitney drove away in a hurry.

She went straight to the restaurant as planned but we never said a word to each other. I was sure she wanted to ask a few questions but didn't know how, and I was still trying to recover from the shock. I'd been standing right in Cameron's driveway and had seen his little family, but I still didn't want to believe it. Yes, it was true that I'd started thinking that he might be up to something, but a wife and two children had never entered my mind. There just hadn't been any reason for me to think that way, so I hadn't. Call me naïve, but how does any woman suspect that the man she loves is already spoken for when she's had a key to his house and car the whole time? And the killing part was that he'd never gotten any strange phone calls whenever I'd visited him. Although now that I thought about it, Cameron was famous for forwarding all of his calls to voice mail, claiming that he didn't want to be bothered with sales calls—specifically in the evenings and on the weekends, all the times when I was there with him.

My God, what a mess this day had turned out to be.

But as bad as it was, I still asked myself that dreadful question.

What could possibly happen next?

Chapter 31

CHARISSE

CHARISSE SAT on the end of the pew, trying to stay involved in the service, but she was having a very tough time doing so. Brandon and Brianna were sitting right next to her but she was starting to feel like she was the only person sitting in the church. Partly because she'd been in such deep thought ever since the start of devotion and partly because her mother's voice kept drowning out everything. *I wish you had been the one who had died and not my sweet Johnny*. Charisse heard the words over and over, time and time again, and they wouldn't stop. No matter how she'd tried to ignore them. And then there was this thing with Whitney. The argument they'd had on Friday as well as the one they'd had in Taylor's room yesterday. It had seemed as if Whitney couldn't wait to get something started and it was the reason Charisse had left when she had. Charisse had decided that she couldn't and wouldn't stoop to Whitney's level at her own place of employment.

But on top of that, there was still the whole Marvin factor. This whole idea that Marvin had pulled rank on her, had moved out of their bedroom and was still threatening to call Mattie Lee. It was almost as if he'd become obsessed and even intrigued by his ability and willingness to blackmail her. But then Whitney was doing the same thing as he was. Her fat ass was threatening to tell Marvin about that thing Charisse had done fourteen years ago, one year after she and Marvin were married. No one knew about that, not even Taylor, and now Charisse was sorry she'd ever confided it to Whitney. But the thing was, Charisse had never thought in her wildest imagination that Whitney might find the courage to deceive her. It just hadn't been something that Charisse had expected to happen, and now she knew that she'd terribly underestimated Whitney. It was the reason Whitney was on her list of people to take care of, the same as Marvin and her mother.

Although the problem she had was figuring out whom to deal with first. She'd played some ideas and scenarios around in her head, trying to organize her agenda, but she still didn't know exactly where she should begin. So, once again, she laid the facts down in order. Whitney was threatening to tell Marvin some things that he would never forgive Charisse for and that would definitely force him to go to her mother. Marvin, on the other hand, was threatening to tell her mother about the way Charisse had treated her brother and also about that insurance policy. But her mother had ruined her life since the day she was born. So, now she wondered if it was better to start from the top and work her way down or do it vice versa. She just couldn't be sure one way or the other. Although she had to admit she was leaning toward handling Whitney right away because it would buy her some time with Marvin. If she could silence Whitney, Marvin would have no urgent reason to do anything foolish. He would keep what he knew to himself and would continue using it as a means to control her. But then there was the fact that she wanted so desperately to yank him down from his high horse. She wanted to show him who he was messing with and that she really could make life unbearable for him. And in all honesty, the only thing that had stopped her up until now was the compassion she had for her children. She just hadn't been able to see taking their father from them. Not when they loved him so much. But now that was basically the least of her worries. She'd decided that she was all her children really needed. And now that she and Brianna were building a more solid relationship, Brianna probably wouldn't care what happened to Marvin. Maybe at first, but eventually she would learn to adjust the same as all children did when divorces occurred. And of course, Brandon had always been a very strong individual. Even from the time he'd been born, he'd shown a certain level of strength and confidence about himself. So, there was no doubt that he would be fine in the long run.

Charisse abandoned her thinking and looked over at her daughter and son, who were sitting next to her. They looked so happy considering they knew their parents couldn't stand each other and that was even more confirmation that they didn't need Marvin. It was confirmation that maybe he should be the prime target because what good would Whitney's news be to him if he was gone?

But then again, she couldn't simply let Whitney get by with the way she'd been speaking to and disrespecting her. Charisse had never allowed or taken that kind of treatment from anyone except her mother, and she was at the point where she was going to stop her mother from belittling her, too. It had gone on for much too long and it was finally time she had a talk with her mother. Charisse was the only child her mother had left in this world and the only person her mother could depend on. That is, besides Charisse's father. So, maybe it was just a matter of Charisse going back over to visit her mother and then apologizing for everything she'd ever done. She would apologize for everything she'd done as a child and even for situations that had happened over the last few years. She would explain that she was going to be a much better daughter and how she would make her mother proud. She would make her more proud than her sweet Johnny had done.

As soon as they'd left the church grounds and started on their way, Brandon and Brianna began laughing about one of the church members. Brandon was in the backseat and Brianna was sitting in the front with her mother.

"B, did you see that humongous hat that woman sitting in front of us had on?" Brandon said to his sister, who was cracking up.

"I could barely see Pastor Damon when he got up to preach. And it was some ugly orange color, too," she said.

"She looked like some overgrown pumpkin," Brandon said, heartily enjoying his own joke.

"And she even had the suit to match it."

"Mom, I sure hope you don't make us sit in back of her again," Brandon said.

"It's not nice to leave church badmouthing people," Charisse said.

"I know, Mom, but you know she needed to quit with that outfit."

"Still, it's not nice. God doesn't want us criticizing or judging other people. Right?"

"Right," he said.

"Pastor Damon gave a good message this morning, didn't he, Mom?" Brianna said.

"That he did," Charisse answered, but she knew she hadn't heard more than a couple of words of it. Although she did know the subject of what he'd been preaching about because he'd told her about it yesterday morning. She'd gone to meet him at his condo right after she'd left from seeing her parents, and they'd had another memorable sexual encounter. Pastor Damon had yelled out some ungodly words, right when he'd had his orgasm, and he'd told her that it was time they saw each other on a regular basis. He'd told her that he was willing to make time for her whenever she needed him to and that all she ever had to do was call him. But Charisse had told him in no uncertain terms that it just wasn't going to happen. She'd told him that every now and then was still the proper protocol and that was all she'd ever be able to commit to. He hadn't seemed too satisfied, but Charisse knew he would get over it eventually.

"What are we eating for dinner?" Brandon asked.

"What do you want?" Charisse said.

"Can we go to Applebee's?" Brianna chimed in.

"Okay."

"What about Dad?" Brandon asked.

"I'm sure he's probably already eaten," Charisse said, and she could tell Brandon was disappointed.

"I'm sorry that things are not good between your father and me, but it won't always be this bad. There will come a time when you'll get used to the way life is for us now and you'll be just fine."

"But can't somebody help you with your marriage?" Brianna wanted to know.

"There's counseling, but right now your dad doesn't want to do that. He did once upon a time, but he's not interested in that anymore," Charisse said, figuring it was time she started blaming Marvin for everything. It was time she turned the children completely against him so they wouldn't miss him when he was gone.

"Well, maybe if you ask him again?" Brandon begged. "Maybe if Brianna and I ask him, too, he'll go."

"I don't think so," Charisse said. "Your father has decided that he doesn't want me anymore and there's nothing any of us can do about that."

"But Daddy was always so in love with you, Mom," Brianna said. "He always did everything you told him."

"I know, but now he's changed," Charisse said, deciding to take her plan even further. "And as much as I hate saying this, your father is the reason you and I weren't getting along with each other."

"Why?" Brianna said.

"Yeah, why?" Brandon added.

"Because he had me thinking that Brianna didn't like me and that she wanted Taylor to be her mother. He used to tell me that all the time, even when Brianna was a baby."

"He did?" Brianna said.

"Yes. And the other thing he's doing is trying to turn your grandmother against me, too."

"Is that why she doesn't like you?" Brianna asked.

"That's part of it. Your father never liked Mama, and because I stayed married to him, she started hating me for it. But I stayed with him because I didn't want the two of you to have to be without your father."

"I can't believe Dad!" Brandon said. "And I can't wait until we get home."

"No, honey. For now, this has to stay between the three of us. We have to stick together until we figure out what move he's going to make next."

"Like what, Mom?" Brianna asked. "What do you think he's going to do?"

"Leave us for another woman and take all the money we have in the bank."

"I hate him!" Brandon said. "I hate him for doing this to you, and now I know why you used to treat him so badly."

"I'm sorry that we've both made your lives so unhappy," Charisse said.

"But it's not really your fault, Mom," Brandon hurried to say.

However, Brianna didn't say anything. Meaning it was pretty evident that it would take a few more dramatics and a few more lies to convince her of whose side she should be on. But Charisse had no problem waiting. As a matter of fact, it was the least she could do.

Charisse drove a few more miles and then turned into Applebee's parking lot. The place was packed but so would most other restaurants in the area be at this time of day. So, they got out of the car, got in line, and were told there was a forty-five-minute wait to be seated.

As they stood there, Charisse decided that after they ate, maybe she would take the children by her mother's house the way her mother had asked her because it would also give Charisse an opportunity to talk to her. Her mother sometimes treated Charisse just as horribly in front of the children, but it was never as bad as when Charisse came to visit without them. Charisse wasn't sure why, but Mattie Lee did love her grandchildren. Which was strange coming from an evil woman like her, but she cared about them a great deal.

Then again, nothing was normal when it came to her mother. Never had been and probably never would be, but Charisse was still going to try to make peace between them. She would try to build a new relationship with Mattie Lee the same as she was now doing with Brianna.

She would try because it was the one thing she had always wanted from her mother but had never gotten.

Chapter 32

Charisse

CHARISSE RANG THE DOORBELL a third time and her children stood a couple of steps below her. Charisse wondered what was taking her parents so long to answer. It would be out of the ordinary, especially on a Sunday, but she was starting to think that they might not be here. However, her father finally came to open the door for them.

"There's my grandbabies," Roy said. "Come on in here," he said, giving both of them huge bear hugs. "Mattie Lee, your babies are here to see you."

"Hey, babies," Mattie Lee said, walking toward them with an enormous smile and grabbing hold of both of them immediately.

"Hi, Grandma," Brandon said, but Brianna only smiled and didn't say anything.

Charisse observed what was going on and wondered why her mother never had a problem cuddling her grandchildren yet had never offered to do the same with her own daughter, not even when Charisse had been a child. On top of that, her mother hadn't even gotten upset when she'd seen Charisse's father shower the children with such strong affection. Which was all so unfair to Charisse, but maybe after she had this talk with her, things would be different.

"It's so good to see you two," Mattie Lee said. "And you look so nice in your Sunday-go-to-meetin' clothes."

"Thank you," both children said.

"Y'all sit down," Roy said, doing the same but Mattie Lee stopped him.

"Babies, I need to speak to your mother about somethin', so why don't y'all go on downstairs to the family room with your grandpa. And me and your mama will be there in a little while."

"Okay," they both said, and Roy put his arms across each of their shoulders and led them out of the living room.

"Y'all hungry?" Charisse heard him ask them when they walked into the kitchen. "I cooked a pot roast, some macaroni and cheese, and red potatoes."

"No sir," Brianna said. "We just came from Applebee's."

Charisse sat down in the chair adjacent to where her mother had taken a seat and waited to hear what she had to say. Although Charisse could tell it wasn't going to be good because her mother's cheerful and loving attitude had vanished. And she now had a nasty look on her face. She was angrier than Charisse had ever seen her.

"Lawd knows I didn't wanna have to clown like this in front of my grandchildren, but this thing I done found out today got to be brought out."

"What are you talking about, Mama?"

"Marvin called me this morning. Yeah, that's right. He called over here sayin' how you had hurt too many people and that it was time he told me a few things."

Charisse swallowed as hard as her throat muscles allowed her and her hands started to tremble. She couldn't believe what she was hearing and now she wished she had taken care of Marvin when she'd had the chance to.

"He told me everything. How you treated my boy Johnny

when he was in his last days, and how you stole that insurance policy right out from under me."

"Mama, Marvin is—"

"Just stop it! Because I don't wanna hear no lies. Marvin already called that insurance company and got proof that that check was *mine*. You hear me? He already got proof of it."

Charisse tried to figure out what to say, what to do, and how she was going to maneuver her way out of this web of duplicity, but she couldn't think straight.

"And to think I couldn't stand Marvin all these years, thinking he was no good for you, when in reality you been sleeping with that pastor of yours. I always figured you was a slut, but to think you been sleepin' with a preacher. Quiet as kept, you ain't nothin' but a worthless little whore who been runnin' to church every Sunday puttin' on a front."

"Marvin is lying, Mama. I'm telling you."

"No he's not. He followed you right after you left here yesterday morning," Mattie Lee said matter-of-factly, and seemed proud of what she knew. "He saw you meet that fool at some apartment and he said you never came back out for three hours. Marvin waited in his car the whole time but you was too stupid to realize it."

"Mama, please," Charisse begged, and wondered why she'd been so careless when it came to Pastor Damon. But in all honesty, she'd never expected even remotely that Marvin would think to follow her. Not when he was acting as though he didn't care anything about her.

"Let me explain," Charisse continued. "I was going to tell you about the money but I wanted it to earn some interest. I wanted to surprise you with how well I've invested it."

"You just a lying, sneaky bitch, Charisse," her mother yelled, standing up. "Which is another reason why I've always hated you. But baby, I promise you this . . . you gone pay. You hear me? If it's the last thing I do, I'm gone make you pay for this. You gone pay for what you done to me and my Johnny," she said, pointing her finger in Charisse's face.

"Mama, please just let me talk to you. We can go to the bank tomorrow morning and fix this," Charisse said, and was glad that she'd already opened another joint account in both her and her mother's name—all thanks to one of her coworker's daughters, who worked at a nearby branch. Charisse had gone to see her the day after Marvin had begun threatening her about the money. "Mama, please just listen to me," Charisse continued.

"Ha! Now, Charisse, do you actually think I'm gone let a stupid bitch like you get over on me like this? Do you?"

"But Mama, this is not all my fault," Charisse declared. "If only you had loved me the same way you loved Johnny. Because if you had, I wouldn't have despised him so much and none of this would have ever happened."

"Look," Mattie Lee said, now touching Charisse's nose with the tip of her fingernail. "For the last time. I will never love your silly ass. Not for as long as I live," she said, forcing her finger farther into Charisse's face and knocking her head backward.

"Now get out of my way," Mattie Lee said, reaching for the phone.

And Charisse started panicking. "Who are you calling, Mama?"

"The police, that's who. So, I'm tellin' you for the last time. Get the hell out of my way," Mattie Lee repeated, and shoved Charisse to the side.

"Mama, I'm begging you . . . please don't pick up that phone."

But Mattie Lee grabbed it anyway and pressed the on button.

And that's when Charisse yanked the wrought-iron fireplace poker from its holder and swung it across her mother's back.

Mattie Lee bellowed out and dropped the phone by reflex.

"You crazy bitch," she said, clearly in pain but still bending over to pick the phone back up.

"I said *no*, Mama," Charisse screamed, and whacked her mother across her back again and Mattie Lee fell to the floor.

But Mattie Lee was far from giving up and struggled to get to her feet. When she did, she made another confession. "That's why from the time you were two years old, I beat your little ass whenever I felt like it. And now I'm gone beat it again for old time sake."

However, when Mattie Lee charged at Charisse, Charisse swung the poker repeatedly. She swung it across every part of her mother's body until finally Mattie Lee dropped down to the floor again, this time screaming for her life and yelling for her husband to come help her.

But Charisse didn't care about any of that and simply started swinging again. She swung back and forth as hard as she could and she was now striking multiple blows to her mother's head.

She did this over and over and over again until her father seized the weapon from her.

Chapter 33

Whitney

Taylor was preparing to lie down for a while, but I was still trying to process what had happened over at Cameron's. It was so totally astounding, and I was now convinced that there was no sure way to truly know a person. At least not completely, and that bothered me. I was troubled because this unfortunate realization had already been proven twice within the last twenty-four hours. First by Rico and then by Cameron, and I feared that this was as good as life was ever going to be. At this point, I just didn't see any reason to be optimistic about anything.

"Can you believe him?" Taylor finally said while easing her body into bed and leaning against two large pillows.

"No," I said, pulling the sheet and comforter over her and realizing how stuffed I was. Taylor had eaten barely half of her dinner, but I had gobbled up every morsel of mine and was happy about it.

"I mean, the man has a wife and two kids and I never even picked up on it. I feel so stupid."

"But you shouldn't. Not when there was no way for you to

know what was going on. He hid his family from you and that's not your fault."

"But I still should have noticed some sort of sign. I should have paid more attention to what he was doing. I should have thought about the fact that he always kept his phone calls forwarded, and now I'm trying to think back to some of the business trips he went on and which cities he'd claimed he went to."

"He forwarded his phone calls? Why?"

"He would tell me how he didn't want to be bothered with sales calls or any others when he was at home. And I guess it never really mattered to me because I always called him on his cell phone anyway. He spends a lot of time at construction sites and with his clients in their offices, so that's the way I usually contacted him. Pretty much, it just became a habit."

"Wow. Well, I will say this, Cameron is good. And so is Rico. Both of them have mastered the art of deception and it makes me sick."

"I just don't deserve this," Taylor said, closing her eyes and covering her face with her hands. I knew she was outdone so I sat on the edge of the bed and tried to console her.

I sat there for a few minutes and then my phone rang. When I pulled it out of my purse I saw that it was that jerk Rico. He'd called while we were driving home but I hadn't answered it. But this time I would end this once and for all.

"Hello?" I said.

"Are you still upset?"

"What do you think?"

"I know and I'm sorry. But the fact that I'm really in love with you should mean something."

"Well, it doesn't."

"So, what are you saying? That you've never made any mistakes. Are you saying that you're perfect?"

"No. But I've also never used someone the way you used me and then lied about being married."

"Okay, look. I know you probably hate me right now, but Whitney, everyone deserves a second chance."

"Not where I come from."

"So, just like that, this is it? This is the end of what we had together?"

"Exactly, and now that you finally realize that, please don't ever call me again."

"If that's what you really want."

"I do."

"Then, Whitney . . . you take care of yourself," he said, and hung up.

But the thing was, I didn't know how I felt about it. I was still hurting terribly over what he had done to me and I was sure that I could never trust him again, but for some reason I was now wondering if I had made a mistake. I wondered if I had dismissed him too quickly and possibly passed up on a man who did love me. I could tell Taylor was thinking the same thing from the way she was looking at me.

"Don't even say it," I said, smiling at her.

"What? That you'll probably regret this for the rest of your life?"

"I doubt it. It'll be hard but I'll get over this the same as anything else."

"I hope so, Whit. Because my gut tells me that Rico was the one. I don't know why, but I just have that feeling about him," Taylor said, and her phone rang.

I leaned over toward the nightstand to see who it was.

"It's Cameron."

"Then don't answer it."

"Are you sure?"

"I'm positive."

"I wonder if he'll leave a voice message."

"I'm sure he will. He'll go on and on with some sob story, but it's too late for that."

I agreed with Taylor but I didn't say anything because I could tell she was becoming emotional again.

"Can you believe we're going through almost the same thing at the same time?" she asked.

"I know. Strange, isn't it. But at least we're able to be here for each other."

"There was a time, though, when Charisse would have been here with us, too."

"Amazing how things change, huh? But that's life."

"I guess," Taylor said, and her phone rang again.

I leaned over again and saw that it was Charisse.

"Speak of the devil. And I hope she's not on her way over here, because she's calling from her cell phone."

"Will you stop being so difficult and just give it to me," Taylor said, and I laughed.

"Hey, Brianna," Taylor said, and then paused. "Sweetie, what's wrong? What? Oh my God, where are you? Where's your dad? Is your grandfather there? Okay, honey, your Aunt Whitney and I will be there as soon as we can and you call me on my cell phone if you need to, okay?"

"Who was that?" I said when I saw the horrifying look on Taylor's face.

"Brianna. And it sounds like Charisse has killed her mother."

Chapter 34

Taylor

When Whitney tried to turn down the street that Charisse's parents lived on she couldn't. Squad cars were everywhere, neighbors were standing and talking nosily on their lawns, and homicide detectives were parading in and out of the crime scene like it was normal. But I guess to them it was normal because they were used to it.

"Gosh," Whitney said. "Why would Charisse do something like this?"

"I don't know. And I keep hoping that it's not true. But after seeing all this . . ."

"Do you want me to let you out and then go park? Because I can tell you're in a lot of pain."

"I'll be fine. Just pull over here."

When she did, I stepped out of the car and walked up the sidewalk. But when I arrived directly in front of the house, one of the policemen stopped me.

"Ma'am, you can't go in there."

"I'm Taylor Hunt, Charisse Richardson's attorney."

"Oh, I'm sorry. Are you also the Aunt Taylor that the little girl inside keeps asking about?"

"Yes."

"Please go on in," he said, and I dreaded walking up the steps in front of me. But I held on to the rail and did the best I could.

Inside, it was a madhouse. Even worse than it was outside and I thought I would faint when I saw Charisse in handcuffs and a black body bag over near the fireplace being zipped closed. Charisse looked at me strangely and I wanted to run to her. I wanted to tell the officers that this was an innocent mistake and that Charisse hadn't done anything. But I could tell from the look on her face that this wasn't true.

When the officers escorted her toward me I got weak. I guess because I was still trying to digest what I was seeing.

"I'm sorry," Charisse said. "I'm sorry for everything I ever said or did to you, Taylor, whatever those things were."

"Don't say another word. Don't say anything to anyone until you hear from Jim Sable. I called him on the way over here and he's going to meet us at the police station."

Tears dropped from Charisse's eyes and I fought hard to keep my composure. It was hard seeing my friend look so pitiful. And while I had always known Charisse to be filled with sheer egotism, she now had straight humility. It was as if she'd become this person I hadn't met before.

"Please don't take my baby," Roy said, rushing toward Charisse and wailing loudly. "She was just defending herself. That's all she was trying to do," he continued explaining, but one of the officers stood between him and his daughter.

And after he did, Charisse gazed at her father, and I stood there *still* trying to figure out why any of this was happening. It just didn't make any sense. I knew Charisse had never gotten along with her mother, but had it been much worse than I had imagined? Were things so bad between them that Charisse hadn't seen any other way except killing her?

"Taylor?" Charisse said as they led her outside. "Please stay here with Daddy and the children until you know they're okay."

"I will, and then I'll see you in an hour or so."

"And one other thing, please tell Whitney that I'm sorry for everything."

"Of course," I agreed, and wondered where Whitney was. But I was sure that the officer guarding the door wasn't planning to let her through.

I placed my arm around Charisse's father. "Mr. Freeman, where are Brandon and Brianna? And Marvin?"

"They in the lower level."

"Well, why don't you come down there with me so I can check on them."

"I cain't. I just don't want them babies to see me like this," he said. "And plus, one of them detectives say he gone wanna talk to me in a few minutes."

"Well, you come and get me when he does. Don't you say a word unless I'm there with you."

"I won't. And thank you, sweetheart."

When I went down the stairs, all I could think was that I would eventually have to walk back up them and how I hoped I wasn't going to be sorry about it. I hoped I wasn't causing internal bleeding or something a whole lot worse.

"Auntie Taylor," Brianna said, tearing away from her father's arms and rushing over to me.

"I'm here," I said, hugging her, and to my surprise, Brandon came over and grabbed hold of me, too. They were both pressing against my stomach too closely, but there was no way I could reject them. There was no way I could disregard the love they obviously needed from me.

"Thanks for coming," Marvin said. "Especially since I know you just had surgery."

"No problem," I said, asking him with my eyes what happened, but Marvin dropped back down in his chair.

"It's all my fault," he said, and the children both turned to look at him.

"I knew it," Brandon yelled. "I knew you had something to do with this."

"Stop it, Brandon," Brianna said. "Stop yelling at Daddy. He didn't do anything and you know it."

"Yes he did, because Mom was just telling us how he was trying to turn Grandma against her. Remember in the car on the way over here?"

Brianna moved away from her father and grabbed my arm, now seemingly agreeing with her brother's thinking.

"I didn't mean it," Marvin said. "I did tell your grandmother some things, but I had no idea—"

"Just stop it, Dad," Brandon said. "They handcuffed Mom right here in front of us and now they're taking her to jail because of you."

I cringed when I heard Brandon's words and I wondered why the police couldn't have waited to cuff Charisse upstairs. I wondered why they'd had to do it right in the presence of her children as if her children didn't matter. I knew the police department had its job to do, but it just seemed so insensitive. Even as an attorney I just didn't understand it.

"I wanna go home with you, Auntie Taylor," Brianna said.

"Well, somebody's got to stay here with Grandpa, so that's what I'm going to do," Brandon announced, and I could tell he was serious.

Marvin looked totally defeated and not at all like the new and improved husband who had purchased that new television without Charisse's permission and then drank beer right in front of her that night I was over there. Instead, he was acting more like the old submissive Marvin again.

Still, I stood there not knowing what to say to anyone about anything, and before long Charisse's father yelled down to me. I assumed the detective was ready to question him so I turned toward the stairway.

But when I did, Brianna asked me a question.

"Auntie Taylor, can I come live with you for good? I promise I won't be any trouble. I'll do whatever you tell me to and you won't ever have to get mad at me."

All I could do was look at her, then at Marvin, and back at her again. I just didn't know how to answer.

Chapter 35

Taylor

WHAT A DEPRESSING FOUR WEEKS it had been. Not just for me, but for all of us. Brandon, Brianna, Marvin, Roy, and even for Whitney, because the truth of the matter was, Whitney still cared about Charisse and had wanted to help her. As a matter of fact, Whitney had even gone with me to see her and the two of them had finally reconciled.

But in the end, Charisse had forgone a trial, pleaded guilty, and the judge had sentenced her to fifteen years with a chance of parole in a few years. I'd been so upset, but I knew this particular sentence was actually lenient and that it had had a lot to do with her father's testimony. He'd told the judge how Charisse's mother had beaten her as a child and how if he'd been a better man he would have stopped it. He'd explained that Charisse had acted in the only way she knew how and that violence and cruelty was the only thing she had seen growing up. Then there had been the testimony of two psychiatrists who'd confirmed that Charisse was somewhat unstable and needed daily medication—medication that Charisse had never had prescribed for her in the past.

I'd been shocked, of course, about everything I'd learned, and all of it saddened me. Partly because I loved Charisse as my friend, but mostly because her children were so miserable without her. They'd been inconsolable and had missed over two weeks of school. And it hadn't been until they'd gone to see Charisse three days after her arrest and one day before Mattie Lee's funeral that they'd finally started speaking to Marvin again. Still, it had taken them another week before they'd moved back home, Brianna from my house and Brandon from his grandfather's.

But thankfully, Charisse had told them the truth—how she'd lied to them that Sunday about their father and how she'd been a terrible wife to him. She'd told them that Marvin loved them more than anything and how she needed them to be a family. She'd explained how she hadn't been a good mother and how she would forever try to make it up to them. She'd told them that it would be her primary mission from that day forward.

Although as bad as all of this was, Charisse murdering her mother and being sent to a state prison, I was still very shocked about something else. Charisse had found the courage to tell Marvin everything. Specifically, why his two best friends had basically stopped contacting him one year after he and Charisse were married. Interestingly enough, Charisse had paid two women to seduce and sleep with both of them and then threatened to tell their wives all about it—that is, if they didn't stay away from Marvin. And so, Ronnie and Charles had respected her wishes. Whitney had told me about this very thing weeks ago, that night I'd returned home from Los Angeles, but I still couldn't fathom the whole idea of it. I just hadn't expected Charisse to confess to something so appalling and I wondered if she was now regretting doing it because Marvin had made it clear that he was filing for divorce. He'd promised that he would bring the children to see her regularly but that this would be the limit of their relationship.

I shuffled through some papers on my desk and realized it was good to be back at work, especially after being gone for so long. Dr. Green, whom, as it turned out, Charisse had also slept with, had released me from his care about two weeks after my surgery, but I'd still taken additional leave so I could assist Marvin and the children. Marvin because he'd never paid a single bill before and didn't know how to budget his money, and the children because they seemed a lot more at ease when I was there with them. But a couple of days ago, I'd decided that it was time I got my own life back to normal, whatever normal was going to be for me. Because there was no doubt that it wouldn't be the same as it had been one month ago. Not with me finding out who Cameron really was and then, within hours, losing Charisse to the penal system. No, life for me would never be the same, but I was still hopeful. I had faith that my world would be better as time went on. Better because my goals and dreams were still intact.

I opened Jessica Harris's file, checking to see if she'd called while I was gone. Her first court appearance for the divorce was in two weeks, so I was thinking I should call to get an update on her husband. Especially since before I'd taken leave, he'd been harassing and threatening her almost every day. But as I flipped through the documents, looking for her number, my phone rang.

"Cameron is in the reception area," Sharon, my assistant said. "So, should I have them send him back?"

"Sure, go ahead," I said, because I hadn't told Sharon or anyone else at the firm about our breakup. It was true that I still didn't want to see Cameron, but if I suddenly turned him away, the rumors would start floating from one office to the next almost immediately. Especially since everyone there knew Cameron because he'd accompanied me to countless office parties.

It took a couple of minutes, but finally there was a slight knock and Cameron walked in.

"Please close the door," I said, and he did.

"Thank you for seeing me."

"Please. I'm only doing this because I'm not ready for my coworkers to know about us yet. But you still have a lot of nerve coming here."

"Well, I wouldn't have, Taylor, if you'd answered my calls or, even better, your doorbell," he said, sitting down. "I've been calling you every day and I know I've been by your house at least five times."

"And you still didn't get the message?"

"I just don't want things to end like this. Not on such a cold and permanent note."

"Well, that's just too bad, because this is the way it's going to be."

"But can I at least explain?"

"Explain what?"

"Why I didn't tell you about Cindy or my boys."

"To be honest, I really don't care."

"Maybe you don't, but Taylor, I was scared. I found myself caught between a rock and a hard place and I didn't know what to do about it."

"Well, guess what? You no longer have that problem now. Do you?"

"But I still love you. I mean, I love my boys. But I love you, too. I've always loved you."

"And what about Cindy?"

"She's the mother of my children."

"Then that's who you should be with. End of story."

"But it's not that simple. I want to be there for my sons and keep you, too. I mean, we wouldn't have to stop seeing each other, and as soon as they're a little older, I could divorce Cindy."

I laughed at him like he was a comedian.

"What's so funny?" he asked.

"You. You're as funny as they come. Either that or you're just plain ignorant. But let me make myself clear once and for all.

You and I are over. You hear me? Over. And I don't ever want you contacting me again. Not by phone, not at my house, not here."

"I don't believe this," he had the audacity to say. "I know I was dead wrong for what I did, but how can you just walk away so easily? Especially when you kept claiming you were so in love with me."

"I really was in love with you, but the important thing is that I'm not anymore."

I could tell he wanted to say something else, but he didn't.

"Now, if you don't mind, I'd like you to leave," I said. "I want you to get out of my office and pretend you never met me."

"Fine, it's your loss," he said, standing up. "Because it's not like you're going to find another man who looks as good as me and who has it going on businesswise the way I do."

"Is that what you think?"

"No, that's what I know. I'm a good catch and any woman would be thankful to have me. I mean why do you think Cindy has been sitting around for two whole years praying that I'll take her back?"

"I don't know, maybe she just doesn't know any better. Because if she did, she would take almost everything you own and find herself a real man."

"Like I said, you won't ever find another man like me and that's why you're lashing out the way you are," he said with a stupid smirk on his face, and without hesitation I did something I hadn't planned on. I picked up the phone and dialed Skyler.

"Are you busy?"

"No, what's up?"

"Can you come in here for a minute? Like as soon as possible?"

"Sure. I'll be right there," he said and hung up.

"So, what are you doing? Calling security?" Cameron asked.

"No. I just want you to say hello to someone before you go."

"This is meaningless," he said, opening the door, but Skyler was already standing there.

"Cameron, my man, how are you?" Skyler said.

"A lot better now that I'm leaving."

"No, wait," I said, still sitting behind my desk with my arms folded. "There's one last thing I need to tell you."

"What?" Cameron said, and his tone wasn't cordial.

"Skyler and I have been seeing each other for over two weeks now and that's why I haven't returned your phone calls. Not to mention he doesn't want me consorting with men I used to date. Isn't that right, Skyler?" I said, and I could tell Skyler was confused. But thankfully, he followed my lead.

"Yeah, I guess I can't deny it. And I hope you don't have any hard feelings about it, man."

"I think both of you know where you can go," Cameron said, and walked out.

"Okay, so what was that all about?" Skyler said, coming in and shutting the door.

"It's a long story and I'm sorry for involving you in it."

"He must have really pissed you off."

"More than you know. We broke up the day I came home from the hospital and then this morning he just showed up here."

"I'm sorry to hear that."

"Hey, it happens."

"So, was this a onetime deal?"

"What?"

"Me pretending to be your significant other?"

"Yes. I promise I won't ever ask you to do that again."

"Well, it's not like I'm complaining, and since we're on the subject, my offer to take you to lunch still stands."

"I don't know, Skyler. I mean, I just got out of this relationship with Cameron and a part of me is still trying to recover from it. He really hurt me and it hasn't been that easy to deal with."

"I understand that and that's why I'm only asking you to lunch. Nothing more."

"Today?"

"Yes, if you're available."

"Okay, make the reservations and let me know what time," I finally agreed.

"Will do."

"But Skyler?"

"Yeah?"

"You know this is crazy, right? You and me treating each other so terribly and then all of a sudden going to lunch together. I mean, what is everybody going to say around here?"

"I don't know, but do we really care?"

"No, I guess we don't," I said after thinking about it. Skyler smiled at me and left my office.

I smiled to myself and realized that for the first time in weeks, I actually had something fun to look forward to.

In all honesty, I couldn't wait.

Chapter 36

Whitney

THE DAY OF MY CLASS REUNION had finally arrived and I was thrilled as all get out. I was thrilled because I had indeed dropped fifty pounds and this black cocktail dress I was wearing was a 14—W, that is. Which was still a huge blessing, since originally, I'd only been shooting for a size 16. Although I knew that this was all because I'd lost a lot more inches than I had planned on and because I'd made what was proving to be one of the best decisions in my life.

I had officially joined Weight Watchers.

Which actually hadn't happened until about two months ago, right after I'd read this study in a medical journal and had discovered that this just might be my ultimate solution. Yes, I'd still been working out on a fairly regular basis and was paying a lot more attention to what I ate, but it had become more and more apparent that what I really needed was something a bit more structured. What I needed was something that wasn't your normal flimflam diet plan but instead was a wonderfully fulfilling new way of life and one that centered on nutrition and fitness. Thankfully, this program was all of that and then some and I couldn't have been happier.

Still, though, this whole process had been a bittersweet journey for me. I mean, sure, I'd lost the weight that I'd wanted to lose, but I'd also lost Rico and was now regretting it. I knew that he had lied to me and that his *experiment* had been heartless, but now I was starting to see what Taylor had been trying to tell me. It was too late, but I understood why she'd insisted I give him another chance. Because if I had, I wouldn't be heading to such an important celebration without him. I wouldn't be standing here getting all dressed up and then waiting for Taylor to come get me. I mean, what kind of hot date was that? It was true that I loved Taylor and would give my life for her, but she wasn't someone I could show off to my schoolmates. She wasn't the person I'd had in mind when I'd first decided I was going to this reunion.

But I guess I should just be happy that I didn't have to go alone and that Taylor was even available. Especially since she'd called me yesterday afternoon practically bragging about her lunch with Skyler. She'd gone on and on, telling me what a great time she'd had and how she was surprised that they had a lot in common. Which to be honest, I wasn't all that shocked about because they'd never really gotten to know each other. At least not on a personal level, and I was glad Taylor was spending time with him. I was glad she had someone else to focus on so she could eventually forget about Cameron.

I did a once-over in the full-length mirror and was glad I'd slipped on a waist whittler. It was sort of squeezing me tight, but the important thing was that I could hardly see any bulges. Still, I had to admit that surgery would eventually be needed. I wouldn't have gastric bypass, the procedure my coworker Renee was still checking into, but maybe liposuction or abdominoplasty. Actually, I was thinking more toward the latter because once I'd lost a full hundred pounds, I knew massive skin would be hanging everywhere. I'd seen it happen too many times on a number of reality shows and I knew I wouldn't be excluded. I knew I would have to find a good plastic surgeon and soon.

When I grabbed my purse and turned out the bedroom light, I heard the doorbell ringing. Taylor was right on time—so I thought—but I about keeled over when I saw Rico. He was dressed in a classy black suit and I just stood there, I'm sure with my mouth open.

"There's someone on the phone for you," he said, passing me his cell, and I took it.

"Hello?"

"Sometimes we don't always know what's good for us or what isn't, so I took it upon myself to help you out in that department," Taylor said.

I was still speechless but Rico smiled at me.

"You're my girl, Whit," Taylor continued. "You're a good person and you deserve to be happy and that's why I called him."

This time I wanted to respond, but I still couldn't.

"Well, aren't you going to say something?" she said.

"I guess I don't know what to say. Except you never cease to amaze me."

"And that won't ever change. Now, go have a good time and call me when you get home . . . or should I say whenever it's convenient," she said, slightly laughing.

"I will. And T?"

"Yeah?"

"Thanks."

"You're quite welcome."

When I passed the phone back to Rico, he said, "So, are you going to invite me in or not?"

"Of course," I said, and he stepped past me.

"Baby, you look like a million bucks."

"Thanks. So do you."

"And you don't know how glad I was to hear from Taylor last

week. She called my company, found me through the employee directory, and we started planning from there."

"Well, I'm glad she called you, too. I mean, I know I said I never wanted to see you again, but after a few days passed I really started to miss you. I started to miss you a lot but I was worried about being hurt again."

"I know, and you had every reason to feel that way. What I did to you was the worst but I'm still hoping that you'll find it in your heart to forgive me. Because Whitney, I don't want to go another day without you."

"And I don't want to be without you either, but I'm scared."

"But you don't have to be," Rico said, pulling me toward him. "I know it'll take a while before you believe me, but I promise you I won't ever hurt you again," he said, caressing my cheek. "I won't ever hurt you again because I love you too much to ever do that."

"I love you, too," I said, and prayed that he wasn't running another game on me.

I prayed that Rico really could love someone like me. Someone who'd struggled with weight her entire life and even now wasn't thin by any stretch of the imagination.

But I decided that I really didn't have anything to lose, that I should give Rico a chance, and that I should hope for the very best.

Because in the end, I knew that hope was all any of us truly had.

Discussion Questions

1. Do you believe Whitney's low self-esteem was a result of her relationship with her mother?

2. Have you or anyone you know struggled with the problem of being overweght? Do you think overweight issues in America are worse than ever before?

3. Did you realize that Taylor's boyfriend was hiding such a huge secret from her in terms of why he wasn't ready for marriage?

4. Do you think Taylor's choice to ignore her symptoms of an illness is typical of many women today? Specifically, when the symptoms might mean a possible hysterectomy?

5. Do you know someone who has the same controlling personality as Charisse?

6. Do you think Charisse's life might have turned out differently had her mother been more loving to her as a child? Or do you think Charisse was born mentally unstable?

7. Were you happy to know that Marvin finally decided that he was going to stand up to Charisse?

8. Which of the three characters could you most identify with, Whitney, Taylor, or Charisse and why?

9. In the end, do you believe that Rico really did love Whitney and that they truly have a chance of having a happy relationship?

10. Do you have friends that you can always depend on the same as these women are able to depend on each other in *Changing Faces*?

11. Do you believe the friendship among Whitney, Taylor, and Charisse is similar to most friendships between women?

Here's a sneak preview of

Love and Lies

by Kimberla Lawson Roby

Available in hardcover
from William Morrow
An Imprint of HarperColllins*Publishers*

Charlotte

IT WAS ALL I COULD DO not to curse my husband out—my husband, a man who was never home more than a few days at a time, a man who didn't seem to care about his wife in the least, a man who was probably sleeping with only God knew whom. Which is why after five years of pleading with him to change and begging him to spend more time with me, I had finally had enough. I was finally in a place where I would no longer tolerate the world-renowned Reverend Curtis Black or the adultery I was sure he was committing.

"So when exactly are you going to be here, Curtis?" I asked now, gripping the phone tightly.

"I just told you. In a couple of days."

"I realize that, but I need to know a specific day. What I need to know is the time your flight will be arriving at O'Hare."

"Well, Charlotte, as much as I hate to disappoint you, I don't know what time."

"*You don't know?* How could you not know?"

"Because I just don't."

"Curtis, please. Do you think I'm that stupid? Do you really think you can get me to believe that you're coming home this week but your travel reservations still haven't been arranged? Do you really think I'm that crazy?"

"Like I said . . . I'll be there in a couple of days."

See, it was comments such as this that made me want to do unspeakable things to Curtis. Made me want to snatch him down from that nice little pedestal that thousands of people nationwide had placed him on. What I wanted to do was show him firsthand that being a *New York Times* bestselling author didn't mean that he could do whatever he wanted whenever he wanted to.

But I decided instead that I would calmly try to reason with him one last time.

"Curtis, have you even thought about the amount of time you spend on the road? I mean, are you even aware of the fact that you've now been gone for two weeks straight, and that once you return, you'll only be here for five short days?"

"Charlotte, why are we doing this? Huh? Because you know just as well as I do that my speaking engagements are very necessary. You've known for the last five years that this is what I have to do if you want to keep living the wealthy lifestyle you so desperately wanted when we were first married."

"But baby, there has to be some sort of balance," I said, remembering just how miserable I'd been before his publisher had offered him a contract with an initial advance worth seven hundred and fifty thousand dollars for one book.

"Look, either you want luxury or you want average," he said, sounding impatient.

"What I want is for you to be here with your family. Matthew and Marissa need you, Curtis, and I'm tired of feeling as though I'm a single parent. Twelve-year-old boys need their fathers."

"All three of my children, including Alicia, know that I love them and that I have a job to do. I've explained to them that it won't always be this way, but for now, this is what I have to do."

"Curtis, all I'm asking is that you please cancel some of your commitments. I need you to spend more time at home."

"It's not going to happen. Not right now, and to be honest, I'm tired of repeating the same words to you over and over again."

"Oh, so now you've got the nerve to be irritated?" I said, my last bit of tolerance evaporating second by second.

"No, I just don't see a reason to continue discussing a situation that isn't going to change."

"Well, maybe the problem isn't your speaking engagements, Curtis. Maybe it has more to do with the fact that you're out there sleeping around. Because, knowing you, you've probably got a different woman lined up in every city."

"You mean like the way you slept with Aaron behind my back? How you slept with that deceitful lunatic even though he claimed to be my best friend? Or do you mean like how you lied about Matthew being my son when you knew full well that he might not be? Or maybe you mean like how because you slept with Aaron, we had to get a paternity test just to make sure Marissa was actually mine? So tell me, Charlotte, which sin of yours are you talking about exactly?"

At that moment, I wondered when Curtis would ever stop wallowing in the past and would eventually forgive me for the way I had betrayed him. Because whether he wanted to admit it or not, it wasn't like any of this had happened one month ago. As a matter of fact, it had been five whole years since Marissa had been born, and to me it was high time for us to move on. Not to mention it wasn't like he'd been this perfect little Boy Scout himself.

"You know what, Curtis, as far as I'm concerned, you need to get over it. What you need to do is stop making all these lame excuses and get your priorities in order."

"No, what I need to do is the same thing I've been doing all along. Making a ton of money so that you can continue living like the queen you *think* you are, and so that I can maintain the type of freedom I've definitely become accustomed to. End of story."

His tone was razor sharp and more than anything I wanted to hurt him back. What I wanted was for him to feel more pain than he was now causing me, but for some reason I couldn't find the words. I was speechless and the only thing I could think to do was slam the phone down on its base.

Which is exactly what I did, and then I covered my face with both hands.

It was so hard to believe that after all the lying and scheming I'd done over the years, making sure I obtained everything I wanted, I was still living in complete turmoil. To put it plainly, I was living a life of pure hell and I didn't know how much more I'd be able to stand before exploding.

I walked out of the sitting room inside our master bedroom suite and over toward the balcony. Once there, I folded my arms and gazed out, trying to settle my nerves. This just didn't make any sense, being so unhappy. Not when we had this massive three-level mini-mansion, a Lexus 470 SUV, a Mercedes S500, and a BMW two-seater. Not when I'd hired a five-day-per-week housekeeper who also cooked our meals. Not when we had an enormous bank account and a whole slew of investments.

Although maybe this overly aggressive attempt at gaining the whole world really was grounds for losing one's own soul, because that's exactly how I had been feeling for more than a year now. I'd tried my best to make things right with Curtis, but no matter what I said or did, he no longer paid much attention to me. And even on the rare occasion when he was home, he spent all of his time with the children and even visited Alicia on her college campus, which was only a couple of hours away. He did everything with everyone except me, his wife of seven years, and now I knew, just at this very moment, that this wasn't going to change. After all, he'd slept with me when he was married to his first wife, Tanya, and his second wife, Mariah, so how in the world could I have ever thought I would be an exception? How could I have ever thought Curtis was going to be the loving, faithful husband until death do us part?

Of course, in the beginning, when we'd first gotten married, I had to admit that Curtis was in fact the loving husband and father. I also had to admit that I was the one who'd blundered into this ridiculous world of insanity the day I'd made the decision to sleep with Aaron Malone—or Donovan Wainright, which we'd learned was his real name. Oh, how this had proven to be an absolute nightmare, and to think I'd almost lost my life because of it. The man had taken the fatal attraction theory to a whole new level, and he'd gone to major extremes to ruin everything. He'd blabbed to Curtis practically every comment that I'd been naïve enough to confide to him, and in the end he'd tried to burn our house down with me still inside it.

Just the mere thought that I'd risked each of our lives for the likes of Aaron, a schizophrenic who'd masked himself as a stable and intelligent born-again Christian, was enough to make me cringe. It was enough to make me wonder if that mental institution he'd been dragged back to was now keeping closer watch on him. Because for the life of me I still couldn't understand how in the beginning he'd been able to convince his psychiatrist that he'd somehow made this miraculous recovery, how he'd been able to leave the state of Michigan, set up shop in Illinois with a whole new identity, and then find a good-paying job. Although Curtis had learned from one of the detectives that this had all been possible because Aaron had been good about taking his medication.

I stared through the window a while longer almost in a daze and then finally walked back toward our California king-size bed. And then it hit me. No matter what I'd done with Aaron five years ago, Curtis still didn't have the right to treat me as if I didn't matter. He had no right because his own history was full of dirt, and as far as I was concerned we were even. He'd gotten me pregnant before I'd turned eighteen, which by law was statutory rape, and I'd committed adultery with Aaron. We'd both committed sins that we would surely have to answer for, but from this day forward, I was going to handle things a lot differently. I wouldn't give up my affluent way of living, not under any circumstances, but I was going to live my life the same as Curtis, any way I chose. At the same time, I would find out who my husband was sleeping with, because no matter what he refused to admit, I knew him better than he knew himself. I knew my husband, the Reverend Curtis Black, couldn't go more than a day without having sex, even if it wasn't with me.

So, starting today, my primary focus would be my own happiness and raising my two adorable children. I would live even better than I had been and Curtis would come to realize that soon enough. He'd learn the hard way, once again, that I truly was his match. He would learn that just because he was the sole provider of our household didn't mean that I wasn't in a position to collect half of everything. Which is exactly what I would do if he forced me.

Over the next hour, I phoned my friend Janine at work, called to speak to my parents, and now I was heading down the wrought iron and wood winding staircase that led to the foyer. I strolled across the black-and-white marble flooring, down the long hallway, and into the kitchen.

I gasped when I saw Marissa playing with fire.

She was standing her little five-year-old behind in front of the stove, switching one of the front burners from low to high, high to low, and then waving her hand through the flame, back and forth and back and forth again.

"Marissa!" I yelled out to her. "Have you lost your mind?!"

But she never even flinched. She seemed almost mesmerized by what she was doing and, strangely enough, fascinated by the whole scenario.

"Marissa!" I screamed louder than before, and this time she snapped out of her trance. "What are you doing?"

Instead of responding, however, my little girl stared at me, turned back toward the stove, politely turned off the burner, and walked right past me. She walked right out of the kitchen and headed up to her bedroom like I hadn't said a word to her. She acted as if nothing out of the ordinary had just happened, and this worried me more than anything else. Especially since as of late, Marissa had begun acting so bizarrely, and I also wondered why at times she was so cruel toward Matthew and me but was always the perfect little angel when Curtis was around. I'd tried to ignore these signs, but I feared that something was very wrong with her. I feared that maybe Marissa wasn't Curtis's daughter after all and that instead she was Aaron's and had inherited his schizophrenia. Because it wasn't like I'd ever actually seen the results of the paternity test. It wasn't like I'd even wanted to see them, because I'd immediately decided it was better if no one, not even I, knew the truth. It had been better that way because as long as Curtis had believed wholeheartedly that he was Marissa's father, there hadn't been a thing for me to worry about.

And the more I thought about it, there still wasn't.

I decided that Marissa *was* Curtis's daughter and that she was merely going through some weird childhood phase—one she would grow out of any day now.

Truthfully, I refused to accept anything different.